CW00516914

the glow

The Glow

jessie gaynor

TINDER PRESS

First published in the United States by
Random House, an imprint and division of
Penguin Random House LLC, New York

First published in Great Britain in 2023 by Tinder Press
An imprint of HEADLINE PUBLISHING GROUP

1

Cataloguing in Publication Data is available from the British Library

Hardback ISBN 978 1 0354 0416 2
Trade paperback ISBN 978 1 0354 0417 9

Offset in 13.11/17.68 pt ITC Galliard Std by Jouve (UK), Milton Keynes

Printed and bound in Great Britain by Clays Ltd, Elcograf S.p.A.

Headline's policy is to use papers that are natural, renewable and recyclable products and made from wood grown in well-managed forests and other controlled sources. The logging and manufacturing processes are expected to conform to the environmental regulations of the country of origin.

HEADLINE PUBLISHING GROUP
An Hachette UK Company
Carmelite House
50 Victoria Embankment
London EC4Y 0DZ

www.tinderpress.co.uk
www.headline.co.uk
www.hachette.co.uk

To my mother, Jude

chapter 1.

Hey, badass bitch! Thought you might be interested in the new line of non-toxic, non-flammable, BPA-free toys from Pleasure Class. C-Sweet toys are designed for the adventurous #GirlBoss. They put the *OHHHHH* in She-E-O. C-Sweet is for all the Nasty Women who work hard, play hard, and c*m hard;)

Sometimes it helped Jane to think of the emails like poems in which she was enacting her own mania, a little more each line.

And just in case you think this is just another basic-bitch vibrator, let me tell you about a couple of my favorite C-Sweet goodies:

- BijOoh, a subtle vibrating ring and necklace set that can take you from boardroom to bedroom

- 1:1, a double-ended dildo that will touch *all* your bases
- The Management, a remote-controlled butt plug for not-so-hostile takeovers

Trust me: These will clit-erally change your life. Can I send you over some samples? And let me know if you're free for some mani/pedi/girl talk action soon!

xxJane

Jane Dorner had never used a butt plug, and manicures made her cuticles bleed.

At first it had been fun, the refining of Public Relations Jane. She was breezy, overly familiar, sexually omnivorous, joylessly joyful, and clever in a nonthreatening way. She was hot, but only with makeup on. She liked her shoulders but hated her arms. She wouldn't steal your boyfriend, but she might fuck his brother and tell you about that dick. She did barre and boot camp, but she was just in it to cancel out the day-drinking. She thought women with visible muscles needed to take it down a notch, even though, obviously, *you do you!*, et cetera. She liked VIP lounges and Champagne-flavored gummi bears and USB drives shaped like baby animals. If your mother died, PR Jane would send you a gift basket a month later—one of her clients, UnBereave, was a subscription box service that focused on self-care after tragedy, including lavender bath bombs they'd rebranded as bath blooms—but she probably wouldn't be able to go to the funeral, because she already had tickets to see her college roommate in LA for the long weekend. She'd post her brunch-themed sign from the Women's March and go to brunch after. She was up for whatever, but she wasn't someone you called in any kind of emergency. PR Jane was twenty-five and she figured she had two more good years before she had to really knuckle down and listen to the answers to her questions.

Actual Jane was twenty-nine. She had $97,000 in medical debt, a limitless capacity for disappointing first dates, and a malaise so deep she wondered if it might just be her personality. Lately, she was becoming increasingly concerned about her career and her future—neither of which seemed like the low-stakes annoyances they once had.

All of a sudden, without warning, the conversation about so-called passion among Jane's cohort had turned from *thinking about starting a band* to *thinking about accepting my manager's offer of corporate leadership training*. Jane didn't begrudge anyone their selling out; she only wished she could have done so more effectively. All she'd done in the seven years since she graduated from college was accumulate an unfinished PhD, a closet full of clothes that all looked slightly wrong on her, and the debt.

She knew that in order to be a participant in capitalism rather than solely a victim of it, she had to have something to sell, but she didn't believe in her own viability as a product and had no ideas for better ones. As an account manager at Relevancy PR, she shilled goods she knew to be third-rate, and her lack of conviction fed her stasis.

When she took the job, she had been blinkered by the impressive title—impressive, at least, compared with "grad student without distinction"—and the idea of the kind of life it suggested. Jane had never been able to envision her life more than six months into the future, so a job with a ready-made identity was appealing. Only when she was already mired in the day-to-day drudgery of Relevancy did she realize that "PR Maven" was, like "middle-class homeowner," an identity on its way out. And while there were plenty of other jobs she wished she *had*, it felt impossible to imagine a job, any job, that she would like to *do*.

"Jane—" Her boss Rand Hagen materialized like a flinch beside her. "Stop by and see me whenever you get a chance. Now would be best."

She followed him into his office, repulsed, as always, by the skeletal shoulders visible beneath his thin white button-down. She sat opposite him and prepared for the intermittent but unrelenting stream of *Hmm*s that was the hallmark of their meetings. Every time Rand Hagen peered at her with his dark button eyes and *Hmm*ed, Jane felt an unmistakable tugging on her second left toe. It always started out as a twinge, but as the meeting wore on and the *Hmm*s persisted, the tug became excruciating. Jane had once read on a yoga store's shopping bag: TRAUMA LODGES ITSELF IN OUR BODIES—RELEASE THE WOUNDS OF YOUR PAST. Though the same bag had also warned that tomatoes were a leading cause of depression, Jane couldn't deny that the trauma of Rand Hagen had lodged itself in her second left toe.

She got the job at Relevancy through a combination of name-brand schooling (her incomplete PhD in poetry from Columbia), a moderately viral satirical essay ("Makeup Tips for the Apocalypse," which she now suspected the Relevancy recruiter had taken at face value), and, she later learned, the fact that two buttons on her shirt had come undone during her interview, fully exposing her bra and convincing Rand Hagen that she was "one of the fun ones."

Her job was to oversee content creation for the firm's Women's Empowerment Sector and manage a team of junior copywriters. Relevancy was a large, multi-armed agency that was forever being re-orged, and Rand had been shuffled from Travel & Leisure to Emerging Technologies to Healthcare Solutions before finally landing in WE. He spoke wistfully about projects and managers past, and had spent the last two years failing to impart his lifetime of leadership lessons to Jane.

Jane excelled at suggesting snappy wordplay to the copywriters, but she was temperamentally unsuited to lead anyone—even toward greater awareness of a remote-controlled butt plug. Her PowerPoints read like personal essays, full of bloated asides and dubious anecdotal evidence, and heading meetings made her sleepy; she had never been able to stretch one past twenty minutes.

Jane had been at Relevancy for two years. For the last two months, since being dumped by a milk-pale poet named Byron, she had completed almost no work. Post-dumping, she gave herself a week to grieve without accountability. She didn't intend to shirk her responsibilities indefinitely, but her team's work carried on much as before, and her grief had manifested mostly as exhaustion. Now she still came in every day, but she pitched ideas she knew she couldn't execute and promised placements in publications that would never touch Relevancy's third-tier brands, no matter how many desperately cheeky emails she sent.

There was something liberating about dereliction. As

the days during which she did absolutely nothing piled up, she wondered if she could, possibly, stop working forever, but continue to draw a paycheck, at least until she paid off her debt. In a way, it would be the more ethical thing for her to do. Her job did nothing to improve the world, and given the volume of microplastics in the products on her roster, her semi-intentional work stoppage was probably a net positive for the environment.

"Walk me through the status of the reFaun campaign," Rand said. reFaun was an at-home fecal transplant kit marketed—like all of Relevancy's products—to the upper-middle-class millennial woman who was her own hobby. Even if reFaun's claims *had* been substantiated by the FDA (the closest thing Jane had to a doctor's endorsement was a chiropractor who said it was "likely" safe, at least in terms of spinal alignment), the product was disgusting, and no one wanted to touch it.

"We're in the weeds right now, but everyone is pulling together to . . ." Jane kept a list of Rand Hagen's favorite business jargon on a Post-it at her desk. ". . . think outside the box. For the reFaun campaign."

"Hmm. And your workload. Is it manageable?"

"We're all working hard, but we're hanging in there."

"Jane, there's no delicate way to say this: Per Relevancy's employment agreements, I—we—have the right to audit employees' computer activity, a right we exercise when the employee's keystroke activity falls below a predetermined number of strokes per minute for four consecutive days, as yours did this month. I just want to read you some of what we found. This was some of the internet activity from your machine for last Wednesday."

Jane's personal best humiliations always reappeared to her at times like this, when she suspected their number was about to grow, a slide carousel of moments *ftt-ftt-ftt*-ing behind her eyes: flickers of misplaced hope—an "O!" where an "O" should have been—or simple bodily obviousness, visible sweat and audible farting and a creeping facial rash, anything that made being alive look like work.

"Rand, there's really no need to—"

"Most alarming here is the number of searches for the name *Iza Brecht*. We have Iza Brecht's Facebook, LinkedIn, Twitter, Instagram, and Yelp accounts, as well as his-slash-her Amazon customer page and Gallatin School student publication archive."

Iza Brecht was Byron's girlfriend now, and had been before Jane, too. Jane had thought Byron's interest highlighted some quality in her that she had been unaware of. The kind of thing that the romantic leads in movies allude to in climactic declarations of love: *You don't even realize how special you truly are,* et cetera. Instead, Jane was the interlude, the blip. Her Iza Brecht tracking wasn't only masochistic. She was researching her own deficiencies. She felt ashamed that Rand Hagen had witnessed this, but also furious. Her instinct was to shout *I'm in here!*

Iza Brecht was thin in a way that was both slinky and heartrending, like a neglected cat, all length and unsubtle bones, and had broken Byron's heart and made him vulnerable to Jane's less-obvious charms. In the many pictures Jane had seen, Iza Brecht was always smiling lazily under thick bangs and long, fashionably clumped eyelashes. She wore expensive clothes insouciantly and looked like she would smell of cigarettes and orange blossoms and leather. Jane had gleaned from the Gallatin website that her undergrad thesis was about the eroticism of John Donne. *Of course.*

Byron had some kind of nebulous artists' grant that, along with a part-time job at a bookstore, allowed him to make a modest living as a poet. He described his own work as "an exploration and amplification of the perceived arcanity of poetry that is by turns frolicsome and melancholy." Byron was irrevocably dedicated to the arcane—whole stanzas of his poetry detailed nineteenth-century cleaning lore, ecstatic descriptions of the taste of rampion root, the smell of liturgical incense. He and Jane met at a reading of a cycle of war poems written with an app that mimicked a cipher machine. She got drunk enough at the after-party to give Byron her real opinion on the poems—that they were farcically opaque and terrifically boring. He called her *refreshing*.

Since dropping out of grad school, Jane mostly avoided poetry-adjacent activities, which reminded her of her failed degree. Her knack for analyzing poetry had been a source of pride in her undergrad days, and she had conflated her aptitude with a deep love for the thing itself. But in grad school—among people who wanted to think and talk about poetry almost exclusively, who gently mocked her not only for watching television but also for reading fiction, who could earnestly debate for forty-five minutes whether *heartsick* and *bronchial* rhymed—she was a rank amateur.

She hung on for three years after she realized how comparatively dull her curiosity for poetry was, but gave up when it became clear how much work even a mediocre dissertation required. When she talked about her time in grad school now, she told people that one day, in the middle of a seminar on the sublime, she had been struck by the realization that she actually *hated* poetry. Which made for a better party anecdote than the truth: that she liked it, just not enough to overcome the grinding shame of her own lack.

The night she met Byron, she had been lured to the reading with the promise of literate single men. When he ended the relationship after five months, he wept. "I'm like a dog. I just want to herd everyone into a room and make them be happy," he told her plaintively. Jane had been happy with Byron. She could make him smile without deviating too far from her real thoughts, and he acted so grateful after she went down on him that she felt secure in his affections.

"But I'm happy now," she told him. "Because of you. You did it."

"It was a metaphor," he said. "I'm sorry."

Jane tried very hard not to roll her eyes, because she still wanted him to like her. Byron was the kind of person Jane wanted people to think she was. Everyone agreed he was brilliant, but he wore his intelligence like his perfect jean jacket—*I stole it from my mom*, he'd confessed on their first date—an effortless afterthought. Being with Byron made Jane feel like maybe she was brilliant, too. Their mutual acquaintances seemed to regard her with a new respect when they learned of the relationship. Byron's attention had made her more worthy of theirs.

She felt smarter when she was with him, too, and more charismatic. He was generous in conversations. He laughed easily, and dispensed compliments, seemingly for no other reason than that they had just occurred to him.

As if he lost nothing by pointing out another person's strengths. As if he had enough of everything to spare.

They took long walks around the city, stopping to eat or drink when the mood struck them, at the first place that appeared in their path, without so much as a quick Yelp check to see if it was any good. The low-level spontaneity was thrilling to Jane, even if most of the meals were mediocre.

When Byron went on a research trip to Berlin for three weeks, he called her every day from the single-stall library bathroom and they had phone sex, which neither of them had ever done before. *You're hot, you're hot, you're hot,* Byron panted when he came, and Jane got off more on her power to render him inarticulate than his middling sexual narration.

She felt like all her previous romantic flailing had led her to him, and just at the moment she'd developed an awareness of her looming thirties. Her uncharacteristic certainty that they would stay together, probably even get married, made the dumping extra humiliating. With his kindness, he'd tricked her into believing it was safe to reveal herself to him fully. Or almost fully. But more than that, he'd tricked her into believing that something could be easy.

For a few weeks after the breakup, she sent Byron emails that were first pleading, then icy, the latter's potency diminished by its proximity to the former. He got back together with Iza almost immediately. Jane imagined him reading Iza her emails, pityingly. *What should I do? I don't want to be cruel.* Since then, she had mucked through Iza Brecht's digital leavings with a fervor she had never brought to her education or her career.

"I was considering hiring Iza to write copy for the reFaun campaign," she told Rand. The plausibility of the lie amazed her.

"Hmm." He consulted his paper. "On April twelfth, fifteenth, and twenty-first, you searched: *Iza Brecht untalented.*"

"It's important to find out whether the people you're hiring are untalented."

"We audited a week of your internet use, Jane, and this is just the tip of the iceberg when it comes to Iza Brecht. Frankly, I'm struggling to see how you got any work done at all."

Jane was excellent at following directions, but when it came to setting them herself, she spun in lazy circles. She did not suffer from a lack of ambition. She wanted plenty. She wanted money and prestige and shiny hair and poreless skin and the envy and admiration of everyone in the room. Any room. Every room. She was hungry, just not in the sense that people applied it to young investment banking analysts who never left the office before midnight, or publishing ingénues who spoke up in meetings with firm but sweet confidence. Her hunger was nonspecific.

A Czech woman in her grad program had once given Jane a word for the way she was: *mlsný. It's the feeling of standing in front of a fridge full of food and you can't decide what you really want to eat,* the woman explained. *You could eat anything and it would be fine. But* mlsný *is the feeling when you know there's one thing, and maybe it's even right in front of you, or you could at least order it or make it, if only you could figure it out.*

Jane was taken with the word, and looked it up later.

The only definition she could find was "finicky, dainty, lickerish." She wasn't fussy. Fussy people were good at PowerPoints. They set goals. They collected data on themselves and used it to iterate on their lives. They added new features all the time—Life 6.0 was going to be their best update yet. But Jane's ambition was lecherous and one-sided. It had no plan for how to manifest itself beyond leering and panting and whistling, only to feel shame when some object—an opportunity to try for more money, a pore-reducing diet—looked its way. Her ambition didn't have anything to offer, after all. It could only ever masturbate itself to sleep.

"Rand, it's true that in the past few weeks I've put some of my existing accounts on the back burner. Obviously I've delegated that work to the junior copywriters, but in terms of my own work . . ." She tried to keep the panic from her voice. She needed her job more than she hated it.

When Jane was in school, she had selected the university's "Brass" health insurance option, which seemed like an adult, budget-conscious decision at the time. She rarely went to the doctor, apart from her annual visit to the gynecologist to renew her birth control pills. She had never considered the fallibility of her body until the day it failed her.

She was on a research trip to Northampton to visit the Sylvia Plath archive at Smith when she collapsed in a food co-op while standing in line to buy the $9 sachet of small-batch saltines she thought might ease the cramps that had come on that morning. The cramps turned out to be appendicitis, and the ambulance summoned by the conscientious store manager took her to the nearest hospital, where an out-of-network anesthesiologist put her under so an out-of-network doctor could extract the offending organ before she woke up and drank an out-of-network orange juice, all of which left her with a $111,000 bill.

At first she thought it was a mistake. The number was so outlandish that she rolled her eyes at the explanation of benefits when it arrived in the mail. She didn't even call her insurance company right away. She was certain that a corrected statement was on its way. She felt a pang of sympathy for people without insurance, but that was the extent of her worry because, after all, she *had* insurance. She was lucky. But when she finally phoned a few weeks later, the flat-accented woman she spoke to made it clear that the only mistake was Jane's, in trusting that her youth and cynicism and name-brand insurance would protect her from anything.

After that first call, she spent hours on the phone with insurance representatives who were always blandly polite and entirely unmoved by her pleas and her tears and her abuse and her subsequent apologies. *Ma'am, if you don't start paying down this debt, the hospital will send you into collections. There's nothing more we can do for you.*

She felt like a fool, but she tried to bluff her way from shame to anger. It helped that when she told people about the debt, they responded mostly with righteous indignation on her behalf. This was perhaps the one story in her life in which she was indisputably blameless. No one asked whether she regretted her actions, as they had when she told the freshman comp class she was teaching an admittedly overly detailed story about her disastrous date the night before in order to illustrate the importance of word choice, prompting one of the more religious students to report her to the dean. When it came to the debt, there was literally nothing she could have done to prevent the catastrophe, aside from choosing a more comprehensive insurance plan, which would have cost nearly half of her monthly stipend. If she had to be a victim, better to be a faultless one.

When she got the job at Relevancy, her $90,000 annual salary felt like both a miracle and a reward for her pain and suffering. It felt like a given that she would be able to pay off the debt. Except then her roommate in Morningside Heights decided not to renew the lease, and Jane decided she could no longer stomach sharing a bathroom with a relative stranger, so she found an apartment that everyone told her was a deal but that still cost $2,200 a month (though for a proper one-bedroom!). And then she rear-ended a car in the U-Haul she wisely rented to avoid wasting money on movers. And then her phone broke when she threw it across her new room after a particularly terrible call with the hospital's billing department. And all her clothes were grad student clothes, not PR person clothes, and PR person clothes were expensive.

She stopped telling people about the debt, and they stopped asking. Her "grace period" with the hospital had ended, and the $97,000 she still owed to Vitalia Healthcare Group was her tether, wrenching her back anytime she got too close to stepping off the edge of her life, and making the kind of reckless decisions that led either to founding a start-up or moving back to your childhood home and buying beer for local high schoolers in the hope of being invited to their parties.

Sometimes, when Jane read a particularly ridiculous

wellness claim from one of Relevancy's clients—"One study finds that virgin walnut oil reduces the size of tumors by 75 percent in certain gerbils!"—she thought of her poisonous appendix and seethed. Which was probably bad for her health, too.

She had the urge to wreck things. There was a power in ruining. It made people pay attention. When she was a kid, her mother took her to see *Annie,* and she couldn't stop imagining herself running onstage in the middle of the performance and singing a song herself, or just standing there in the middle of Daddy Warbucks's foyer and screaming.

Aren't they worried someone is going to run up there and ruin the play? she asked her mother at intermission, pointing to the staircases at either side of the stage.

Her mother looked concerned. *Why would anyone want to do that? Everyone worked so hard to put it on. Aren't you having fun?*

Now the urge was upon her again, to ruin her career, such as it was, with the truth. Instead, she thought of her debt and steadied herself. One of the posters on Rand's office wall was an illustration of two white hands holding a crystal ball that looked like the Earth and the words THINK BIGGER. It hung just to the left of his head, and she often stared at it when she was trying not to make eye contact with him. Now was the time to pivot. "May I be honest with you, Rand?" She thought maybe if she said his name enough, he would forget Iza's. "I've been trying to think bigger," she said. "Products are our bread and butter. But I've been doing some market research, and I think the future is in experiences."

"Hmm."

"Millennial women are spending more money on experiences. It's called the experience economy." She had seen the headline on BuzzFeed when she was taking a quiz about which *Sex and the City* boyfriend she was (the gay-straight pastry chef Charlotte dated in Season Two). "So I've been spending time researching promising leads in that space. I didn't tell you because I wanted to wait until I had something more concrete. Now I see that I should have been more transparent, Rand."

"And do you have something concrete?"

"I'm closing in on something." She could tell he wasn't going to fire her. He looked irritated, but not resolute. "I'll have a business plan for you early next week." She'd google it. "I'll make a PowerPoint."

chapter 2.

The unfortunate side effect of Jane's successful lie to Rand Hagen was that now she actually had to find a prominent lead in the experience space. It was surprisingly difficult to find something low-profile enough that it would be unlikely to have a PR person but sleek enough that it had any hope of attracting "the Relevancy girl," as Rand referred to their demographic. A yoga retreat/gem mine looked promising until Jane got to the part of their manifesto where they claimed interracial relationships upset the spiritual balance of the universe. (Relevancy's target demographic was almost entirely white, but Rand always hastened to point out that this wasn't *by design,* it was just "the market.")

First, she searched *wellness getaway* (which yielded expensive private rehabs) and *beauty retreat* (eating disorder recovery clinics) and, in despair, *hot adult summer camp* (porn). Then she tried Instagram, which had surpassed books, television, and her pore-magnifying mirror as the number one thing she stared at. *It's research,* she would tell herself. *I'm keeping up with the tastemakers.* It was true that she was making a study of the lives of beautiful and inexplicably wealthy women, but the only end to it was a stiff neck and a hollow sadness that lasted all day. (She had to stay away from Twitter, because that was where all the poets hung out, and being ignored by people who actually knew you was worse.)

Sometimes she looked up from her phone, alone in her apartment, and felt so ashamed of herself that she had to read a punishment book, like *Walden,* which made her feel chastened but also a little smug, because everyone knew Thoreau's mother had done his laundry. Jane might not do her own laundry, but she at least paid someone else her own money to do it.

Instagram also made her want to move to the woods, but an Instagram version of the woods where all her pots and pans were copper and all her sweaters were chunky oatmeal-colored wool and it was always late fall and her bearded husband (*My whole <3*) made a fire in their wood-burning stove every day. Eventually she would get pregnant but she would only gain weight in the perfect orb of her belly and everyone would comment about how glowy she looked, like a mystical orb herself. The baby (Hesperia, or Benedictine, or Ethel) would be born in a cedar birthing pool inside their living room and even the screams would be captured artfully, in black and white so the gore was less obvious. The family would all wear chunky wool sweaters (#gifted by the eco-fashion version of PR Jane) that were complementary but not matching and sit on the screened-in porch and read books (#screentime) and make their own brooms and drink from speckled enamel mugs and maybe Thoreau's mom could stop by and do their laundry sometimes.

Jane had once spent €250 (plus international shipping) on one of those sweaters. It was itchy from the tiny pieces of hay poking through the weave, and it smelled like a herd of goats.

What she most envied was how the people in her phone had built their own small worlds. They had banished ugliness and loneliness and accidental excess. They had pared down their lives just to the #gifted products that were absolutely essential. Jane wanted that control, that certainty that she had chosen right. She wanted to feel like a selector rather than someone always waiting to be selected.

Jane suspected that seeing so much manicured beauty all at once, unbroken but for the internal misery of her own human condition, was warping her in some fundamental way. The only beauty secret was a combination of genetics and money, but if you looked at enough beautiful faces, sometimes you could convince yourself that yours could be in the mix, with a little tweaking. You forgot what you looked like, even.

While she was growing up, she kept waiting for the moment when her beauty would become indisputable, instead of something only her mother noticed. She would study her straight nose, which sometimes looked enormous and sometimes normal, lips that were thin but not skinny, a chin that didn't recede into her neck, eyes that were average in everything but their bright blue. She knew which girls were the pretty ones and which ones were the ugly ones, but the in-between was a wide and unknowable chasm. Every time she collected a compliment, she would turn it over in her mind like a clue.

Now Jane searched for #wellness and #namaste on Instagram, but the return was overwhelming. By then she had put in a good fifteen minutes of work. She was planning to give up when a picture on her *Explore* tab caught her eye. It was a photo of a woman so undeniably beautiful that she looked like a new and exciting species. She stared into the camera, a slight smile on her face like she knew exactly how much you must hate her but had no hard feelings about it.

The bones in her face were at once delicate and strong, like a lace woven from copper wire. Her jaw and shoulders were covered in a colorless down that caught the light, as if the light were an employee whose job was to highlight her beauty. Jane clicked through to the account, @FortPath, which had under 20,000 followers and described itself as "A Spiritual Retreat in the Heart of New Jersey." In wide shots the woman was long and lean, with mathematical curves. Sometimes she wore her sun-shaft blond hair knotted on top of her head with a careless radiance that was the promise of every hair product ever sold. Sometimes it streamed down her back like a silk banner. There were other people in the pictures, too, but they barely registered beside her.

Whenever Jane saw an extremely beautiful woman, her first reaction was antagonism, followed immediately by resignation: *What, you think you're better than me? Well, you're right.* There was something different about this woman, though. Her beauty felt, somehow, inclusive, inviting, like a beautifully laid table with an extra place. At the same time, Jane felt almost proprietary, as if the woman were a dress she had to have. She wondered if this was how very rich men felt about their third wives.

She tapped the picture once, but no tags appeared. She screenshotted the picture and tried a reverse image search, which only led her back to the FortPath account. Women this beautiful were rarely so traceless. Jane felt her heart beating in her hands. She felt like a truffle hunter whose pigs had started going berserk.

The pictures of FortPath itself made the place look like a low-budget summer camp, with patchy fields fading into the woods and an overgrown vegetable garden. They were all taken outdoors, though sometimes a corner of a house was visible. In one, the woman stood in the middle of a circle of people in flattering yoga clothes, wearing the kind of shapeless linen caftan that the very beautiful wear to prove that their beauty can overcome any sartorial obstacle. In another post, she was alone, sitting cross-legged and staring into the camera with an expression that was somehow both entirely neutral and incredibly sexual. Jane bookmarked that one.

Besides the woman's beauty, the most appealing thing about the page was the clear ineptitude of its curator ("curator"). Every fifth photo was a poorly lit still-life of zucchini. A number of the pictures were just inscrutable quotes, poorly typeset in some cousin of Papyrus: *The Fear is Finished—it is Time to simply Thrive*. With a less attractive woman at its center, @FortPath would have been a slide in Rand Hagen's annual PR Fails slideshow.

"A Spiritual Retreat in the Heart of New Jersey" was

a tagline inelegant enough that Jane was pretty sure there was no branding master behind it. She followed the link-in-bio on the Instagram page to a website that looked like it was created circa 2006. She wondered if the beautiful woman had made it herself, and introduced the system of haphazard capitalizations; if so, the strangeness might be hip.

She sent an email in her best PR Jane voice, tweaked slightly toward the website's tone:

> Good evening!
>
> My name is Jane Dorner and I am a "PR guru" at Relevancy, a large firm in Manhattan with numerous clients in the prestige wellness space. I came across your website while researching exciting new wellness experiences and I would love to learn more about FortPath! Could you possibly send me your press kit, or provide me with a bit more information about what goes on during a typical weekend there?
>
> Namaste,
> Jane
> P.S. Your Instagram had me craving zucchini!

She went to get a Diet Coke from the fridge. When she returned to her computer no more than three minutes later, she had a response.

> Dear Jane!
>
> YES of course WE are happy to answer any and ALL of your queries about FortPath. Of course, some parts

of the Process are 'proprietary,' meaning we cannot explain them fully to you over email correspondence. If you choose to join the FortPath 'family,' of course you will understand ALL aspects of our Methods and OUR Visionary Program.

As to the activities for the three-day Seminar, there will be plenty of exercises of the mental and physical variety, but nothing more strenuous than a short hike or daily yoga practice. All TOXIN-FREE meals ARE PROVIDED, as well as very comfortable, semi-private sleeping accommodations.

Transportation will be provided in the form of a van service departing from 39th St. and 10th Ave., Manhattan, NY.

Yes! It is true that *Zucchini* is the most SPIRITUALLY NOURISHING VEGETABLE. This is because it GROWS WITHOUT FEAR and because it is ANCIENT and a member of the revered Squash Family.

Yours,
Tom Bradstreet

She hadn't realized how much she wanted to hear from the woman until she got to the signature and realized that she was reading someone else's words. But of course the woman wouldn't handle something as mundane as answering emails. Jane wanted to ask Tom Bradstreet about his relationship to the woman, but couldn't figure out how to make obsession sound professional.

Hello Tom!

Thanks very much for your speedy response! A bit more about me: I work with companies to help them reach their most valuable potential client base, and serve as a "right-hand woman" as they continue to grow. As I'm sure you know, reputation is everything when building a business!

I noticed that most of your outreach seems to be in the influencer sphere. Would you be able to tell me a little more about the "VIP clients" your website mentions?

Warmest regards,
Jane

This time, he replied so quickly that Jane reflexively glanced over her shoulder, as if he might be there in the room with her.

Dear Jane!

WE are delighted to hear from you again! Your continued questioning suggests that you treat your Spiritual Future with the appropriate gravity.

Of course you will understand why WE cannot release to you the names of any of FortPath's 'distinguished alumni,' but WE can assure you that they include board members of Fortune 100 companies, successful entrepreneurs, Hollywood-types, and of course high-ranking politicians.

As you have seen on the Website, we have a collection of testimonials about our Process. They are only anonymous to protect the privacy of our Members, being that it is of the utmost importance to them.

WE hope that you will come 'see for yourself' what FortPath has to offer!

Yours,
Tom Bradstreet

Tom's *WE* was so unsettling that Jane went back to her own email to make sure her curiosity about the woman hadn't somehow leaked through her veneer of professional neutrality. Or, even more terrifying—what if Tom's spiritual acumen allowed him to feel Jane's desire all the way in New Jersey? She tried to strip her words of all subtext.

Dear Tom,

This seems like such an exciting time at FortPath, and I would love to experience the program for myself! Do you offer an industry rate? No worries if not!!

Cheers,
Jane

Dear Jane!

We deeply admire your commitment to Fearlessness.

We are Of Course happy to waive our fee for an Industry Professional.

We can in turn assure you, Jane, that FortPath's labor is one of love, and not of greed. You are the gift to US!

WE hope to see you soon!

Yours,
Tom Bradstreet

Jane had already made up her mind to go—to commit to fearlessness—when she googled him and found an eight-year-old article on a neighborhood crimewatch site about someone named Thomas Bradstreet getting arrested for assaulting an information professional at the Brooklyn Public Library.

Her stomach lurched at the word *assault,* but the article's description of the violence was a portrait more of ineptitude than of rampage.

> Thomas Bradstreet, 24, repeatedly yelled, "Listen to me," before reaching across the information desk and wrapping his arms around the computer terminal, knocking it to the floor. Library security officers subdued Bradstreet and held him until police arrived, when they found "a small bag" of cocaine on his person.

She was glad to learn that no one had actually been hurt, and also that Tom was thirty-two. She always preferred to be the youngest one in a situation, professional or not.

> Bradstreet was charged with second-degree harassment, destruction of property, and possession of cocaine. Reached for comment, his lawyer called the charges "absurd" but declined to elaborate.

Jane wondered what happened to Tom after his arrest. His lawyer sounded confident in a way that suggested wealth and whiteness, so he had probably gotten off easy. Still, the image of a man standing in a library begging an *information professional* to listen to him was unbearably sad. It made Jane like him more. At a distance, it was easy for her to confuse pity with fondness.

chapter 3.

The next evening, Jane had a first date with a lawyer named Adrian. Since Byron had dumped her, Jane's attitude to dating again had been one of grim determination, like an unemployed head of household at a job interview.

Though the Idea of a Boyfriend was only a small part of what she liked about being with Byron, in the wake of their breakup, she'd become obsessed with her singleness. Byron had robbed her of five critical months. Every newly announced engagement or cohabitation or even accidental pregnancy that crossed her feeds—no matter how tenuous her connection to the parties involved—was a personal attack.

Her failed prospects had included the aspiring comedy writer who spent half an hour describing the plot of an episode of *The Simpsons*, the physicist who revealed as they sat down for a drink that his wife had died so recently that a tub of her Greek yogurt was still in his fridge, and the magazine editor who said he found books by women "too contrived."

The latest false start was a self-styled tech entrepreneur. They went out four times, which was more than enough to realize they liked each other better as strangers. He was an early adopter and an early ejaculator, the former by far the more irritating quality.

Adrian-the-lawyer's only social media presence was a Twitter account where he re-tweeted serious political articles with lengthy, smart-sounding commentary that began "we should all be terrified of this: THREAD (1/x)." His bio read *Attorney. My favorite movie is* The Lake House. Jane loved when men were unapologetic about liking the terrible things marketed to women. In college, she once gave a guy her number because he was eating a Luna Bar.

~

"So, *The Lake House*. I don't want to alarm you, but the time-travel conceit in that movie is a goddamn mess." Jane was drunk enough to obliquely admit that she had lurked in Adrian's internet shadows. He wasn't handsome, exactly, but he had picked a bar with lighting that suited his angles. He had a pointy face that looked a little like the cartoon fox version of Robin Hood.

"But the time travel's not the point, really! I have a whole thing about it. But look, it's getting me all riled up! Also, I think maybe I have had a few drinks. So I'm not going to do the *whole* thing, but let me just say I think it's actually about the excuses we make for our own paralysis. I'm prepared to admit that I'm projecting, but I promise it's more convincing when I explain the whole thing." Adrian flushed endearingly. Jane had the urge to kiss his cheek, so she kissed his cheek.

"Oh God, I'm sorry," she said. "That was a weird thing to do. I don't usually do that on dates. I mean, I do weird things on dates sometimes, and weird things in general, but that particular one was sort of like . . . I don't know. I guess it actually wasn't that weird, was it? *You're* the weird one! You really like *The Lake House*! Haha, no, just kidding!" Jane had a keen sense of when to shut up, but only when she was sober.

"Want to get out of here?" Adrian asked, offering her his hand.

~

The sex was a solid "fine," which she upgraded to "good" in her head because it was only the first time, and because she liked him. "That was *amazing,*" she said.

"Yeah, good job us."

The first person plural made Jane's belly flutter. She turned her head to look at him. She'd already decided she could love him. On the walk to his apartment, he kept grazing her ass with his hand and lingering there. She'd had sex with him partly because she wanted to, but mostly as a favor to him, so he'd feel like he owed her something.

"We should do it again sometime," Jane said, aiming for jokey-sexy. "Except I'm probably going away for a few days soon." She tried to hedge her desire—want was only sexy if you were already sexy. "I'm going to a very weird leadership retreat. It was either that or getting fired from my terrible job, so I figured, leadership retreat."

"Good instincts," he yawned. "That sounds more fun than getting fired. Quitting has its charms, though." Jane was grateful he had picked up her tone. She hated when she tossed out self-deprecation and got whacked with pity. Adrian wriggled up onto an elbow. "What's the deal with the retreat?"

"I work in PR—I know." She rolled her eyes elaborately, in case he thought she took herself even a little seriously. "And I have to drum up new business. So I found this bullshitty spiritual retreat place on Instagram that seems sort of on-brand for us, or whatever." She didn't want to tell him about the beautiful woman in case it invited comparisons. "And I've been emailing with this one guy there. His emails read a little like computer-generated poetry, and I sort of like that more than, like, bro guru earnestness. Also they *really* like zucchini."

"Wait, shit. What's it called? Is it—"

"FortPath," they said in unison.

Adrian sat up straight. His voice was suddenly serious. "Yeah, that's just straight up a cult. My cousin is in it. She did that seminar shit last year, and was just, like, *weird* after. She goes back all the time. But it's really freaky. She just *talks* weird. She was in a theater MFA, but she dropped out, probably because it was too expensive to pay for that and keep going to these retreats."

Jane didn't point out that dropping out of an MFA program wasn't exactly moving to a compound in Guyana. When she dropped out of her PhD program, most of her friends seemed relieved for her. She waited for Adrian to say something definitively damning—something beyond *my cousin recently cut her losses on an impractical dream before accruing further student debt.* But that was apparently all he had.

"But . . . she's happy? Like, it doesn't sound like they're one of the *bad* cults. I think *cult* is one of those words that's losing its potency, anyway. When you think about what it really means." *Cult* made no sense with the photos of the woman. Cult leaders weren't beautiful. In the documentaries, people spoke of their magnetism and their charisma and their raw sexual power, but they were usually deeply average-looking men with unflattering haircuts. She felt almost offended on the woman's behalf.

On the other hand, she really wanted him to like her. "Anyway, aren't a lot of things low-grade cults these days? Like CrossFit? And *The New Yorker*?"

"*The New Yorker*?"

"Don't you think it's sort of creepy how *everyone* has that one tote bag?"

"Look, I know we just met and it's not my place to give you life advice, but I'm going to exercise the rarely invoked Cult Clause in the First-Date Codes and Statutes and strongly urge you to find another potential client. Hey, my sister is really trying to get her YouTube makeup tutorial career off the ground." He gripped her wrist. Jane wondered if a search of *earnest concern + proprietary physical contact* would turn up anything on Pornhub.

"Maybe I can just—" She tugged at the waistband of the basketball shorts he had put on after they fucked.

"Oh yeah. Just . . . I guess I should probably have said this before. I'm not really looking for anything serious right now. We can definitely keep hanging out. I just didn't want you to get the wrong idea." He looked at his erection sheepishly. "I think you're really cool, though."

chapter 4.

Adrian's postcoital pre-rejection hurt in a dull, familiar way. Jane's dating life suffered from the same affliction as her professional one. She was a try-hard in love, but one who lacked the kernel of talent necessary to grow her enthusiasm into anything like proficiency. She had been a boy-crazy kid who became a man-mentally-ill adult.

When Byron went to Berlin, they had only been dating for a month, and the degree to which she missed him alarmed her. Ordinarily, she would have tried to keep the feeling to herself, allowing it to ooze out around the edges as a few too many text messages, or else a feint at coldness. By this time, though, Byron had tricked her into trusting him, so instead she assembled an elaborate care package for him. She would later cringe to remember the level of thought and preparation that went into it.

At a used bookstore, she found a copy of James Joyce's children's book *The Cat and the Devil,* and though Byron had never expressed a particular interest in Joyce, it felt like such a perfect combination of whimsical and literary that Jane didn't blink at the $75 price tag. More humiliating even than the book was the novelty carrot-sharpening device she found at a Danish general store. She was charmed by its uselessness, and the fact that it was shaped like a large pencil sharpener. It only cost $2.50, which somehow made it worse—why had she sent it across an ocean? Did Germans even eat raw carrots? She added a small box of Q-tips, which he had once mentioned he used every day but never remembered to bring on trips, and an interesting rock from his favorite part of Prospect Park. (Three weeks. He was gone for *three weeks.*)

In an effort to add some summer-camp-ish levity she included a homemade Mad Lib about how much she missed him. Instead of signing it *Love,* she left the valediction blank with the specification "amorous noun."

Byron was gracious about the package, but there was a reservedness to his response that raised her hackles. After that, she made an effort to hold something of herself back, but she couldn't—not in any essential way. He never said *I love you,* and she never said it out loud.

Jane was lonely, but more than that, she was afraid of all future loneliness, and afraid of what her aloneness said about her. She was afraid of having to learn to do the things she'd been putting off, like figuring out exactly what a 401(k) was, because learning felt like acquiescing to the aloneness.

When she was in her early twenties, Jane sometimes fantasized about an ill-advised first marriage, a city hall wedding and a rooftop reception, the guests talking mild shit because she and the unnamed groom barely knew each other. She never considered how awful the inevitable divorce would be, only what a good story it would make later. She would be able to tell future dates about it and they would know that she was the kind of girl whose irresistibility inspired terrible decisions.

Now Jane was at an age where the weddings were assumed, and only shit-talked behind closed doors. She still had no idea what she wanted from an actual marriage, only that she wanted one, because the alternative was too dire. She knew there was no possibility of being happy alone, or even being able to fake it confidently. Parties would be out of the question.

~

Despite her skepticism about Adrian's cult claim, Jane kept thinking about it. In truth, she had long suspected that some part of her was constitutionally suited for cult life. Not a murderous cult, though she felt some sympathy for Patricia Krenwinkel, the homeliest Manson girl, who said she followed him because he called her beautiful, which seemed like a better reason than thinking he was Jesus Christ.

Jane thought about the number of men she'd fucked in gratitude for compliments (or approximate compliments; she once gave a guy a hand job because he said her hair looked long). It was the flattery, of course, but not only that. Jane wanted the truth, too. She needed more information about her parts, and their quality. She wanted to be a reliable narrator. She couldn't decide how to live in the world until she knew what kind of person she was.

In college, she decided she liked poetry because the professor of her Romanticism seminar wrote *Good insights!* on her final essay about John Clare. She dutifully narrowed her focus and eventually applied to PhD programs once she heard you didn't have to pay for them, and that in fact, they paid *you.*

Though she came to hate the program, she liked having a shorthand for her essential self, even if she knew it was a lie. She was still looking for the real elevator pitch for Jane.

She wanted to be brainwashed with compliments because that sounded nice, like a long, hot shower, but she also wanted to be slapped with the truth of herself. She imagined it like a platza scrub at a Russian bathhouse, abrasive but also greasy. Embarrassing, but ultimately refreshing. And on the other side, she would smell like earth and blood and extra-virgin olive oil.

chapter 5.

On Saturday, a week before she was set to leave, Jane woke up with the beginning of a pimple on her chin and some overall dullness in her T-zone. She thought about the FortPath woman and her glowing skin, and wondered if the secret really could be the combination of zucchini and fearlessness. Like everyone, Jane wanted to have the skin of an infant—preferably the only child of a wealthy older couple.

Having flawless skin was about more than natural beauty. If your skin glowed, it didn't matter as much what the rest of your face looked like. Good skin signaled discipline and prosperity and health and virtuous contentment and, above all, being cared for, like that rich infant, whose good fortune had been assured from the moment of implantation in the office of a very expensive reproductive specialist.

In the pursuit of good skin, Jane spent hours on internet message boards, reading about the morning routines and night regimens and scarring and sebaceous filaments and hyperpigmentation and damaged moisture barriers and hormonal acne and age-related inelasticity of internet strangers.

She was better equipped than most to see through the hype. She worked in the industry—albeit in the damp basement of the industry—and she knew that skincare lore was the result of women like her puffing up their cheeks and blowing gusts of hot air and claiming they were acts of a god who was finally ready to gift you with the skin of your dreams. Still: *maybe*. She was like a cultural Catholic who no longer believed but went to church because she claimed to like the ritual and stained glass but was still secretly hoping to see a statue cry.

In the mornings, she applied a gentle micellar water that had a French name but was produced by the largest consumer chemical manufacturer in America, followed by an alcohol-free toner, to maintain her skin's delicate pH balance and possibly shrink her pores (though there was some dispute about the latter). She then smeared on a sticky vitamin C solution that promised to fade her skin's dark spots (she didn't really have any—maybe because of the serum?) and impart a dewy glow. After that, she scrubbed on an exfoliant with gentle upward circles that didn't make it sting any less. After the exfoliant, she used a few drops of a retinol serum, which cost $135 a bottle, promised to halt the aging process indefinitely, and smelled like those trees that smell like semen.

The routine was always in flux. Anytime she read about a new ingredient she folded it into the regimen, but nothing ever got cut. It seemed safer to keep using everything, just in case her face operated like a garden, its secret radiance waiting to burst forth. She was cultivating. She couldn't afford to pay a doctor to inject her with face-reshaping agents, but her email drafts folder was cluttered with the names of new "miracle fillers"—Hebederm, Catavol, Leyoxin. It was only a matter of time.

~

Jane called her mother while she walked to the dry cleaner's to pick up the violet peplum dress she hated but that always got her compliments at PR events. She didn't especially want to talk to her mother, but she wanted to talk to someone, and her mother was the only one with any obligation to her.

Her mother was unflaggingly supportive, but in recent years a distance had grown between them for no reason other than the fact that her mother's life had expanded since Jane had left home, and Jane's had only contracted.

Jane had a constellation of friends, but no unifying group, and no aptitude for maintenance. She hadn't had a best friend since Eleanor. They met when they both showed up at an open call for hair models (Eleanor was selected, Jane wasn't) and rattled through their early twenties together, sleeping off hangovers in each other's beds, pathologizing the guys that didn't text them back, and GChatting through the drudgery of their incidental office jobs. They stayed close when Jane was in grad school and Eleanor began to take her work in book publishing seriously, but they hadn't spoken in over a year. There hadn't been any ceremony to the friendship's end, no obvious blowup or confrontation, just a fading that felt violent only in retrospect, in the lonely late-night moments when Jane forced herself to concede that it was mostly her fault. Sometimes Jane still had the urge to reach out, but her last two texts (*omg, just saw roller blades joey on the subway!*; *ru ok?*) had gone unanswered.

Jane tried not to think about how much she missed closeness in general and Eleanor specifically, but her mother still asked about Eleanor every time they spoke.

Sometimes Jane couldn't bear to hear about the fullness of her mother's days and so she called less frequently, and her mother called less frequently because she was inevitably taking an improv class or working at a CSA for low-income families or having a date night with Dave.

Jane was abstractly happy for her. Dave was the first man her mother had dated since Jane's father had left twenty years earlier, and he was very *nice*—even his humorlessness was perfectly amiable. Her mother told her often how much Dave admired Jane's social conscience and work ethic, which was *nice* even though it struck her as complete bullshit because Dave's daughter was a teacher at a therapeutic preschool for children with PTSD.

Dave had slightly more money than her mother, who herself had slightly more money than she'd had during Jane's childhood, when she was studying for a degree in social work at night and working as a receptionist at their small city's third-best podiatry practice.

There had usually been just enough, but the atmosphere in the house was always just a little tense, like at any moment something could go terribly, expensively wrong. Which, of course, it could.

Jane's mother didn't pressure her to achieve—she'd

found her own moderately paid bliss later in life, after all—but the financial friction of Jane's childhood made her long for smoothness. Smoothness was what the Instagram women had, whether by money or beauty or beauty-dependent money.

Jane had, miraculously, made it through college without having to take out the kind of crushing student loans that were her generation's defining accessory. Her mother's social worker salary was low enough to qualify Jane for a generous financial aid package, and her mother took out loans herself to pay for Jane's room, board, and books. Jane knew she was lucky, but mostly she resented having to believe she was lucky.

Jane's mother didn't know about the medical debt. When Jane told her that insurance covered everything, her mother's long, long sigh of relief told her she'd done the right thing. But she didn't know how much more not-knowing their relationship could withstand.

"Sweetheart!" Her mother sounded happy and distracted when she picked up the phone—the Dave effect. "What's doing with you?"

"Nothing. Errands." She hadn't decided what to say about FortPath. Jane was never sure if she wanted to provoke her mother to worry about her, or reassure her she was fine, so she usually went with some combination that left both of them edgy.

"How's work?"

"Busy," she said. Her mother claimed to think Jane's job was interesting and glamorous, just as she had claimed to think graduate school was impressive and noble.

Her mother had grown up with some money—enough for brand-new cars and middling private schools. Jane's grandfather was a pilot until he and her grandmother decided to open a travel agency together in the 1970s, which failed almost immediately, taking their savings with it. They both died before Jane was born, and apart from occasionally fact-checking a TV show's in-flight stagecraft, her mother rarely talked about them.

Jane suspected her mother had access to some secret money-having codes that would have made Jane feel less uncomfortable in expensive stores, but she seemed to have scrubbed them from her memory.

"I'm going to a work thing next weekend, actually," she told her mother. "A spa thing. Or more like a spiritual retreat, I guess."

"That sounds *great,*" her mother said, suddenly serious. "I think it's a great idea for you to take care of your mental health. How's Eleanor, by the way?"

"She's fine, Mom. And this isn't therapy."

"Did I say therapy?"

Jane had tried therapy a few times, but it never stuck. She always wanted the therapist to give her the secrets to becoming a different person. She wasn't interested in a belief system that told her she was already enough, that the bare facts of her were not the real problem. She wanted action items. She wanted a chemical peel for her personality.

"It's more about skincare, really," she told her mother.

"Well, I think your skin is beautiful."

Jane heard the smile in her mother's voice. She didn't remember her mother smiling much when Jane was growing up. She was affectionate, but more fiercely than playfully. Her hugs were vacuum-tight, like she was afraid Jane was on the verge of splitting apart.

Maybe she'd started getting happier before Dave, once she finished school and started doing the work she loved, but Jane still blamed Dave for turning her mother into someone less familiar to her, someone for whom calm was the default. Now Jane's constant worries felt inappropriate, like a maudlin toast at a wedding.

"Sweetheart?" her mother said. "Anything else you need? Dave and I are headed to the farmers market."

In the background, Dave called, "Rhubarb season!"

It was possible she hated Dave.

chapter 6.

The FortPath shuttle turned out to be just a livery cab, with a wonderfully taciturn driver whose name, according to the laminated license on his back seat, was Emanuel. Tom had offered her a choice of two departure times, six-thirty or eleven-thirty, and registered surprise when she selected the latter.

The farm was two hours from New York. She scrolled through the Welcome Packet that Tom had emailed her. This is *YOUR* Time to Thrive! You need only bring a Waiting Soul, a Fearless Curiosity, and an Open Energy (open to both Giving and Receiving!). **Please note that even if your visit is in the summer months, the Farm gets chilly at night, so you may Wish to bring a sweater/jacket. She tried to doze, but she was too anxious. She hadn't brought any snacks (Please! No Outside food or drink. Nutritional Mindfulness is essential to Your FortPath Experience.), and she was already hungry.

She wondered if the food was part of a brainwashing. Nutritional Mindfulness sounded menacing, but maybe no more than other kinds of mindfulness—sustained attention of any kind made her nervous. Despite Adrian's warning, it seemed unlikely that FortPath was a cult. If it were a cult, someone would already have made a podcast about it.

~

As the cab turned into FortPath's driveway, Jane felt something like the first-day-of-camp hopefulness of a fresh start, undercut by a pang of fear over the amount of effort she would have to expend to convince these people she was a PR professional worthy of their business. She breathed deeply and tried to summon competence. An enormous mint-green Victorian with a turret and a wraparound front porch towered over her. It looked like a dollhouse that had sat in someone's attic for too long. From closer up, the paint job was disastrous—large swaths had flaked off, revealing Pepto-Bismol-pink paint underneath that looked like diseased skin. There were half a dozen large geese perched on the roof, like sharpshooters.

From certain angles, the house was supremely Instagrammable. From others, it looked like a feral child's art project. Fields stretched behind the house, but Jane could see only a few rows of green leaves and little yellow flowers growing there. There was a small circle of people sitting on the front lawn. They looked relaxed, and not obviously brainwashed. Jane cracked her window and heard their laughter. She wondered if they knew one another from before or if all this bonding had occurred in the early van. She felt like a fool for choosing extra sleep over potential inclusion.

A woman in yoga pants who looked like the second lead in a supernatural teen drama—tiny and forgettably hot—wore a sweatshirt that said NORMALIZE MAGIC. One man wore a saffron caftan, which read more fashion than faithful. A guy in a snug cream henley approached the driver's side. He passed a wad of bills to the driver through the window and said, "Thank you, Emanuel." He sounded stilted, like a child actor in a local TV commercial. "We really honor the work you do."

He turned to her. "Jane. Welcome to FortPath. I'm Tom. We're so happy you've joined us."

She smiled her bright, PR Jane smile at him; he was just shy of handsome, with long eyebrows and a wide mouth with deep brackets at its sides. His skin was otherwise unblemished and radiant. Jane wondered if the house stood in a microclimate of good lighting, but when she glanced at her arm it looked the same as always. Emanuel got out of the car and took Jane's canvas duffel from the trunk, gently launching it onto the yellow lawn, right into a pile of goose poop, before driving away.

"Before lunch, I'll give you a brief orientation," Tom said, picking up her bag. "Follow me."

~

He led her through a door at the side of the house and into the kitchen, guiding her to a large weathered picnic table in the middle of the room. The wood felt damp through her leggings when she sat down. Tom retrieved a large binder from the counter and sat down across from her.

"Jane," he said. "Welcome to your life."

In spite of herself, Jane felt the same tingling in her sinuses that overtook her when she saw a blandly inspirational TED Talk, or one of those commercials where a dog welcomes a veteran home—her body's small, humiliating rebellion against cynicism.

"I'm *so, so* thrilled to be here," she said. "What an incredible space."

"I'm going to give you a brief personality assessment to help us establish your Fear Zones," Tom told her, leafing through the binder. "Question one: Please describe your primary life force."

She caught her laugh just in time, but ended up coughing for so long that Tom silently poured her a jar of water from a carafe in the middle of the table. She'd assumed that the green disks floating inside were cucumber, but when she took a sip she realized they were zucchini, and began coughing again. By then, she could only remember that the question had been ridiculous, and had to ask him to repeat himself.

"Is there . . . could you give me an example of a life force?" she said.

"There are no right or wrong answers here. This is just a way for us to get to know you a little better," Tom said. He seemed a little thrown by her question. She couldn't have been the first one to ask for clarification, could she?

"Okay, well, I guess . . . love?" It seemed unassailable. It might even be true. Tom made a note in the binder.

"And would you characterize yourself as inward-manifesting or outward-contemplating?"

"Probably inward-manifesting?"

"Great. And do you perceive the world as fundamentally open or fundamentally still?"

"Are those opposites?"

"Do you perceive them as opposites?" Tom said, either perplexed or annoyed.

"That's why I asked. The question sort of sets them up as opposites but . . . are they opposites?"

"I sense that you're trying to answer these questions with your conscious mind. It's better if you follow your heart center."

Jane's skepticism was not bone-deep. It seemed possible that other people really could answer questions from their heart centers, and that her inability to do so said something more damning about her than the exercise. She tried to picture her heart, its muscled center.

"Fundamentally still. I guess." Her voice came out gruff, like she was doing a dad impression.

"Any food intolerances?"

"No!" she said loudly, excited to be sure of an answer. Tom looked at her like he was trying to suss out a trick. She smiled back in a way she hoped was professional and nonthreatening.

"I'm going to give you a brief overview of the weekend. Unfortunately, you've missed the Healing Welcome."

"There were options for two departure times."

"Yes?" Tom said without looking up from his binder.

"I took the later one. I just think maybe you shouldn't

give people an option if they're going to miss something by choosing one of the choices."

"Life is a path through a garden of choices, and every choice is a compromise." He paused. "Did you just roll your eyes?"

"No! I'm just disappointed I missed the Health Welcome."

"*Healing* Welcome." He rolled his eyes.

"Did you just roll *your* eyes?" she asked. He rolled them again, then broke. The exchange felt sweetly, chastely flirtatious. Jane was almost entirely sure he was gay. There was something appraising in how he regarded her, but with no detectable microexpression of sexual evaluation, no flicker of hostility that might signal attraction or its opposite. He could have been comparing different brands of cottage cheese.

There was something else about Tom, too. Working in PR had sharpened Jane's skill at demographically assessing people. She could usually clock sexual orientation and income bracket via careful observation and reliance on stereotypes, which she told herself wasn't offensive per se, but made her more efficient at her job, and didn't all advertising rely on stereotypes anyway? Sitting across from Tom, she noticed that he didn't seem comfortable in his skin, but his self-consciousness seemed unmoored from some of the social trappings of masculinity, possibly because he'd already transcended them.

Jane gravitated toward gay men, though not for any kind of fetishistic reasons (at least not in the traditional sense). She just liked being around men whose implicit rejection didn't feel personal. Being friends with a straight man who had chosen not to try to fuck her seemed humiliating. She might have considered a friendship with a man who had tried unsuccessfully to fuck her, but it had never come up. She liked being around men, though, because she didn't constantly compare herself with them. That all of her friendship decisions were made based on not upsetting the delicate balance of her self-détente was a problem she tried not to think about. With Eleanor there had been more parity. Eleanor was plagued with doubt, too, which offset the threat of her shiny, fast-growing hair and tiny waist.

"Next is lunch, then the Honor Circle, then Humbled Silence, then Unguided Reflection, then Dinner, then Rest. Tomorrow morning is Rise, then Mindful Spatialism, then Earth Communion, then Breakfast, then Active Silence, then Self-Structured Manifestation, then Lunch, then Power Grounding, then Dinner, then Rest," Tom said.

It was almost impressive how little sense the words made. At least there were three meals a day. She was already hungry.

chapter 7.

Lunch was "a nest of spiralized zucchini and activated pistachios sprinkled with bee pollen, shiitake shavings, and sprouted heirloom microgreens." It was mostly flavorless, but texturally fascinating—like eating a whole garden, dirt and vermiculite and worms and all. It looked beautiful. She thought about Instagramming it but in the end her hunger won out. She finished in four minutes and was somehow hungrier than before she ate.

There were six of them at FortPath, not including Jane. Or Tom. Or someone named Cass, who was meditating somewhere. ("Cass has to meditate for at least four hours a day, sometimes longer," Tom said.) Jane had been awaiting the arrival of the Instagram woman since she pulled up. She hadn't wanted to ask Tom in case he took it—as she would have—as a comment on his orienting abilities. The thought had also occurred to her that the Instagram woman could be a trap, a paid spokesperson intended to lure the envious strivers. But of course Cass was she. The name fit her photos perfectly.

Everyone was between the ages of twenty-seven and forty, and their studied insouciance said they were rich, or knew how to fake it. Individually, they weren't all beautiful, but together they looked like an ad for a segregated yoga studio: slim and radiant and unambiguously white.

Everyone around Jane was deep in conversation. They were all so easy with one another that she wondered if she had been years late rather than hours. She made an inventory of everyone: To her left was a man who had late-stage Nicolas Cage eyes, sad but not pitiable. He wore an artfully moth-eaten cardigan over his caftan. She knew his name was Josh because the man he was speaking to kept saying his name, like an incantation, in response to a horrible story Josh was telling about his ongoing acrimonious divorce.

Across from Jane, a translucently pale redhead who would have been pretty if she had a chin was whispering to a very handsome man in a wide-brimmed hat, who kept looking around like he couldn't decide if there was a better conversation to be had elsewhere. His eyes alighted on Jane several times, but in a way that suggested short-term amnesia more than flirtation. The redhead seemed determined not to notice his inattention.

Farren, the sharp-featured pixie in the yoga pants, was to her right, feet tucked under her on her chair. She had only eaten half her bowl. She was talking to a woman with very long, very fine blond hair about heart fires and cauldrons of change. Eventually, the blond woman stood up, and Farren turned her attention to Jane.

"We don't really do the small-talk thing here, but I think it's helpful to know what people *do* because it says a lot about your soul's mandate. Also"—she lowered her voice—"this place is seriously *amazing* for networking. My friend came here last month and she met an angel investor who fully funded her direct-to-consumer dairy project."

Farren was the social media manager for a start-up that connected people who wanted to sell their airline tickets with people who had their same names.

"Sky/twin facilitates commodities transfers, essentially. We've actually disrupted the entire air travel market. Imagine if all your tickets were fully refundable, with no extra fees whatsoever. Except the small fee that we charge for the service," she said. This was her second stint at FortPath. "Our founder knows Cass from boarding school or Burning Man or something."

Even though Jane's own reasons for attending were purely professional, she hated Farren, with her naked ambition and her slick elevator pitch, immediately. *What is it about her that you don't like about yourself?* her mother, with the wisdom of an in-progress social work degree, would ask her anytime she complained about a girl at school. She had resented it at the time, and now that she was older and found the sentiment to be true again and again, she resented it even more.

"Wow, that sounds *incredible*!" Jane said. "I'd love to hear more about what drew you to FortPath specifically. Have you ever done anything like this before?"

"I go on, like, five yoga retreats a year. I was in Costa

Rica last weekend. It's really important to me to improve myself. But not, like, *selfishly*. If I'm the best version of *myself*, it inspires everyone around me to be the best version of *themselves*."

"Oh, wow, totally!" Jane said. "So you must do a lot of volunteer work, too." She couldn't help herself. Farren looked at her with suspicion. Jane smiled back encouragingly.

"I'm a little tired right now," Farren said, and walked out of the kitchen.

~

If she hadn't been so hungry (could she really be the only one?), the Honor Circle would have felt like an auspicious start to the weekend. They gathered on the lawn after lunch. It was warm for May, high humidity and blazing sun. The grass was wet and studded with little piles of goose poop. No one was wearing shoes except Jane. She wondered if she could take them off without anyone noticing, just casually, like *Oh yeah, I always take my shoes off right before the Honor Circle, just one of my little quirks!* But she decided not to draw more attention to herself.

Tom explained that they needed to recognize their strengths as well as the strengths of others, and honor those strengths. Jane loved compliments with a fervor that embarrassed her. This didn't translate to being an expert complimenter of others—she homed in on too-specific details that made people feel observed rather than appreciated, like the pronunciation of a certain letter, or the way hair looked tucked behind an ear. Even in poetry world, land of maddening specificity, it unsettled people.

Compliments could be dangerous (see: ill-fated PhD decision), but she continued to chase them. She still enjoyed the sense of recognition she'd once gotten when a high school friend told her she was funny. Actually, what he'd said was *You're the funniest girl I know,* though it didn't occur to her to be offended on behalf of girls. But since then, she allowed herself to believe that yes, she was funny. So she started to collect laughter, too. The problem with relying on others to define her was that others were only slightly more reliable than she was. She had to stay vigilant in case someone got her wrong.

"Jane, you took the step of coming here, which is so honest and important. And you have nice table manners, which is also super important for thriving. Like if you have to do a breakfast with someone. And also I feel like you've really figured out what kind of clothes work for your body. And I honor you for all those things." Farren pressed her prayer hands to her sternum and gave a shallow bow.

"Hello, my loves."

The woman from Instagram floated over from the trees, loose-limbed in linen pants and a threadbare tank top. Jane sat up straighter as she watched the woman whisper something in Tom's ear. He gave a single nod. "In gratitude to Cass for sharing with us the clarity she gained from her meditation time today, I'd like to gift this time to her."

Jane heard someone breathing hard and thought, *How embarrassing,* before realizing it was her. She had both hoped and feared that the pictures were enhanced, that the woman didn't actually glow as she appeared to on Instagram. Weren't people always insisting that Instagram wasn't real life? Cass was even more captivating in person.

Cass beamed, then locked eyes with Jane across the circle and stared at her with a newlywed's intensity. Jane had wanted to continue staring at Cass unobserved, and the reciprocity felt almost unbearable. Still, Jane was determined not to blink first. It was only after Cass broke the gaze that she realized it wasn't a staring contest. Instead, Cass was going around the circle, making some variation of the eyes at everyone. Some of the moments seemed to have a *Meet me in the bathroom* dirtiness, while others appeared tenderer. When she was finished with their eyes, she sat down on the ground and invited them all to join her.

"When I was a child, my greatest love was trees," she began. "I also loved crystals and truth, but trees: They were these perfect, alien beings. And everyone I knew ignored them. I would sit next to them, and touch their bark, and bring home the leaves that had fallen. And then one day, I saw a group of children climbing one. At first I was shocked. It seemed disrespectful to me, treating a tree like a jungle gym, there for your amusement."

When Jane was a child, *her* greatest love was Marshmallow Fluff. After her father left, she could convince her mother to buy it a few times a year. Jane would sneak into the kitchen in the middle of the night and bring it into bed with her so she could eat spoonfuls under the covers. Once she fell asleep with the lid off the jar and woke up with her hair so sticky and matted that her mother had to cut chunks of it out.

"But the longer I stood there watching them, the more I yearned to share the experience. I tried to convince myself that climbing the tree was a way to commune with her. In my mind, I asked the tree, and I made myself believe that it had told me that being climbed was one of life's great joys for a tree, that she truly loved getting kicked by those dirty little sneakers. The next day, I climbed a tree. I didn't even ask her permission; I was so certain of my right to do it. I climbed until the branch I was standing on cracked. While I was lying on the ground, the tree began to scream at me. She told me I was a burden, a weight, a stranger.

"*We are not your great friends,* she said. *You thought you heard us, but you were always speaking to yourself alone. We hear you, and we choose not to answer. We deign to speak to you now only because we can't bear you anymore. The children who climb us thoughtlessly are forgivable, but you are arrogant. Humble yourself.* My arm was broken in two places. I didn't look at a tree again for two years. When I passed them, I lowered my eyes. I humbled myself. At the end of the first year I permitted myself to look at their shadows." She smiled. "But I didn't deceive myself into thinking the trees had given me that permission. I knew I was giving myself permission. On the second anniversary of my fall, I decided I had been adequately humbled. Now I look at trees all the time. But I never, ever speak to them."

The story was so bizarre that Jane was almost impressed. She had expected Cass to speak in generic Yoga Instagram quotes. Vengeful Tree Fable was much more interesting. It was also the preface to Humbled Silence, two hours during which they would sit in a circle without speaking or moving.

"This won't be a directed silence," Cass said. "But I may be pulled to adjust you if I feel you're on the brink of something." She explained that the optimal Humbled Silence position was Dandasana, but Sukhasana was also acceptable. Jane had never done yoga and was hoping one of those meant lying down, but everyone was upright, with their legs either crossed or extended. Her stomach grumbled loudly. Farren scowled at her.

It had been two years since Jane had taken a shower without listening to a podcast. Once her phone died on the subway platform late at night, and the only reading material she had was a pamphlet from her gynecologist about cervical cancer screening. By the time she got home, she had committed most of it to memory.

It wasn't that she was afraid of being bored; she was afraid of being alone with herself. Even when diluted by media, her thoughts were cruel. No one had ever been able to talk her out of what she knew for sure: Her meanest thoughts were right. Acknowledging them only made them louder.

Yes, I know, I wasted every moment of my education by being too timid to ask questions and too lazy to find the answers myself. Of course, I understand, I'll never be in a relationship because my needs and expectations are unreasonable for someone who is me. Got it. Check. Oh and yes, I do realize that an ability to remember everything anyone has ever said about me is not the same as a sense of self.

Her only defense was distraction. Wasn't that why podcasts were so popular? Wasn't everyone trying to escape themselves? Evidently not—ten minutes into Humbled Silence and the faces around her suggested serene satiety.

Her eyes were supposed to be closed. She wanted to feel serene. She wanted not to feel so goddamn hungry. Jane often feigned fullness when it seemed appropriate, when everyone around her was complaining about how much they had eaten (usually not that much), but at least she could follow it up with a secret snack. Still, it seemed impossible she was the only person in the circle who hadn't been sufficiently nourished by the meager portion of pollinated zucchini crunch.

When she was younger, adults had always told her how *healthy* she looked, as if the badge of honor for a woman weren't the opposite. But now that people like Cass were claiming *healthy* for themselves, what was left for the sturdier women? *Healthy* now meant *smug and highly oxygenated and glowing and reed-like and able to be silent for days at a time without being psychologically murdered by my own thoughts.*

How long had it been? There was no way of knowing. She cracked an eye; across the circle, Cass was sitting behind Josh, legs spread, as he lay back into her. She embraced him, and he started to shudder with silent sobs. So maybe it had been longer than it seemed? How long did it take to get to the sob stage of Humbled Silence? She wanted to be comforted by Cass, but what if she sobbed and Cass didn't come to her and she just had to cry alone in a circle of strangers?

Maybe Cass would touch her even if she didn't cry. Maybe Cass could see something special and interesting in her that no one else saw. Maybe that was part of her power. Jane wondered if Cass and Tom were fucking, or, again, if Tom was gay. After some amount of time, she felt Cass behind her. She sat down, back-to-back with Jane. Cass leaned into her, pushing her forward, face to feet. It felt good at first, like a stretch. She tried to feel the stretch as more than just a stretch, to allow herself to be pushed over the edge of whatever Cass had sensed in her. She suddenly felt something in her gut. But not a good, spiritual something. She opened her eyes; they were at least a hundred yards from the house.

"Um, Cass," she whispered. "Sorry, I really have to go to the bathroom. I think something from lunch isn't sitting right."

"Physical discomfort is a manifestation of spiritual sickness," Cass murmured. "The best thing you can do for your body is to sit with the Humbled Silence. Don't talk. *Listen.*"

"Right, of course, it's just that right now I think my body is telling me it needs a bathroom immediately." She was starting to sweat. Her stomach suddenly felt like a knot of snakes, roiling and malevolent.

"Don't enforce order on your body. Sit deeply in your experience."

Did Cass *want* her to shit herself? She weighed the risk versus reward of running. Cass was still leaning hard against her. Jane dug her fists into the ground and pushed back, clenching her butt like a vise. Even more than usual, not shitting herself felt like a question of honor; she couldn't let Cass win this one. People like Cass won all the ones. *You may be beautiful and charismatic, but I have control of my bowels.*

Cass leaned harder, until they were both hovering an

inch above the ground. Jane wondered if she realized that if Jane did "sit deeply in her experience," Cass was squarely in the splash zone. "I'm going to shit on you!" Jane hissed. "That's not a threat, it's just what's going to happen if I don't go to the bathroom right now!" In response, Cass hummed. It began as a *Hmm,* like *What an interesting fact you've just shared!* but as she drew it out, it reverberated throughout her body and Jane's until they were vibrating together.

The pressure was relentless. Jane's eyes filled from the combination of exertion and restraint. Agonizingly slowly, they rose together, back-to-back, until they were close enough to standing that Jane could break away and trot toward the house. "Let's give thanks to the silence," she heard Cass say behind her.

chapter 8.

Jane emerged from the bathroom feeling an unfamiliar kind of peace within her. The relief of having been spared the humiliation of shitting herself in public was the truest kind of gratitude she could fathom. Maybe that was Cass's whole point. She did feel fairly humbled. The fact that Cass might be willing to teach that lesson even if it meant she was covered in another person's feces was both scary and impressive.

Everyone was still outside. She walked through the house slowly, examining its spare décor. Upstairs, three of the five bedrooms were completely empty; two had mattresses on the floor. In the turret room was an unmade bed, and Jane smelled a brothy, bodily odor, like maybe the sheets hadn't been washed in years. She realized this was probably where Cass slept, because of the piles of gruel-colored clothing on the floor, and so the smell became intriguing rather than repellent.

She walked over to the bed, as if she were just casually

investigating, as if she had no intention of lying down in it. But then she was lying down in it. She pulled the uncovered duvet over her head. The light from outside came through the downy patches. Did everywhere Cass had ever been retain remnants of her good light?

Under the duvet there were also a few loose wooden beads, a thin paintbrush, a small nest of grass, and what looked like shards of magazine paper. Jane rested her cheek against the mattress and breathed in the smell of Cass's humanness.

She heard voices outside, signaling the end of Humbled Silence, and scrambled up. She did her best to restore the bedclothes to their previous state of disarray, though she doubted Cass would notice either way.

~

None of the rooms on the first floor of the house appeared to have a defined function. They were all fair game for anything, or nothing. Blankets, pillows, and foam sleeping mats were piled in the corners. The largest of the rooms—just off the kitchen—was Spartan in a fashionable way. The walls were yellow, and cobwebbed with macramé wall hangings that looked interesting from eight paces, amateurish from five.

A few dozen plants thrived in whitewashed terra-cotta pots: *Monstera deliciosas,* fiddle-leaf figs, clusters of succulents. There was an Eames-style dining chair draped carelessly with a sheepskin rug, and a tall, narrow whitewashed bookcase, whose books were arranged by color, and which was topped with a bust of a woman who might have been Aphrodite. It was the kind of room Jane always had in mind when she shopped for her own home, but the effect was slightly marred by the small piles of cricket husks Jane found everywhere—they were sprinkled around the floor like seasoning—and the aroma of old zucchini, wet and fishy.

Despite the diarrhea and the crickets and the smell, Jane was hungry. She went to the kitchen, determined to eat something, even if it was a fistful of shiitake shavings. Jessica, the redhead, was sitting at the greenish picnic table.

"How was it for you?" she asked. "My first Humbled Silence was so intense. But, like, *great*."

"*So* great, ohmygod!" Jane said, trying to match Jessica's enthusiasm. "So, do you do a lot of meditation usually? What's your spiritual practice like?" In moments like these, Jane felt good at her job.

"I use a meditation app *every day*," Jessica said.

"That's *amazing*."

"Cass says most people treat their brains like lab rats going through a maze, when really we should treat them like wild rats. The way they want us to live makes us blind, *literally blind*, to possibility. And it makes us really sick. A lot of us are sick already. Brando is here because of his chronic pain. He thinks it's a combination of unresolved trauma and black mold, but doctors keep telling him he's fine. Cass says most diseases were fully invented by drug companies."

"Most?"

"Probably sixty percent, at least."

The confidence required to claim that more than half

of diseases were drug company inventions was unfathomable to Jane. She wondered if Cass actually believed it. Somehow, she hoped so.

"So, is he feeling better? Brando?" Jane asked.

"Oh, definitely. I mean, the food *alone*. It's so healing. Almost no one in America is getting enough kelp."

"Is there anything I could eat right now?" Jane asked in a *just between us girls* way. "I'm, like, really hungry."

"Cass says snacks wreak havoc on our satiety signals and put our brains and bodies at odds." Jessica smiled. "I missed them, too, at first. But I'm basically in complete brain-body alignment now."

"Ohmygod, wait. Are you a Scorpio?" Jane asked.

"No, Pisces. Why, do I seem like a Scorpio?" She sounded alarmed.

"Ooh. A little," said Jane, who knew nothing about astrology.

~

Dinner was more zucchini ribbons, this time with "matcha marinara" and kelp dust. "Kelp is most potent in its resinous form," Tom said.

Because Rise was at five, everyone went to bed at nine.

"Have a fruitful rest, everyone," Tom said as everyone picked up a bedroll from the pile in the corner and carried them off to different corners of the house. There were no other visible bedtime preparations, no changing of clothes or brushing of teeth. Jane hated brushing her teeth, and wondered if the FortPath diet rendered fluoride unnecessary. Cass, of course, had beautiful teeth.

By the time Jane had chosen a spot near the door to

the kitchen, the house was quiet except for the sound of breathing, almost uniform, like she was inside a bellows. She could see bundles of the others in shadows, and the particular loneliness she always felt in the presence of sleeping people began to set in.

The crickets didn't swarm her bedroll as she had feared, but they softly bumped her fingers, like they were all on a full subway together. The bedding's thinness made her uncomfortably aware of her bones. It was hot. God, it was hot. The heat that had seemed pleasant during the day was now soupy and suffocating. Hadn't Tom's emails claimed it was chilly at night?

Jane prided herself on being able to sleep under almost any circumstance, but the prospect of another eight hours on the floor without food was untenable. She hadn't been this hungry since her grad school days when she tried to subsist on capers and mustard every day as both a weight-loss and a money-saving technique. After years of self-soothing with free office candy, she was out of practice at hunger. There must be something in the fridge. Or the cupboard. Or she would dig up the fucking lawn. She was going to eat something. She rose in slow motion and crept to the kitchen.

"Jesus!" She didn't see Tom at the table until she was close enough to blow on his neck.

"Please be quiet," he said sheepishly. He was holding a piece of pizza in one hand, and the other was palm-down on the table, tensed like he might make a run for it. There was a DiGiorno box open before him, hoary with frost. She decided that she definitely liked him, this guy who snuck forbidden dietary toxins in the dark.

"Sorry!" she whispered. "I couldn't sleep. I'm just

really, really hungry. Any chance I could have some of that pizza?" She usually hated inviting herself to anything, but Tom was eating secret pizza; this was mutually assured desperation. He nodded warily.

"Fair warning, though: This pizza is pretty old. And still frozen."

"So . . . come here often?"

"Only sometimes. When I get too hungry and I can't master it. Cass tries really hard to help me with it, but sometimes I slip," he said.

That Tom was hiding his own reserves of need made Jane feel both pity and familiarity. If he had been a shade more pathetic she might have hated him for his resemblance to her, but instead she almost loved him.

She remembered that he was older than she was and felt a pleasant tinge of superiority. They might be kindred losers, but he'd had an extra three years to figure things out.

"I don't think having a snack is so bad," Jane said. Tom didn't respond. Jane picked up a slice and took a small bite. It tasted like almost nothing, like a memory of pizzas past.

"I read an article about you. About the thing at the library. What's the deal with that?" she asked. The darkness emboldened her. Tom was silent for a long time. She was about to apologize when he cleared his throat.

"After college I lost my way. I made some bad choices and started doing too much cocaine. I lost my job and I spiraled. I was spending a lot of time at the library, and I snapped one day when I felt like the librarian wasn't paying attention to me. I know," he said, though Jane was careful to keep her face neutral, even in the dark. "I take full responsibility for my actions." The words were well worn, like he had recited them over and over through the years.

"I went to court-ordered rehab, which was the best thing that ever happened to me. That's where I met Cass. For the second time. We knew each other when we were kids. Cass was a counselor at the facility."

"Wow, the criminal justice system really does reward whiteness."

Jane was a great unpacker of the privilege of others. She was obsessed with the lengths of everyone's head starts. The ostentatious success of rich people's children made her stasis more forgivable, noble even. Her own moderate privilege was of less interest to her, but sometimes she recited her advantages like a penitent Hail Mary when she felt her self-pity veering toward ridiculous.

But she still thought about the time, seven years earlier, when she had gone to dinner with a college friend whose parents were in town. The girl was really a friend of a friend, little more than an acquaintance, and Jane had been surprised and flattered when she invited her to a family event at an expensive restaurant, the kind where the servers are surgically attentive and present you with a wrapped package of flower-flavored cookies at the meal's end.

When she arrived, she realized almost immediately that she was there as her friend's buffer, and likely fourth-string. The father was the head of a major record label, but except for a thin gold hoop in one ear, he looked more like a Republican senator, and spoke like one, too, monologuing about the injustice of tax codes for hardworking people like himself, while his wife and daughter sent messages on their BlackBerries. When they were finished eating, when Jane tried to make herself useful by stacking her friend's empty plate on top of her own, the father snapped at her. *No stacking!* She wondered how everyone else knew things before it was too late.

Terrible as the evening had been, Jane felt strangely at home in her discomfort. The father was saying out loud what she suspected everyone thought: *You don't belong.*

Tom certainly had some kind of a head start. He was a white man, and something about him suggested wealth—there was an effortlessness even in his awkwardness. And his shirtsleeves. He was wearing a blue chambray button-down with the sleeves pushed up in a way Jane had often tried to replicate, at home in front of the mirror. Hers always looked wrong, too labored somehow.

"My lawyer was a friend of my father's roommate," Tom continued. "From Harvard. He knew the judge from somewhere. I got probation and rehab. The lawyer called the place I went the Yale of rehab. I think he meant it as an insult."

"So you guys grew up together?" Jane asked. She thought of Cass as a child, in love with trees and truth.

"My family moved to Little Rock for my father's job. Her mother was our housekeeper. Cass was my best friend."

"Cass is from *Arkansas*?" Jane knew that the choice to

ask about Cass instead of Tom, when he was right there, offering her slivers of himself, was a kind of irrevocable dismissal. But she couldn't help herself.

"She is. Her mother, too. And her mother's mother, I think, but she died before Cass was born." It occurred to her that he might like talking about Cass as much as she did.

"Where's your family from?" she made herself ask.

"Connecticut."

"Siblings?"

"No siblings."

"Does Cass have siblings?"

"Does she seem like she has siblings?" Tom said. Jane shrugged carefully. "Only child. She lived with her mom, but then her dad took her. After my family moved back to Connecticut."

"Took her like, *took* her?"

"He took her to Aruba for nine months."

Jane felt a shameful pang of envy that Cass's father had gone to such great lengths to spend time with her.

"Was she okay?" Jane asked, because she knew she should.

"She's always been how she is now, even back then. She's like her own universe. Cass is short for Cassiopeia, you know." His words were moony, but his tone was matter-of-fact. Tom felt familiar to her, only slightly off, like if someone rummaged through a drawer of your things and tried to put them back the way they were.

"Isn't everyone kind of their own universe?"

"I think most people are just looking for a universe to join," he said, not unkindly. It was indisputable, and Jane had nothing to say to it. For a few minutes, they sat quietly together, the only sound the squeak of the pizza against their teeth.

"Can I ask you another question?" she said finally. "What's up with the emails?"

"What do you mean?"

"Do you really write them? Because they don't sound like you."

"Your emails don't really sound like you, either," he said. "They're slightly more chipper."

"Yeah, well. I'm usually trying to sell people on at-home fecal transplant kits, so a little chipper goes a long way," she said before she remembered that she was also meant to be selling Tom on Relevancy's PR sovereignty. "But your emails are more than just *slightly more chipper.* They sound sort of like . . ." Jane trailed off. She couldn't think of a nice way to say *computer-generated religious propaganda.*

"Can I ask *you* a question?" Tom said, his volume startling them both. He lowered his voice to a sharp whisper. "What are you even doing here? You said you wanted to work with us, whatever that means, but all you seem to want to do is question everything about what we do here. Do you want to try while you're here? Do you want to learn anything? Are you open to the possibility that there are things you *could* learn here?"

Jane tried to remember how honest she had been in the emails they exchanged. Had she told him she was worried that she was constitutionally incapable of trying and kept running up against the limits of her natural abilities and just quitting? If not, how did he know? She thought she had done a good job of hiding her cynicism, but maybe he could sense her desperation.

She knew he was likely only returning her own fears back to her. But after months—years—of aching to be known by another person (no point in trying to define that abstraction for herself; she only knew what *being known* was not), the questions felt close to closeness. It felt like part of an argument that had been going on for years, vital and benign.

chapter 9.

In the grand scheme of shitty dads throughout history, Jane knew she had gotten off easy. Easier than Cass had, certainly. Really, the worst she could claim was hurt feelings, which, her dad would have angrily joked, didn't even exist until the 1970s. Jane's mother used to say he was the most sensitive man she'd ever met (which, in Jane's experience, usually manifested as giving Jane the silent treatment if she didn't call him early enough on holidays).

The worst thing he did was leave, and the other things barely seemed like anything when Jane said them out loud. Like describing a dream you were sure had been fascinating.

Her parents split up early enough that Jane didn't remember much of the close-quarters acrimony. Once she heard her father tell her mother he would have stayed if she'd had another child. For years, Jane nursed an inchoate hatred for her theoretical sibling, who didn't even need to exist to be the favorite.

Jane's mother mostly stopped eating after he left, and when he came by to pick Jane up he complimented her new figure. *You couldn't have lost the weight when it would have made a difference?* he said, winking at Jane. Jane had smiled up at him, because she liked to be in on jokes.

After her father left, he always seemed to have a new girlfriend, who would usually try to curry favor with Jane by reading her product descriptions from clothing catalogs or letting her try her lipsticks. All the girlfriends were pretty in a way that made Jane think *Pretty!* reflexively.

When Jane was nine, her father moved to Colorado because he knew a guy that could help him get a better job. Jane visited him in August, when the tickets were cheapest. On the plane, she had to wear a plastic tag around her neck that read UNACCOMPANIED MINOR. The younger flight attendants were nice to her and brought her extra sodas, but the older ones treated her with suspicion, like being alone was a sign of her unruliness.

Her father's apartment building was so old it skipped the thirteenth floor for superstitious reasons. The windowsills were mass ladybug graves. The area behind the building was wooded, and sometimes when her father was on the phone Jane took the elevator downstairs to explore. She kept hoping it would be magical, like the woods in books, but instead it was just a patch of trees with a highway on its outer edge and a lot of broken glass everywhere.

When she came home and her mother asked her how

her trip had been she always said it was the most fun trip ever. She wanted her mother to miss her father, so maybe he would come back. But Jane usually gave it away by crying when her mother asked, too enthusiastically, what they had done together. Her mother never pushed further, just quietly gave her back scratches.

When Jane was twelve, her father introduced her to his friend Nikki. The three of them went to Bennigan's for dinner and he told Jane that Nikki was having a baby, and the baby would be Jane's half brother or sister. *Sister, I hope,* Nikki said, holding up crossed fingers. Then she said, *I remember you when* you *were a baby, Jane,* and Jane didn't wonder until much later how that could be.

They named the baby Jeanne, which made Jane think of how much worse it was when people got your name just a little wrong.

Jane couldn't always peg things to Before and After. Had she always been a needy child, or only After? She cringed when she thought of her child self, always asking other girls to declare their allegiance to her, to call her their best friend, to talk for hours on the phone after school. At least now she knew enough to flee at the first sign of lukewarm attention from other women. She could channel all her obvious need into the men she pursued. She didn't have to risk dismissal from friends. With Eleanor, at least, it had been more complicated. They had dismissed each other.

Jane's father hadn't disappeared. She knew where he was. If she needed to talk to him, she could eventually talk to him. Her complaints were so puny. She wished there were something more horrible to explain why she needed so badly for anyone—no, everyone—to tell her that she had some redeeming qualities, and what those might be. She used to tell guys she had daddy issues to be funny, but she stopped when she realized only the terrible ones were ever going to laugh.

The last time she spoke to her father, it was to tell him she had dropped out of grad school and was going to work in PR. She thought he would be disappointed, since he put a premium on brand-name education, but instead he told her about a woman he used to go out with who worked in PR. Besides the accomplishments of Jeanne, he most loved talking about his ex-girlfriends.

I think she might have been the love of my life, he said. *She was gorgeous. It's a pretty image-obsessed business, to be honest with you. I guess your boss saw something special in you.*

She couldn't tell whether he was implying that she got the job because of her looks or in spite of them, and she hated him for making her wonder if her father found her attractive.

chapter 10.

Jane was aware of the stirring and morning sounds around her, but by the time she opened her eyes at 5:04 A.M., everyone was already somewhere else. She put on yoga pants and a T-shirt she had always thought made her look sort of thin and went outside. The group was seated in a loose circle on the lawn, Cass included. She wore a colorless sack dress and a perfectly worn red flannel. Jane knew if she wore the same thing she would look like a too-on-the-nose interpretation of a psychiatric patient.

"Will someone bring Jane a cup of mushroom tea? It's wonderful for intestinal distress," Cass called, sounding entirely sincere.

FortPath seemed like the kind of place where people spoke frankly about their bowels. Jane was surprised by how little shame she felt about the previous day's nearmess. Three people scrambled up, but Jessica was fastest and returned less than a minute later with a cup of warm gray water. It tasted like very weak broth, but not unpleasant.

Jane sat between Farren and Brando, the man with the hat, who was maybe deeply ill but getting better because of the kelp. Brando was the kind of handsome that tricked you into thinking you were the only one who noticed. He didn't look sick at all. He was slight and angular, with light-green eyes and a wide, thin-lipped mouth and a single deep dimple when he smiled. *There's just something about him,* a thousand girls had probably thought. *No one else sees it because he has no lips and his ears sort of stick out and he's short.* She pitied these imagined girls, and hated them, because she definitely would have been one of them at a different moment.

"This morning, your spirits are all asking for guidance," Cass said. "I'm going to lead you through a Mindful Spatialism exercise. We'll be in Balasana." Everyone doubled over into child's pose, foreheads pressed to the grass.

"Mindful Spatialism is the unifying of imagination with reality. Nothing we speak of here is metaphorical. We trust the mind and body to create these objects and spaces. Reality is not linear." One of Jane's professors in grad school said that every metaphor in a poem was, by necessity, true, which itself sounded metaphorical. He also pronounced Beyoncé *Bay-AHWN-say,* which made him easy to dismiss, but here it was again. Maybe her imagination was just shit. Thinking of Tom, she resolved to try.

"You're in a room you know well. The room has no furniture, only shapes made of light. You remember the room because of the feeling it evokes in you, not because you have been there before. You feel safe, but not secure. You feel powerful, but you know you must create the power for yourself. You feel compelled to act. You approach a large light-shape, indistinct but possibly rectangular, and even though you're not tired—you have more energy than you've ever had—you lie down on it."

Jane closed her eyes and imagined her bedroom. She saw her unmade bed and her milk crate side table and her chair piled with clothes. She tried to transfigure them into shapes of light but she couldn't remember what light looked like, so she just pictured everything as a sickly yellow. She didn't feel powerful at all. She felt like her mind's eye was broken. She wanted to stop trying. She ran through one of the few poems she remembered from her grad school memorization, Milton's Sonnet 7: *How soon hath Time, the subtle thief of youth, / Stol'n on his wing my three-and-twentieth year! / My hasting days fly on with full career, / But my late spring no bud or blossom shew'th.* She used to like the poem, but now it just made her feel old.

But she had the sense that Tom would be disappointed if he knew she was failing at the exercise. Or else validated in his skepticism of her. She wasn't sure which would make her feel worse.

"Lying on this bed of light, you become very aware of your body. You begin to pay attention to all parts of your physical being—your fingertips, your chin, your vulva—as never before. This is not a critical attention, but a delighted attention. You're not giving your body a performance review; you're sharing the light with your body. You're delighting in your power together."

Love your body, girl! was somewhere in the text of

nearly all Jane's PR campaigns. The subtext being: *eventually*. Once she had accidentally sent a joke-campaign to Rand, one she had written out of sheer frustration at the number of notes she'd received from a client who made laxative smoothies. *For a look of such radiant health, everyone will ask if you just got out of the hospital!* Rand had called her into his office for a discussion about Relevancy's mission statement. "We *empower* women," he said gravely. "We don't want harm to come to them." (Which Rand may honestly have believed, though it didn't change the fact that he once rubbed her foot with his foot under the table for the entirety of a two-hour staff meeting.)

Jane filed the phrase *Delighting in the power of your body* away for future professional use. She wondered what genuinely delighting in the power of her body would feel like. She could only imagine it in a sexual context, her power gifted to her by some man when he was feeling generous.

She enjoyed sex sometimes, but the physical sensation had always been secondary to the pleasure she took in having a clearly defined end-goal, and an obvious measure of success. If she had sex with someone for whom ejaculate wasn't assumed, she was pretty sure she would never stop wondering if they were faking. The ability to summon cum gave her certainty, and the look of dopey adoration that followed was her afterglow.

"As you lie there, you reach down beside you and scoop up a handful of light. You bring it to your lips and taste it." Jane tried to imagine the bed. The light was slippery as silk. She imagined reaching down, scooping up the light like a bear with honey. Her imagination didn't feel unified with reality. She imagined eating the light. She wished she had some real honey.

"The taste of the light begins to overwhelm you. Even as you eat it, you feel the fear of never being able to taste it again. You take another scoop, just to have one waiting for you when you're finished with the first one. It's the fear you're eating. With every bite, you destroy more and more of the fear, with the teeth, with the throat." Cass would probably be very good at poetry.

"You begin to smear the light on your face. You feel the light fusing to you, a second skin. You take another scoop and cover your neck in it, your breasts. The light covers your breasts like an invisible armor. Your breasts are glowing orbs." Jane's real-life breasts were shaped like pattypan squash. She tried to imagine them as Jell-O molded into perfect spheres.

"You're using both hands now, scooping light over your belly as if you're at the beach, burying yourself in the sand. The light has weight, but it doesn't weigh you down. It changes the composition of you. You spread. You fill the room. Now you reach for one last scoop of light, before your bodily form diffuses. You know that this is the way to satiate yourself. This is how you will be able to taste the light perpetually, because the light will replace your blood and viscera. You gently cup the light in both your hands and bring it to your sexual center. Bring it to your sexual center. Bring it—"

She hadn't noticed the voice getting closer, but all of a sudden Cass was just behind her. She jerked her head up but kept her eyes closed. "—to your sexual center." She felt wet breath in her ear. Cass ran her hands down Jane's outstretched arms and held her at the wrists, lifting them off the ground. Jane sat upright, but Cass let go of one wrist and placed her palm against Jane's back, smushing her cheek against the grass. She guided first Jane's right arm, then her left, between Jane's legs. Jane cupped both hands over her vagina protectively. She remembered the light. *I hope I don't get an imaginary yeast infection from all this fear-honey.*

Cass was quiet now. Jane heard a noise like wet leaves hitting a window. Then a whimper, then a low moan just beside her. She realized what was happening the moment before she raised her head two inches and opened her eyes to confirm it. The moaner was Farren, who was rocking back and forth against her hands vigorously. The wet-leaves sound was coming from Brando, who was spreading imaginary light on himself with methodical intensity. Jane was the only one not visibly masturbating. She wondered how they all knew. Did every morning begin this way? Had anyone ever resisted? She looked for Tom, but didn't see him.

She was horrified, but undeniably turned on. The peer pressure was a gift—however afraid she was to expose her softest underbelly, she was more afraid to be the outsider, arms folded in lonesome judgment. She gave herself an experimental rub through her pants. She closed her eyes and tried to return to the light-filled room. She shoved her right hand into her leggings and began to finger her clitoris defiantly. She wasn't used to masturbating without a vibrator. Or outdoors. Or in a group. The others around her were starting to come, at varying volumes. Farren's moaning had turned to keening, so unsexy it had to be genuine.

"The light courses through you. You can taste it.

Every time you swallow, it gives you a rush of renewed power and energy. You slowly sit up, and open your eyes, leaving the room behind for now." Jane's sudden frustration felt like fury. She had fucked enough careless men not to cry over a lost orgasm, but she felt sure that Cass had deliberately concluded the exercise when Jane was just on the brink. When she opened her eyes, everyone was already standing, mostly looking at their feet, avoiding one another's eyes and hands.

"This bliss will infuse the plants as you tend to them. Remember that at all times."

~

The masturbatory meditation signaled a hedonism that Jane hadn't so far sensed from the group, though she wasn't great at picking up on sexual signals. She was terrified of revealing attraction without confirmed reciprocity.

The strangeness of the morning, and the silence around the strangeness, made her feel like an outsider in some cosmic way, and she had a sudden yet familiar pang for home. Not her apartment, which she hated in a low-grade, manageable way. She had come to expect the late-autumn mosquito infestations, which left small red flecks on her walls all year from where she slapped the blood-lazy bugs in the mornings. She missed, instead, the idea of home.

Even before her mother moved out of the tiny, slanty house where Jane grew up and into Dave's aggressively modern condo ("I don't know how they do it, but I swear this place doesn't get dusty!"), the home feeling of that house had dissipated. Lying in her childhood bed was like trying to remember the taste of something delicious that she hadn't eaten in years. Now the unspoken promise of every new place was: *Maybe this is home.* And then, *Maybe if this is home, everything else will fall into place.*

Her greatest ambition in life was for everything to fall into place.

~

Tom led the next activity, Earth Communion, which was just gardening chores. The combination of alfresco circle jerk and manual labor was, she knew, exactly the kind of thing Adrian had warned her about. She wondered if now was the time to get the fuck out of there. She could find a different kind of Experience to present to Rand, one with massages and affirming counselors and a mineral pool. She would probably leave after breakfast, she decided. Depending on what breakfast was.

Most of them were tasked with weeding, but everyone had their own ideas about which growths were weeds and which were part of the zucchini. Tom was sloshing buckets of water over the unoccupied rows. There was no hose, and he kept having to go into the house to fill them.

Jane felt shy around him after the previous night's encounter. She liked him. And his closeness to Cass, whatever their relationship was, gave him an extra dimension. If this were her other life, she would have spent a few hours crafting an off-the-cuff email so he could see she was cool and smart and interested but not overeager.

"Tom," Jane said when he clanked past her on his way to the kitchen sink. "Just wondering—isn't there a garden tap or anything you could hook up a hose to? I think the buckets are a little uneven. Also seems like kind of a pain in the ass for you." She wondered if this counted as trying; his obvious irritation suggested that it did not.

"The outdoor faucet doesn't work," he said. "It's rusted or something. Anyway, I think the buckets are actually more like the rain. You know, inconsistent. Like weather."

"I think maybe rain is more like a hose than a bucket."

"Well, we don't have a hose," Tom said, and walked off to refill the bucket that may or may not have been like weather.

Jane glanced at Jessica, who had been silently weeding next to them. She decided to take a stab at networking.

"Tell me how you discovered FortPath." She had found that saying *tell me* instead of just asking made people think you found them captivating.

"A friend of a friend followed Cass on Instagram, so then *I* started following her and after that it was like, how could you not? She's just so . . . *fearless.* And obviously fear is a poison in my work, specifically. I'm a theater director."

"How many times have you come here?" Jane asked. The group had a lived-in feeling, which she assumed was a result of all the previous masturbatory teambuilding she had missed out on. But she wondered how long they had been knitting themselves together.

"I first came in the spring, and I loved it so much that I try to come back every other weekend, or whenever I need another reset."

"How do your, ah, friends feel about you being gone so much?"

Jessica rolled her eyes. "All my friends care about is if I cast them in shows. I'm happiest when I'm here. I seriously needed to reframe my thinking. And my skin has been looking *amazing*." This much was true—her face was taut and glowing. "When you think about it as an investment in your face, it's actually really reasonably priced. Not that it's just that at all. Not *at all*. I'm learning so much from Cass. *So* much."

"What kinds of things are you learning?" Jane asked.

"I mean, everything. *Everything*." Jessica looked at her meaningfully.

"No, *exactly*. Can you give me an example?"

"I mean, obviously, yes, I can give you an example."

"I mean, can you?" It never took Jane long to adopt the verbal tics of the people around her. It happened against her will, as if her unconscious mind had taken her desire to fit in too literally.

Jessica ran her fingers through her lustrous hair (how was everyone's hair so lustrous?) and sighed. "Really the main reason I came here was because of my ex-boyfriend. I know, so basic. I date women, too, obviously. But this guy just really fucked me up. His mother was a theater critic for the *Times* who came to see my company's production of *Lysistrata* and told him it was *profoundly bewildered*. And then right after that he dumped me. He said he couldn't be with me because he didn't want to risk losing his mother's respect."

Jane remembered that Adrian's warning had included a theater-afflicted cousin.

"Wait, are you Adrian's cousin?"

"Jesus Christ, did my mother send you?"

"No. What? No. I just went on a date with your cousin last week. Actually he sort of convinced me to come here. I mean, he didn't mean to, but he sort of said it was like . . ." Jane trailed off, embarrassed for them both.

"A cult? Yeah, I know. My family thinks everything I do is cult-related because *one time* I accidentally joined a cult," Jessica said.

Jane made a sympathetic face and nodded, trying not to look too curious about the other cult.

"I thought it was a theater clinic. I actually learned a lot about improv. Non-comedic improv, which is way more productive. Anyway, then they started trying to get me to recruit other people and asking for more and more money. Not like this place at all. Cass is very transparent about pricing. She's, like, barely breaking even every month."

It was true that FortPath was suspiciously inexpensive—only $250 for the whole weekend. Jane had actually wondered if this was somehow part of a larger grift.

"So, you came here to get over your bad ex?" Jane prompted.

"I was in pain for a long time. It had consumed my life," Jessica said. She didn't specify whether the pain was physical or emotional. "Then I saw Cass on Insta and I just thought, *Okay, this girl just looks so centered. I want to be like that.* And then I saw that her workshops were about regaining control of your narrative and I was just like, *Fuck yes, I'm going to take control of my life and my art and my body.* And then obviously my first weekend here was completely transformative. But *then* I went back to the city and I ran into my ex at a party and I was so confidently standing in my truth that he practically begged me to take him back."

Jane didn't know exactly what standing confidently in her truth would look like when it came to Byron, but she loved the idea of him begging her for anything. She knew then that she would stay.

"Did you get back together?" she asked Jessica.

"No. But I still send him nudes sometimes so he knows what he's missing."

chapter 11.

For breakfast, they ate cultured kelp porridge with bee pollen and turmeric, which tasted like low tide at a saltwater taffy stand, but which was also possibly the best thing Jane had ever eaten. Cass floated around the table, perching in between clusters and saying things in a low voice that Jane couldn't make out. Did Cass eat? Maybe she photosynthesized instead.

Jane sat between Brando and Farren again. Farren kept craning her neck in Cass's direction while Brando told Jane about his wellness journey. Jane had noticed that all conversation at FortPath revolved around Cass, with everyone vying for the purest and most meaningful connection to her. It made Jane want to hate her, just to prove it was possible. But maybe it wasn't.

"I had these intense migraines every day for years," Brando said. "And some days my body just felt so heavy I couldn't get out of bed. Then other times I would feel okay except I had these jolts of electricity in my arms and legs. I went to all these specialists. In six months I saw a neurologist, an allergist, a rheumatologist, an endocrinologist, and a hematologist. Most of them just thought I was nuts." Jane nodded, wondering if he was. She wanted to ask what kind of insurance he had, and whether it covered all his specialist visits and if so, whether the two of them could get married so she could have access to it, *hahajustkidding!*

"I'm not crazy," he said, sounding more weary than defensive.

"No, I know. Obviously," she said.

"Anyway, so I started doing the alternative medicine thing. Sound baths were so-so. Past life regression was amazing, but as soon as I would return to the present plane I started to feel like shit again. I saw a shaman for a while and I started to feel a lot better, but then he stole my identity. Then I heard from a friend of a friend that Cass was the real deal. My friend's friend had IBS and as soon as Cass told her to only drink water at body temperature, she was basically completely healed."

Brando paused and took a very long, very slow sip of his (body-temperature) water. Jane wondered if he was signaling the end of their conversation. She hoped not. She wanted to hear more. She would pay good money for Brando's one-man show about Cass. She would follow an unlimited number of CassUpdates Twitter accounts to gather wisps of information about her—*Cass spotted strolling next to the zucchini! Cass tells* Glamour *her favorite food is water!*

Finally, Brando put down his clay tumbler and continued. "So anyway, I've done five or six sessions here and I just feel so much lighter. Before, it was like a giant hand was pressing me into the earth. Now it's more like it's hovering above me. Cass helped me see it. She's helping me free myself."

Jane was skeptical of the diseases that manifested bafflingly and roamed the body and debilitated the sufferer for years without diagnosis, at least partly because she couldn't think of anything worse. She pitied Brando even as she doubted him, and she feared that one day she, too, would be unwelcome in her body.

"How is Cass helping you free yourself?" she asked.

"She's teaching me to honor the pain," Brando said.

Jane hadn't realized how much she'd wanted to believe his answer until she didn't.

After Brando began an earnest conversation with Jessica about experimental theater, Jane turned to Farren, who snapped to attention when Jane mentioned that she worked in PR.

"Do you know Jordana Fisher?" Farren asked. All of her questions sounded like accusations.

"I don't think so. Should I?"

"She started this amazing app that lets you track the periods of women in Africa."

"Wow, that's so cool! What, uh . . . What do you do with that information?"

"So you know when to send them tampons and stuff when they need them. I mean, you can send them a cute little tampon care package through the app. You do know that a lot of women in Africa don't have access to tampons, right? It's like a pretty big problem." Jane stared, at a loss. "So, who *do* you work with?"

She tried to summon PR Jane. She pressed her palms

together and launched into jazzed-but-earnest pitch mode. "We work with a ton of exciting up-and-coming wellness brands! Obviously, in this political climate"—Relevancy's mandate was to proceed with a soft assumption of liberalism, but never to take an overt stance—"self-care has become more important than ever, and our founders are very attuned to that."

Farren was looking just over Jane's shoulder. She knew that even if she could somehow convince Farren she was worth talking to, nothing Farren had to say would be of the slightest interest to Jane. Still, Farren's transparent boredom at their conversation made Jane desperate to hold her attention, maybe out of a simple desire to be the one who walked away for once. Based on Farren's looks and general demeanor, Jane decided to pivot to juicy bitch session.

She leaned in conspiratorially. "Honestly, a lot of them are, like, truly awful. Like there's this one, reFaun. It's for at-home fecal transplants." Farren grimaced. "I know, so gross, right? Like, I'm all for a coffee enema every once in a while"—Jane had learned that it was always a mistake to alienate the enema crowd—"but I draw the line at putting someone else's poop inside me *from the comfort of my own home.*"

Farren's face looked like it couldn't decide between righteous anger and an elementary school tattletale's smug disapproval. "My dear friend Rohan started reFaun. She's an incredibly strong woman who has dealt with so many health issues and made it out the other side because of the power of fecal transplants. I'm sure she'll be happy to know her PR person is slandering the company she built from nothing. You know, there's a special place in hell for women who tear down other women's business ventures."

Jane's heart pounded in her head and her cheeks burned. The degree of her miscalculation made her whole body cringe. Farren's perfect eyebrows dared her to defend herself, but she had nothing.

"You're right," she said. Farren rolled her eyes at the obviousness of it all. "I think sometimes I envy the . . . She-E-Os we work with. Because they all built something of their own, and I haven't." This was sort of true, though Jane also despaired when she read about prolific serial killers younger than she was—H. H. Holmes was halfway through his murder castle at her age—and envied almost anyone who had accomplished anything, no matter how small. She hated that Farren was forcing her to admit this, even if the apology was a sham.

"I'm working on my negativity," she said. "I'm sorry."

"It seems like your personality isn't really serving your best interests anymore." Farren tucked her knees to her chest and spun around on the bench in one fluid movement. It was the most graceful picnic table exit Jane had ever seen. She wondered if Farren had splinters in her ass. Farren left her bowl on the table for Tom to bus and walked out the door without another word.

Jane looked up and saw Cass watching her from across the table, while Jessica enumerated to her the phases of her vegetable milk journey.

"What a fertile moment for you," Cass said to Jessica.

~

Jane didn't remember her mother ever worrying about doctors' bills growing up, but then, she couldn't remember her mother getting sick even once. Jane had been a shameless malingerer through middle school, but before her appendix trouble, she was rarely truly sick, either. Ever since then, though, she'd felt intermittently *off* in a way that felt like a combination of pre-flu and generalized dread. She had finally experienced a failure of the body, and its financial ramifications, and she kept waiting for it to happen again.

At first she thought that paying off her debt would help, but every time she sent in a check, she felt worse, like she was complicit in the injustice of it all. She missed payments even when she had the money. She refused to remind herself. When it was time to make a payment, she bought expensive jeans that looked terrible on her or became a Sustaining Member of her hometown's NPR affiliate. She felt a little bit sick most of the time but didn't go to the doctor. She went on Instagram and found the wife of the surgeon who removed her appendix, and liked pictures of their toddler. She sometimes remembered to drink water.

Now, with the possibility of losing her source of income and the health insurance she was too afraid to use, Jane felt the full force of the debt. She sat in a rocking chair on the porch rocking back and forth fervidly, rubbing the scar on her belly and trying to figure out whether there was any flavor of apology that would appeal to Farren.

After breakfast was an hour of Active Silence, which was different from Humbled Silence because it involved a series of gestures. Cass demonstrated all of them, silently, from the center of the circle, like they were all performing an experimental modern dance.

Once they were finished, a few people lined up for showers. Jane walked to her sleeping corner and sniffed her armpit. She smelled like chicken soup. Jessica sat on a cushion in the main space, in a posture of meditation, scrolling on her phone.

Jane willed someone to approach her, to ask her about her life or compliment her silences or offer some casual physical contact. She stood in the shower line for a few minutes, but no one turned around, so she pulled out her phone and checked it.

She had an email from Rand, subject line A CONCERN.

> Jane, I received a troubling message from one of our clients. Let me know when you're available to speak today.

She locked her phone screen instinctively, as if that might prevent the bad thing from escaping her inbox. Could Farren have worked this quickly? Even if Jane begged for forgiveness now, the message had already been passed on. The only thing she could do was distract Rand from her fuckup with a promise of future success.

If she could convince Cass to hire Relevancy, it might make up for how terrible she was at relating publicly. She wondered if there was a way to highlight the group masturbation without making herself complicit in Rand's fantasy life.

She still wasn't sure if FortPath had the money to hire a PR firm, and she couldn't imagine having a conversation with Cass—or Tom, for that matter—about anything so pragmatic. She wished so hard she could just preemptively quit her job and move somewhere remote and charming but still somehow undiscovered by rich New York people, where no one would ever find her. Anyone who said "quitter" sounded worse than "failure" was a liar or a life coach.

But neither quitting nor failing was an option, so she went to find Cass, who was sitting at the edge of the trees.

"Sit with me," Cass said, then closed her eyes. She made sitting cross-legged in the dusty grass look like a fashion statement. Jane glanced behind her to make sure she was alone, that the invitation wasn't directed at someone else. Cass's glow was so spacious that she could host others inside it. As she sat, Jane felt the warmth of having been chosen.

"You should let go of your anger at not being more beautiful," Cass said. Her eyes were closed. Jane didn't wonder how Cass knew about her insecurity, though *angry* wasn't one she heard often. Jane wondered how much of Cass's mystery was based on her ability to use precise non sequiturs to insult people.

"You are beautiful," Cass continued. Jane thought she felt a bug crawling up her back, but when she tried to brush it away, nothing was there. "But you'll never be as beautiful as you want to be. You think life would be so different." Cass opened her eyes and smiled, with what could have been pity, or sympathy, or something more complicated.

"No, I don't." Jane knew Cass was right, but she thought she had buried the feeling deeply enough that other people couldn't see it. Had it been so obvious?

"You're embarrassed." This observation was less impressive, as Jane's face was radiating heat. "And you think I can't understand what it's like to be you because I'm very beautiful. But understanding takes many forms, not all of them direct."

When Cass spoke, Jane had the same feeling she got while reading a particularly obfuscatory poem in grad school, when she couldn't be sure whether the work was brilliant or meaningless. She felt it when she read Byron's poetry, like there might be an incredible secret world just underneath, or else the whole thing was a joke based on asymmetrical information.

"Tell me your thoughts," Cass continued. Jane shrugged with one shoulder, petulant, hating how childish she must have looked. Cass looked like an enchanted girl-princess.

"Jane," she said, with unbearable tenderness.

In desperation at Jane's early difficulty winning friends and influencing people, her mother had once left a copy of *How to Win Friends and Influence People* on her bed. She read it cover-to-cover but was too self-conscious to follow any of its advice, especially the thing about saying people's names a lot. Saying a person's name even once unnerved her—it felt intimate, presumptuous. When Cass said her name, though, she understood. She felt important. She felt chosen. Insulted, then chosen. Her exact kink.

Jane struggled to regain the upper hand, even as she blinked hard against tears. "I know what you're doing. I mean, no, I don't know *exactly* what you're doing, like I don't know what your endgame is exactly, but I know you're not actually *interested* in me and this is just part of the whole . . . thing."

"Which whole thing?" Cass sounded genuinely interested, like Jane was describing an unusual hobby.

"You know. Whatever you're doing here. Breaking people down by saying mean things to them and then building them back up with circle jerks, and using them for free labor on your farm, and, like, *barely* feeding them. And part of that is you being hilariously charismatic. Or whatever."

Articulating the contours of her skepticism made Jane retreat from it. Her irritation deflated and she just felt ashamed, especially when she saw the concern on Cass's face.

"You don't like the food?" Cass said.

"No, I—well, actually I do, there's just not enough of it." She tried not to sound as ashamed as she felt.

There was a contingent of beautiful women poets in the Iza Brecht model in Jane's graduate program who wrote poetry and wrote about poetry and talked about poetry and sublimated all their hunger to poetry so they never had to eat at all. They were brittle and brilliant and terrifying. Once she heard them discussing Emily Dickinson's weight. The most petite one of them had just gotten back from the Emily Dickinson Museum and was surprised by the size of the dead poet's white dress. *I just thought she would have been . . . smaller.*

Since then, Jane had occasionally wondered whether *passion* was code for "the thing that makes me desire actual food less." Cass's very being seemed to validate this.

Cass was looking at Jane intently, studying her. "Since

you've been here, your skin has transformed," Cass said. "Like your body has been crying out for exactly this all along. Everything we do here is about expelling toxins. Not just the physical nourishment, but telling the truth, hearing the truth. Transformation is often uncomfortable, but your light has become much stronger in the last twenty-four hours."

Jane touched her face instinctively. She tried to play it off as a gesture of contemplation, but her cheek did feel more taut. She restrained herself from opening her front-facing camera to check.

"Fine," she said, trying to sound strong and measured, like a woman who used drugstore moisturizer on her skin but nothing else because she was too busy living a fulfilling life. "So you're making people's skin better. So why don't you just say that? People want good skin much more than they want to be spiritually satisfied. Or, they'll take spiritual satisfaction, but only if their skin also looks amazing."

"Public messaging isn't my strength. I thrive on the energy of people, face-to-face. Tom has cultivated the digital side of my work here." It was jarring to hear Cass admit weakness. And use the word *digital,* which she pronounced with a hard *G.*

"You do want more people to come here, though?"

"I want everyone to come here."

Jane suddenly wondered if they were going to kiss. Cass's effect on her felt like a prolongation of that pre-kiss moment, when you've just become sure it's inevitable, and you're both inching closer. You're giddy, but not impatient. You trust the moment, for once.

Cass smiled thoughtfully. "You have a generous spirit." She stood up. "When you don't feel wounded."

Joke's on you, Jane thought. *I always feel wounded.*

Cass looked down at her and nodded with such intensity that Jane wondered if she had accidentally spoken the words aloud. "What are you afraid of?"

Cass probably asked some variation of this question a hundred times a day, but it hit Jane with an unexpected force, like understanding the literal meaning of a cliché for the first time. She was afraid of being alone forever, obviously. She was afraid of losing her job and never being able to find another one, and of the looming specter of her financial debt. She was afraid of being desperately poor despite all the opportunities she'd had. She was afraid that someone, somewhere might once have called her a loser, and been right. She was afraid her entire personality was a patchwork of traits and phrases stolen from people she met briefly and thought were cool. She was afraid she had no ambition beyond impressing anyone who had ever wronged her. She was afraid she was too self-absorbed to fear anything real.

"Nuclear war," Jane finally said.

"I heard you speaking fearlessly at breakfast today."

This was not the conversation Jane wanted to have. "I had a misunderstanding with Farren. It was nothing."

"Farren?" Cass frowned.

"You know, the girl I was talking to?" Cass looked vaguely interested, as if Jane were describing a strange dream. "Small face?" She wondered if it was possible that Cass would know her name but not Farren's. She was alarmed by how much she wanted it to be true.

"You were speaking from the center of your truth."

"Yes. I was," she admitted.

Jane was surprised Cass would describe the petty, ungenerous parts of her as truthful. She felt simultaneously grateful and offended, like when someone conceded to her self-deprecation instead of responding with knee-jerk polite denial.

Then Cass walked toward the house without so much as a goodbye nod. Jane couldn't tell if this was a bad sign, or a good one, or just another of Cass's many quirks.

She sat on the grass for a while, watching the activity in the garden and on the porch. She had failed even to propose her services to Cass, and now she struggled to think of what those services might be. As much as she hated Farren, she knew that what FortPath needed was dozens more Farrens, women who hated specific things about their appearance mostly out of habit, but who had internalized the idea of themselves as *Badass Boss Babes* enough to feel some shame about that hatred. Scary Women.

Unlike Jane, the Scary Women had fully realized ambition. She envied them so much she had actually convinced herself that she didn't want to be one of them, because they never seemed to have any fun. Which was true, except Jane never really had any fun, either. The Scary Women had long- and medium- and short-term goals. They were trying to eat more but they *just kept forgetting to eat!* Their trainers were going to kill them, but nothing else would kill them. All their hobbies were passions, and all their passions became start-ups successful enough to earn back the seed money from their father-husbands within a year. The Scary Women were the subjects of profiles that remarked on their surprising sweetness. But they were not sweet. They were ruthlessly effective. They were the way forward.

Right now, the beauty aspect of FortPath was too effectively cloaked—the male-to-female ratio was all out of whack. A fleet of Scary Women could transform it into an empire.

Rand Hagen had given a presentation early in Jane's tenure at Relevancy about the challenges of marketing beauty products to men. *Women are easier to shame,* he said. One slide was a chart of different male demographics, ranked from most to least susceptible to shame. It wasn't even in the top five of Rand's most offensive PowerPoint presentations.

Her proposal might sound more impressive to Rand if she presented FortPath as a way into the elusive male market, but it seemed safer to focus on women, whose shame was more understandable and therefore easier to exploit.

Less exploitable, though, was Cass herself. Jane wasn't sure what *want* meant, to Cass. It was almost like the things she desired came to her so immediately that the desire itself never had a chance to pick up speed. As soon as it existed, it was extinguished. Maybe people like Cass needed people like Jane to act as ambition proxies for them. *Vessel of want* wasn't a search option on LinkedIn, but it was the position for which Jane was best suited.

chapter 12.

Just before the call she had reluctantly scheduled with Rand, Jane ducked into a closet, empty except for an atlas that looked like it was growing fur. He called the moment her phone's clock switched from 12:59 to 1:00.

"Jane. Hello," he said.

"And this is Sasha from the people team on the line, too," another voice piped up. "Hello, Jane," Sasha added, a little too brightly for the occasion. "Just so you're aware, this call is being recorded."

Jane felt herself flush. How easily the power of HR could snuff out her little plan.

Rand explained that her recent performance coupled with the possible slander of one of their clients constituted gross misconduct and was grounds for immediate termination. She would no longer be permitted in the Relevancy offices—the company would mail her personal effects to her, along with information about COBRA coverage.

“I’m disappointed,” Rand said. “I faced resistance in hiring someone with so little experience.”

“What if I could bring you a new client? Someone with enormous growth potential with our most engaged demographic?” She knew it was probably hopeless but she took a shot anyway, trying to keep the supplication from her voice. “Cass—Cassiopeia—she’s the CEO of the wellness retreat I’ve been exploring this weekend for Relevancy, and Rand, I think she could be huge. Her brand needs refining, of course, but I’m prepared to take the lead on this and do whatever it takes.”

The momentary silence on the line gave her hope, but as soon as Sasha cleared her throat, Jane knew there was only one way the call would end. There was no reasoning with HR.

“Hm,” Rand said. “Jane, this morning I woke up to an email from Rohan Cooper’s team, telling me that the lead on her account had been spreading malicious lies about the product she was meant to promote. Threatening to sue us for breach of contract. I’ve been on the phone with our legal team trying to ascertain *if* she has grounds to do so in the event that she pursues this. I find it offensive that you would even ask me to keep you on at this point.”

Jane was so embarrassed that she had to hold the phone away from her face for a few seconds, as though it, not her actions, was the source of her mortification. She wanted to cry, but she summoned every drop of capitalist shamelessness she had.

“I’m sorry, Rand. And I’m sorry, Sasha,” she added. “But, please. Please, I really need this job. I know I made a mistake, and it was a really bad mistake, and I’m definitely not minimizing that, but just human-to-human, to humans, I have all this medical debt. From a procedure I had." She thought *procedure* made it sound like maybe she had an ongoing issue, one more worthy of sympathy.

"Rand," Sasha said. "I think we've given Jane all the information she needs at this point."

Jane wondered if Rand was in trouble, too. The thought made her feel a little bit powerful. She thought about how uncomfortable Rand made her with his stares and his expectant silences.

"Sasha, I just think you should know that Rand said something really creepy to me in my interview." As soon as she said it, she realized it had sounded more compelling in her head.

Sasha made a sound like a balloon letting out all its air at once. Rand said nothing. The worst part was that Sasha would never not think she was lying. "I'm not lying," she added, for the cosmic record.

"Jane, as I mentioned, this call is being recorded." Sasha spoke slowly, enunciating each syllable. *REE-COR-DED.* "I understand this is a difficult situation. But I'd like you to think about the way this conversation has gone, and imagine how these accusations might sound to an objective party.

"You were told that your employment at Relevancy was being terminated, and your response was to accuse your former supervisor of sexual harassment. To that objective observer, this might sound quite a bit like a threat. And frankly, Jane, as a woman, as a *feminist,* I'm a little disgusted by the implication of that. Now, I know you're upset, so I'd like to give you the opportunity to do the right thing here."

Jane wondered what a braver, less tired person would do in her situation. She knew there were dozens more Sashas at Relevancy, and that even if her true goal was the noble one of protecting future Janes from Rand, she would fail. It had never even occurred to her to say something about it until this moment, and now she felt ashamed of that, too.

"He told me he hired me because he could see my bra," she said.

"You showed your supervisor your undergarments in a job interview?"

"It was an accident," Jane said, gritting her teeth so hard that they squeaked.

"It's not appropriate to speak about this right now," Sasha said. "Take the rest of the weekend to think about it, and if you want to file a complaint on Monday, send me an email. But you should know, Jane, that it wasn't Rand's decision to terminate your employment. And no matter what happens with this matter, you won't have your job back."

Fuck, she thought. *Now he'll never give me a reference.* But she also felt briefly triumphant. What if some part of her had done it on purpose? Maybe she had hurtled herself over the edge because she was a visionary rather than a fuckup. Why else would she have been so candid with Farren? Surely not just for the approval of a mean stranger?

She imagined herself in a year, sitting on a panel about successful women, talking about her work as the creative force behind FortPath's growth, explaining that sometimes in life, you have to cut your own safety net—that her body knew that before her mind did. That the only way out is through. That if it was easy, everyone would do it.

Then she started to cry.

~

She stayed in the closet for what felt like a long time. It smelled like rotting fruit and unwashed hair. Jane had recently spent a few days researching the "no-poo method" at work, trying to figure out if there was some way Relevancy's clients could capitalize on the idea that if you stopped using shampoo, your scalp's oils would eventually balance themselves out. She had tried it out, but the smell of her own scalp had overwhelmed her almost immediately. It wasn't so bad when the smell was someone else's, though. It was almost interesting.

She was afraid that if she left her hiding place she might see Farren and cry in front of her, or—even worse—that she might say something she imagined was cutting and Farren would just roll her eyes.

What if she never got another job? She would have to move back in with her mother and Dave, whom Jane maybe didn't hate but didn't really like. She would never be able to pay off her debt and pay her rent and pay for COBRA. Maybe she could chance it without insurance, but what if she needed another surgery? What if she got sick from not eating enough kelp? Or eating too much kelp?

A guy she fucked on and off before her appendectomy once told her that when he felt really low about his student debt, he just thought about how many people in the world would gladly pay $130,000 to be him.

I'm quite tall, definitely more attractive than average, and I've never scored under the ninety-fifth percentile on any standardized test. He pointed to ads in Columbia's student newspaper offering top dollar for the eggs of tall, high-achieving Scandinavian women. *If people would pay that much to have genetically superior kids, imagine how much they'd pay to be genetically superior themselves,* he'd said.

Setting aside the creepy eugenics-boosting inherent in his argument, Jane found his confidence fascinating. Even though she was sleeping with him, Jane had always thought he looked a little like a lesser Frankenstein's monster, square-headed with dug-out features. She had tried it out when she fell into debt of her own: *I have a desirable waist-to-hip ratio. I won a regional Halloween poetry contest in fifth grade. One time a barista called me "interestingly attractive."* Even for the sake of argument, none of her qualities ever seemed to add up to $97,000.

"My energy is urging me to run," she heard Cass say from outside the closet door. Cass, who was a font of untapped growth potential and possessed skin like an Uncanny Valley infant and could maybe be convinced that Jane was the kind of PR genius who could bring the world to FortPath (or at least the optically optimal segment of the world). Jane didn't need Relevancy. All she needed was Cass.

It was so easy to be disdainful of capitalism when she didn't have any good ideas. Not that this was even her idea—she had just recognized the insufficient commodification of a commodity. Which was probably even better, actually. The tech bro she'd briefly dated had invested in an app called Fittd, which provided on-demand bed-making. After they broke up, she read that Fittd was valued at $500 million. Cass was a much safer bet than giving a stranger the key to your house and free rein to touch your pillows. All Cass needed was a handler—a semi-competent cynic who knew how to harness her unwieldy charisma.

~

When she heard Cass's footsteps receding, she crept out of the closet, grabbed her sneakers, and ran out of the house. *It's fine if I don't see her, actually,* Jane thought like a protective incantation. *I'm going for a run. I do it all the time.* In the time it took her to reach the road, Jane was already beginning to shuck the shame of losing her job, like a crunchy, nutrient-rich skin.

Though she recognized herself to be a grudge-nurser and failed-relationship-ruminator, in some ways Jane was highly adaptable. For example: There was something wrong with the shower in her current apartment; unless she made small, constant adjustments to the faucet handles, the water would alternate between icy and scalding. It had been like that for over a year, and she had never asked the super to fix it. She made the small, constant adjustments. It didn't even register as unpleasant anymore, except when she burned herself.

Jane had no idea what working for Cass would look like, beyond presumably taking up residence in the house of a thousand cricket corpses. Maybe the shells were somehow good for the skin, too. (*Move over, mucus! There's a new insect by-product that's about to become the exoskeleton of your skincare routine!*) And Cass's Cass-ness gave the project an air of start-up-ish legitimacy. As a minimum viable product, she was practically market-ready. Maybe Jane could call herself the chief creative officer. Maybe word would get back to Byron and he would feel a flash of disdain for Iza Brecht, and her parochial poetic ambition.

With Cass as her product, she would make enough money to pay off her medical debt. She would look into insurance options for small businesses and buy the most expensive one. The platinum tier. The diamond tier. The plutonium / black rhino horn / shaved truffle / free insulin tier.

Or maybe she would just move to the farm and never file a change-of-address and hide from her debt collectors forever.

She spotted Cass about fifty yards ahead, wearing a mid-thigh-length tie-dyed dress and leather sandals and running like she was delivering a joyful message—the end of a war, the birth of a savior. Jane felt heavy and labored in comparison. Cass was as thin as an Olympic distance runner, but her thinness appeared cosmetic rather than performance-based. Whenever Jane ran in the park, she took special pleasure in passing lithe, graceful women. *You think life would be so different,* Cass had said.

She sped up until she was nearly sprinting. *"Cass, hi!"* she yelled, emptying the reserves of her lungs.

Cass turned and cocked her head to the side, smiling. "It's a beautiful day to move," she called in her bell-clear voice, sounding un-exerted despite her speed. She bent over, placing her palms flat on the gravel. Jane trotted up to her.

"Totally," Jane gasped. "I-love-it. Out here."

"My body doesn't always respond well to the violence of running," Cass said from upside down. "But today I felt called to exuberance. Would you like to stretch with me?"

"Oh. Sure!" Jane tipped forward into a little lunge. Cass stood and lifted her arms toward the sky. "I wanted to talk to you about something. About living in my truth." She took a deep breath to steady her voice. She knew she had to ask for what she wanted, straight-out. "I think my truth is—" She paused, in case Cass wanted to jump in and offer what she wanted. "I should work here full-time."

It was almost exhilarating, the *just saying* it. She barreled ahead.

"I think the time has come for me to disentangle myself from my job. My former job. It isn't serving my spirit anymore. But I think if I worked here, with you, I could be a real asset to FortPath. To building your brand." She wondered if Cass could be sheepdogged into Job Interview, the opposite of Emotional Honesty. Jane had been on enough first dates to have mastered the pleasant, studied dissembling necessary to convince someone of her worth.

"I admire your commitment to growth. Of course, not every plant can thrive in every soil. Do you feel you've been thriving here?"

"Well, as you pointed out, I had a fearlessness breakthrough this morning," Jane said, smiling her professional smile. She folded her hands across her belly, then changed her mind and lifted them over her head in a stretch. How did people ever know what to do with their hands? Cass's hands rested on the small of her back, the perfect place for them.

"I've noticed some resistance from you. Are you resistant to me?"

Jane paused and breathed slowly through her nose. "You know, that's a great question, and I understand why you asked it. In the short time I've been here, I've realized some things about myself that I don't like very much. I've realized that my personality isn't serving my best interests anymore." She felt a thrill at claiming Farren's slight. "Naturally, that has caused me some discomfort. But without discomfort, we aren't, um, changing at all. We're just comfortable."

She thought this was probably true, though she didn't clarify that she would never willingly subject herself to discomfort, unless it made her more beautiful.

"Tell me what you don't like about yourself," Cass said.

Maybe this was like in an actual job interview, when you were supposed to say that your weakness was perfectionism, but again, the power of Cass's full attention made her want to be honest. "I can be mean," she said. "I think mean thoughts."

"What mean thoughts do you think about me?"

The trick would be to reel in her honesty impulse just enough. Jane made her face pensive. "I think . . . you're more aware of your power than you let on." She paused to gauge Cass's reaction, but her face remained open, pleasant, and totally unreadable. "I think you understand the effect you have on people, and you use it to your advantage."

"I stand in my power," Cass said, lifting her left leg to her right in tree pose. "Do you feel threatened by that?"

"Yes," Jane said. "But I'm trying to confront that fear. You are a *very* strong produ—" She faltered, worried that Cass wouldn't appreciate being referred to as a product, but she had said too many syllables to back down. "Product. Woman. A very strong soul. I needed to come here to feel it. And I want to help more people experience your strength."

"Even when you disagree with my methods?" As they talked, Cass had sunk into a full split on the road's shoulder. Jane wondered if her disdain had been so obvious.

"On a personal level, I find some of your methods . . . challenging. But I never shy away from a challenge," she lied. "And on a professional level, I respect that you're building your brand. And I think I would be an asset in furthering that brand."

"And how would you describe my brand?" Cass's tone was neutral-to-pleasant, like they were just having a conversation. With a less exceptional face, she could have had a brilliant career in HR.

"Glowing. You are lit from within. That's not attainable, of course, because you're the nonpareil." She said it like *non-Perrier.* Why, at this moment, did she choose a word she had only ever seen written out? But Cass was nodding. "It's not just about skin," Jane said, "but the skin is shorthand for everything else. Can I be honest?"

"There is only truth, expressed in different registers."

All the habitual liars Jane knew just wanted to make themselves sound interesting. Every lie revealed them. She wondered if that was what Cass meant.

"Okay: You are the strongest manifestation of your

power," she said. "Your face. Your, ah, body. People just want to look like you. They want your skin. Or, that's what they *think* they want. But when they're here, they'll learn all the other things you teach. Like truth. And . . ." *Group masturbation*? "Self-reliance."

At some point, Cass had tilted her face up toward the sky, as if reacting to Jane's slight veering off-message. Apparently, neither of them cared about self-reliance. Jane rerouted.

"But you have to be at the center of everything. Your website has too many words. Your face is the proof. It should be *everywhere*. If I worked for you, my first order of business would be reaching out to my media contacts to secure a profile of you. *Vogue*, probably," she said airily. As if anyone at *Vogue* had ever returned one of her impertinent pitches. For once, though, she didn't feel like she was over-promising. Cass was born for *Vogue*.

Cass was clearly aware of the effect she had on anyone in her presence, but she didn't seem to appreciate how easily that effect could be commodified. There was something almost touching about her seeming innocence of a world in which Jane was so reluctantly versed. This was part of Cass's allure: Jane found herself wanting to protect Cass, even if she suspected Cass might have the capability to kill her. Not like a child, or a baby animal, but like a cursed diamond, dangerous but of undeniable value.

"I don't demand belief, Jane." Cass uncoiled her legs in front of her and doubled over, lacing her arms under her knees, and stayed there for so long that Jane wondered if she was asleep, or in a trance. It sounded like a *but* was coming, but none came.

"I believe in you," Jane told her. "I believe in your *power.* You have the power to reach people. I don't know what you'll do once you have their attention."

Throughout her life, Jane had tried to believe in things—astrology, Catholicism, change, herself, intermittent fasting, love, life after love, mindfulness, Pilates, poetry, recycling, retinol, tarot. Her belief in Cass's power felt urgent in an unfamiliar way. She willed Cass to understand that although she didn't believe zucchini was any better than eggplant, or that ice water was reckless, she believed the power was real.

She longed for a full conversion, for the certainty of zealotry to wash over her. And if belief was a matter of effort, Jane told herself now, she was ready to try.

Cass didn't move, beyond maybe breathing more deeply.

"You have devotion. From Tom. From pretty much everyone here. But I'm skeptical. I'm kind of an asshole. You want the devotion of a skeptical asshole."

When Cass didn't respond, Jane wondered if dangling the promise of future allegiance had been the wrong play.

"Also, I'm desperate. Which I think is an underrated quality in employees," she said, hoping Cass would appreciate the radical honesty.

Cass unfolded herself. Her face was flushed, in a way that suggested expensive blush rather than partial inversion. She rose to standing and extended her left leg at a ninety-degree angle to her body, lightly holding her toes in her outstretched hand.

"I agree that desperation is powerful. I'm very sensitive to its odor. It smells like milk just beginning to turn. Not sour, but on the edge. Your odor is different." Jane allowed herself relief that she didn't smell like old milk. "More chemical. Your desperation is synthetic. You created it yourself. It may have the same effect, but I'm not sure."

"Okay, but isn't all desperation sort of created by the person who's desperate? Desperation is a spectrum."

"No," Cass said. She switched legs. "Desperation is not all created by the person who contains it. Some people are captives of their desperation. You're in an unlocked room and you refuse to leave."

"I lost my job." Jane felt sad for herself then, but in a distant way, like she was talking about someone else. She remembered how hungry she was. Sometimes in the mornings when she felt an inchoate sadness different from her usual inchoate sadness, it turned out to be hunger. Sometimes it went away when she had some toast. But this felt different—like she was hungry for toast in a place where no one had ever heard of toast, and she was trying to explain what toast was to people with no concept of bread or radiant heat.

"Is that all?" Cass asked.

For the second time that day, Jane felt the weight of her debt. This time, she spoke it aloud. She told Cass about the pain she'd felt, lying on the floor of the food co-op, and how she thought maybe she would die there. She told her about waking up in the recovery room and understanding, really understanding for the first time how entirely possible it was to spend a life alone.

She told Cass about getting that first bill and being so sure it was some kind of clerical error that she didn't even call her insurance company right away. She waited a few weeks, certain she could clear it up with one phone call, because after all, *she had insurance*. She told her about shouting at the blameless customer service representatives and feeling terrible about it until she did it again.

She told her about the waves of utter exhaustion that washed over her whenever she spoke to one of the representatives, who were human, but bureaucratically incapable of overriding policy with humanity, because they, like Jane, were entirely without power in the face of corporate impassivity. She wanted them to help her, but she figured they were afraid to, maybe even more afraid than most people because they understood worst-case scenarios better than anyone.

She was surprised to find that telling Cass the truth, whole and unvarnished, felt good.

Cass listened to it all, her expression unreadable. At some point she stopped stretching and just stood there, perfectly straight and still.

"So that's all, I guess," Jane said when she was finished.

"Did you sleep in my bed?" There was nothing confrontational or even teasing in Cass's voice; she might have been asking Jane if she'd read any good books lately.

"No," Jane managed to say levelly. She wondered if Cass had cameras hidden around the house, but figured it was more likely that she had a better-than-average sense of smell and that Jane hadn't been especially sneaky. "I lay in your bed."

"Thank you for your honesty. Go speak to Tom."

With that, Cass turned back toward the house and began to run. Jane's schoolyard instincts kicked in with surprising force and she gave chase. Cass ran faster, as if pushed by a strengthening wind. Jane began to sprint.

Then they were both sprinting. The house was a hundred yards away. Jane's lungs burned, but having enthusiastically debased herself in front of Cass, it seemed important to at least run faster than her. She would swear she touched the side of the porch a quarter second before Cass, though by the time they made it her vision was clouded with staticky spots.

"Okay." She tried to contain her heaving. "I'll speak to Tom." But Cass was already gone.

chapter 13.

"She told you there was a job?" Tom kept repeating the question, the way characters in movies did, a performance of incredulity, though he didn't seem to be performing. She had found him in the walk-in pantry, surrounded by boxes of powdered mushrooms and Mason jars of almonds and large bags of unidentified yellow dust. The door was ajar, and when Jane gave a little knock Tom had shouted, "I'm in here!"

"I'm out here," Jane had replied, hovering on the threshold. "It's Jane. Cass said I should come talk to you." Tom made her nervous, though she wasn't sure why. It wasn't the same way Cass made her nervous; with Tom, the power was slippery, shifting. She wasn't quite sure if he was the pathetic one or she was. It had to be one of them.

Tom was strange in an unselfconscious way, like if you told him people thought he was strange he would probably turn red and think about it for a long time, which she appreciated. People who were comfortable with their strangeness unnerved her. She was almost thirty and she wondered when she would stop caring so much about things like this. She could tell Tom still cared, too.

"Okay. Come in." He had sounded wary. She told him she wanted to work at FortPath, and that Cass had said to talk to him about it.

"There are no *jobs* here. I mean, this isn't, like, an office. It's not a place with jobs," he said when she finally convinced him that Cass had indeed sent her. His understanding of jobs seemed about thirty years out of date. What did he think he was doing there if not working?

"I think there could be jobs, more than one. I think FortPath—well, really Cass—could be an industry. You've been doing a really amazing job," she said in an attempt to be generous. "But you need help to really grow this thing."

"You don't even like it here," Tom said.

She thought about denying it. It annoyed her that Tom couldn't see that she was trying. She was trying to figure out if she could like it, if she could buy what Cass was selling, even if only so she could sell it more effectively. She decided he would respect the truth more.

"So what," she said. "I'm talking about a job. People who say they like their jobs are usually lying. And anyway, I'm not the target demo." She was impressed with her subconscious mind, and a little disgusted, too, by how fluently she spoke PR without even trying. If she had lived in Paris for two years instead of in the bowels of Relevancy, maybe she would be able to speak French by now.

"I *understand* the target demo, though," Jane continued. "She's twenty-five to thirty-five, or even forty-five, and childless. She's college-educated. She's urban/suburban." She was parroting one of Rand's pitches, which she knew by heart. She was almost certain *urban/suburban* was his oblique code for *white,* and she wished she hadn't said it. The reality was that everyone who worked at Relevancy was white, and every brand they worked with did everything they could to describe their customer base as white without saying *white.* Jane had always felt ashamed of this, and now felt ashamed of having planted that seed with Tom—though, in fairness, everyone at FortPath that weekend was also white. At work, she had decided that bringing more diversity to at-home fecal transplants probably wasn't a worthy goal, that maybe it was better for the world overall to distract white people with the question of their gut biomes, to prevent them from doing harm elsewhere. In this way, Jane let herself off the hook for direct action, if not for guilt.

"She spends between $1,000 and $4,500 a year on skincare products and treatments, and she earns more than $70,000 annually. She has at least one meditation app on her phone. She identifies as spiritual, but not religious. She lives in a city but has thought about rehabbing a farmhouse.

"She buys organic when it's easy and she's thinking of going vegan for a month, just to see how it feels. She goes to yoga a few times a week and she doesn't lift weights because she's afraid of getting too bulky. She's on a diet, but she doesn't call it a diet, she calls it eating clean. She's disappointed with her life, but she's certain the problem is her. She's privileged but she feels powerless. She thinks maybe vitamins will help. It doesn't matter if she's shopping for a mattress or jeans: She's looking for the One Perfect Thing. She wants to change her life without changing anything at all. She wants to be led while still feeling like a leader. She wants Cass, she just doesn't know Cass exists yet."

"And how is that not you?"

"I already take vitamins," she said. "And guess what, they don't do shit."

She felt the urge to remind him of their conversation in the kitchen the night before. She hoped he could think of her as a friend, both because it would make it easier to convince him, but also because she wanted them to be friends.

He didn't seem hostile, just suspicious. Jane realized that she might not be the first person to attempt to insert herself into Cass's tiny inner circle. She wanted to reassure him in some way, but she couldn't discern the exact contours of his fear. She didn't want to offer him a general reassurance that she wouldn't ruin everything, because she knew she might, in fact, ruin everything. So she just barreled forward with her pitch.

"Look, the landscape has changed. This demo wasn't nearly as defined when you guys started. I mean, I assume." She realized she had no idea how long they had been at it. She didn't even know how old Cass was. Twenty-eight? Seventeen? Two thousand eighteen, and Jesus Christ's little sister?

"But now they're incredibly powerful, and Cass is exactly what they're looking for. They're *hungry* for her."

"The things you're saying have nothing to do with Cass," Tom said. "She's not some kind of *smoothie* you can trick people into buying."

"Of course not," Jane said, thinking that Cass was much more like a serum. "But I thought you would want her message to reach more people. I mean, if you really care about her." She only felt a little bad about the lowness of the blow.

"You've known Cass for twenty-four hours, and you're already trying to see how much money you can get out of her. I'm trying to protect her."

"Well, I'm trying to make her dreams come true!" It might not have been the stupidest thing she had ever said, but it was certainly in the top 10 percent. Still, it wasn't untrue. She wanted Cass to be impressed by her, and in her cosmic debt—not so Jane could call in the favor, but because it would represent a profound connection. Not like Jane's connection to Vitalia Healthcare Group, of course—different from that.

She didn't want to meet Tom's eyes so she stared at a jar of nuts to the left of his head, hoping the effect was arch and steely. He wasn't saying anything, though, and after what felt like a long time, Jane forced herself to look him straight in the face.

At first, she couldn't tell whether he was laughing or crying. Whichever it was, he looked as if something was being forcibly, painfully extracted from deep within him. He yelped a little, which didn't clear things up, then barked. Laughter. Kind of.

"Are you laughing at me?" she demanded.

He nodded vigorously, slapping the shelf next to him so hard that he bounced a glass bottle of honey onto the floor, where it shattered.

"Oh fuck," he said. "That honey costs like eighteen bucks an ounce." Then he laughed some more.

It seemed like a good moment to prove her worth to Tom—sure, she might be an unworthy would-be exploiter of Cass, but she could also help clean up spills—so she bent down and picked up a large shard of the sticky glass. She didn't mean to cut herself, exactly. It was more a deliberate carelessness. She wanted to be in a different moment. It was like the waking equivalent of pinching yourself to stop dreaming. The glass sliced into the meat of her palm. She watched the blood pulse out rhythmically, dripping onto the pooling honey like a heavy-handed metaphor.

"Hey, Tom," she said. He wasn't laughing anymore. "Could you get me a rag or something? And maybe, like, a salve?" She wasn't in too much pain, but she felt strange, like her head was swaddled in rough cotton.

He left without a word and returned with a batik sarong and a bottle of Bragg's apple cider vinegar. "I'm not sure how clean this is, but I think the vinegar is an antiseptic. It cured my plantar warts, anyway. We don't really have anything else because Cass doesn't allow anything that disrupts the body's bacterial biome." He splashed about half the bottle onto Jane's wound. It felt like a slap on a sunburn, times a thousand. She gritted her teeth and sucked in tiny breaths, which made her even more light-headed.

Tom knelt next to her and wrapped the sarong around her hand until the whole bundle was the size of a football. The room was close, and the smell of honey, blood, and vinegar was overwhelming, but neither of them made a move to leave.

"Thank you," Jane said finally. "I know you know Cass better than I do. I know you guys have a very special friendship . . . or, relationship? Family . . . thing? Sorry, I have no idea."

"Actually, we're married." Tom rubbed at a splatter of honey on the floor with one finger. The depth of Jane's disappointment surprised her. She had no choice but to wildly overcompensate.

"Oh wow, cool! That's . . . wow! Do you, um. You guys don't wear rings, huh? That's cool. Kind of modern. I've heard a lot of couples are doing, like, watches or tattoos now."

"Wait, so your *whole job* is trying to convince people that you're telling the truth about things?"

"Okay, fine. I think it's weird that you guys don't act like you're married or tell people you're married. And also I'm a little surprised you're married to a woman. If I'm being honest."

As soon as it slipped out, she knew that this was more garden-variety snideness than radical honesty. The truth of it was beside the point; she'd said it to prove she knew something about him that he tried to keep hidden.

"So you're saying I read as gay? Hey, thank you for that unique assessment of me! You're really holding a mirror up to my experience!"

He sounded angrier than she would have thought possible, and she was ashamed. She didn't even know him, not really, and she had treated his sexuality as a point she could score on him. She wanted to apologize, but she found that the words were just out of reach.

He was looking down at the bottle of vinegar in his hands, his face shuttered.

"I'm really sorry, Tom," she said finally. "That was really presumptuous." Except it came out *prezumshshz*.

She blinked slowly, and the pantry reappeared before her clouded with fuzzy spots. "Also, I think I might need to go to the hospital."

~

The car was a piece of shit, but Tom was a preternaturally good driver. Jane, a nervous driver herself, had never noticed someone's skill behind the wheel before, but Tom drove like it soothed him. His jaw relaxed. He gripped the wheel like he was holding a kid's hand, firmly but gently. He changed lanes at the exact right moment. Jane wondered if he knew he was exceptional.

He didn't speak, and didn't offer to play any music. Jane was exhausted from the blood loss and sorry for how glibly she'd spoken about Tom's sexuality, so she didn't speak, either. The silence felt mostly companionable, though she had a sense that Tom was just on the edge of saying something, but kept pulling himself back.

Ordinarily when someone greeted her with even a whiff of animosity, she treated that person coldly for the rest of the time she knew them, just in case. She didn't want to humiliate herself by expending unnecessary kindness. Despite his recalcitrance, though, Tom felt safe. She felt protective toward him, instead of just toward herself.

Her hand was throbbing. She was light-headed and her mouth was slicked with horrible pre-vomit saliva. The car had manual windows, and by the time she had cranked hers down, it was 10 percent too late. Most of the puke landed on the car's exterior side, but about a quarter cup splashed into the window well. Jane held her head out the window for as long as she could stand the wind and the smell. She feared Tom would ask her if she was okay and his voice would betray his annoyance because realistically, how was he ever going to get that vomit out from the inside of his car door?

She used the blade of her hand to try to clean as much of it as possible, and then her hand was covered in vomit, too. Tom reached behind him silently, keeping one hand on the wheel and his eyes on the road and the car perfectly even within its lane, and handed her an old white T-shirt.

"Thank you," she said after she had done her best to mop up all the visible chunks. "Sorry."

"Your body was responding to trauma in a reasonable way. You don't need to apologize," Tom said, with no trace of irritation. "We're nearly there."

He took the next exit and drove them down an empty thoroughfare past a window-tinting place and a tire place and a candle store and at least three express motels, with no visible cars in any of their parking lots. She wondered if the promise on which they were built was yet to come, or had already collapsed.

The hospital had the lazy brutalist style of most for-profit health facilities. Tom parked outside the ER, where a sign announced that the operation was A PROUD MEMBER OF THE VITALIA HEALTHCARE FAMILY.

"Tom. We have to go somewhere else." Jane pressed the heel of her uninjured hand into her temple, trying to keep the panic from her voice.

"There's literally nowhere else, so," Tom said. He turned off the car and looked over at her. "Why?"

"I owe them money. Vitalia Healthcare."

"Everyone owes them money," he said.

"You?"

"No, not me," he admitted. "But a lot of people. And you really need to see a doctor."

As Jane stared at him, dark spots began to obscure his face.

"Fine," she said.

Sasha had told Jane her health insurance was active until the end of the month, after which time she could apply for COBRA, which at least had the courtesy to embrace a villainous acronym. She wrote her Brooklyn address on the intake form, wondering when, if ever, the bill would find her. Among the form's many questions was "Has anyone ever hurt you emotionally," which Jane refused to dignify with a response.

There was a poster on the wall with a graphic of a white person's hand and a Black person's hand, each forming one side of a heart. VITALIA HEALTHCARE GROUP: FOR YOUR HEALTH. FOR THE COMMUNITY'S HEALTH. FOR SOCIETY'S HEALTH.

After what felt like ten days, the receptionist called her name.

They waited another forty-five minutes in the curtained-off exam room. When the impossibly young doctor finally arrived, he applied a topical anesthetic to her hand and examined it for broken glass, then closed the wound with five stitches. Jane couldn't look, so she focused on the poster of a smiling blond baby with a Band-Aid on her arm. It read VITALIA HEALTHCARE GROUP: FOR HER FUTURE.

chapter 14.

On the drive back, Jane tried to apologize again for what happened in the pantry. The way he'd responded to her admittedly shitty comment suggested that she'd bumped up against something already precarious, and caused more damage than she could have anticipated.

"It's fine," he said, in the universal language of not-fineness. But then he glanced over at her and half smiled. "Really. It is."

The rest of the drive was silent, but a more companionable silence this time.

It was dusk when they pulled up to the house, so at first Jane didn't see that everyone was lying on the grass, spread out haphazardly like there had been a massacre. She had a moment of panic seeing them all there. She wondered briefly if Cass had gone full Jonestown because Tom hadn't been there to make dinner.

As soon as they slammed the car doors, though, she saw a few heads pop up. They walked to the edge of the scene. She heard Cass's voice, serene but with a slight edge. "We are relaxing deeply into our intentions for this fast. We are silently contemplating our bodies' innate fecundity, in times of *great* scarcity as well as abundance. We are as fallow fields, preparing ourselves for growth."

She stood up, like a time-lapse video of a flower unfurling, and stared at Jane and Tom as she continued speaking. "We understand that in order to cultivate *loyalty,* we must at all times remain *loyal* to our bodies, the vessels of our spirits. We show respect to ourselves only with *absolute honesty* and *commitment.*"

There was something familial in Cass's tone, like a mother reprimanding a child who was old enough to know better. Jane glanced at Tom. She felt guilty for the tension her injury seemed to have caused, and a little excited about her role in the drama.

"We'll spend the rest of the evening in silent reflection, and tomorrow morning we will break our fast with words of gratitude, and bone broth."

The figures on the grass roused themselves slowly and walked back toward the house, some of them bowing to Cass as they passed her, others embracing her. Tom pressed the top of his arm against the top of Jane's, giving her a gentle shove away from him and Cass. She feinted toward the house, but when she was sure neither he nor Cass was focused on her, she doubled back and tiptoed behind a large tree, feeling like a Looney Tune.

"She cut herself. She needed stitches, so I had to take

her to the hospital." Tom was speaking softly but his voice carried across the lawn.

"As long as you're at peace with your decisions, you will be in balance."

"I'm sorry I didn't make dinner. We had enough in the fridge, though. You didn't need to make them fast."

"Of course no one is ever required to fast. They chose to fast because it was the anti-nourishment they required," Cass said.

"Well, we don't have any bone broth."

"But we have bones." As was often the case when Cass spoke, Jane couldn't tell if this was a koan or a statement of fact.

"Okay, well. It takes twelve hours, so I guess I should get started."

"Sit with me first," she said.

Jane peered out from behind the tree. Cass sat on the grass and extended her legs in a *V* before her. She held up her arms. Jane strained to see Tom's face, but it was too dark. He sat down between her legs and reclined into her. Cass wrapped her arms around him and leaned close to his ear, whispering something that sounded to Jane like *Swish swish swish.*

She knew she should go inside. The moment was too intimate, like peeping on someone's water birth. She couldn't look away. After a while, Tom sat up and turned toward Cass. He lifted her caftan to her hips. Unsurprisingly, she wasn't wearing underwear. More surprisingly, her vulva appeared, at least from Jane's vantage point, entirely bare. Jane couldn't decide if Brazilian waxes were entirely at odds with Cass's whole thing, or perfectly in keeping with it.

Tom ducked between her legs, his head bobbing and swiveling vigorously. Cass didn't make any noise. She inclined her head toward Jane, quickly, like an animal that's heard a sound. Jane stood perfectly still. Cass's eyes were the only bright things in the deepening night. Jane felt them find her own and hold them. They stared at each other across the lawn until Cass shuddered gently and gave a tiny *mew.*

She stood up immediately, leaving Tom on his knees and Jane breathing so loudly she could barely hear it when Tom spoke.

"I love you," he said to Cass.

"I love you, and everyone." She walked toward the car. At some stage she must have taken the keys from Tom's pocket. "I have to go see a friend," she said. "I'll be back in time for the break fast." She paused for a moment. "Have a beautiful sleep, Jane."

Tom looked around, startled, but gave Jane a tiny nod when he met her eyes. She nodded back, *Oh, hey!* like they were in a crowded restaurant. Tom got up as soon as the car pulled out and walked back to the house, giving Jane's tree an unnecessarily wide berth.

Jane wondered where Cass had gone, and to whom. They were miles away even from the nearest farm stand. Where would she even have met someone? Jane imagined her barefoot at a gas station mini mart, sensuously examining a bag of beef jerky. Had she told Tom in advance that she was leaving? Probably not—Jane suspected that Cass didn't tell anyone anything in advance.

Jane had never seen a marriage up close, but she got the sense that after a time, most of them were held together by convenience, at least in part. Cass could have married anyone, but she chose Tom. Tom could have found a partner who would respond to *I love you* with *I love you, too,* but he chose Cass. Jane wondered about the conveniences that kept them both there.

She stayed put until the mosquitoes became too much to bear. When she walked inside, everyone was sleeping already except Tom, who was in the kitchen alone. She found an empty corner where someone had already laid a mat down, and fell asleep immediately.

~

The smell woke her. At first it seemed like it was coming from everywhere—the walls, the floor, her hair. It smelled like decay, like she was in the middle of a mass grave. When she sat up on her knees, she could see everyone from the night before, still sleeping. Or dead. She crawled over to Jessica and nudged her with her elbow. Jessica groaned and rolled over.

She heard a clang and a "Fuck!" and then a quieter "Fuck," from the kitchen. She remembered the bone broth. When she'd seen bone broth in health food stores, she'd never considered what boiling a pot of bones would smell like. A wall full of corpses, it turned out.

When Jane walked into the kitchen, she found Tom leaning against the cabinets under the sink, crying a little, like the despair hadn't yet decided if it would take. The smell was unspeakable. Her urge to escape it felt primal, not-to-be-reasoned-with.

"We have to stop meeting like this," she said, like an idiot.

"Sorry about the smell." Tom didn't look up. "I don't usually make this stuff when people are here."

"Is this your punishment for helping me?"

He flinched, like the question was a blackfly. "That's not how Cass thinks. She just wants to give everything a sense of purpose. It's really beautiful."

"You don't think that's a little . . . calculated?" She knew she sounded like a man who claimed he *just loved playing devil's advocate* when he was baldly insulting you, but she couldn't stop. Not until he admitted that Cass had some ugliness, somewhere. It was partly territorial, though she knew she had no claim to Tom, whom she had known for fewer than forty-eight hours, especially over his actual wife. The other part, though, was wanting to protect him from the danger of idealizing anyone, and especially someone like Cass, whose tether to other people seemed as thin as onionskin.

"It's a lot of responsibility, running this place with just the two of us. If one of us isn't pulling our weight, it can derail a whole weekend."

"Sure. But Cass meditates for like . . . hours a day," Jane said.

"That's *her work.*"

"No, of course." She was still learning how far she could push him.

"Cass is the love of my life," Tom said. His cadence made the words sound rehearsed, like a mantra. Did people ever describe someone as *the love of my life* spontaneously? "I didn't ask her to marry me, you know. She asked me." He smiled to himself. "She knew my parents weren't big on positive reinforcement."

He told her he could only remember his mother saying *I love you* one time, at her own mother's funeral. He called his grandmother Boop, which was when Jane understood that he came from serious money. Jane was fascinated by people who grew up very rich, and she could usually spot them, but Tom was a tricky case. She had sensed he was privileged, but he didn't move through the world with the ease of the extremely wealthy—the sense that everything from cars to cobwebs would clear the path for them.

Boop had lost one vocal cord to laryngeal cancer, he told Jane, so everything she said sounded like an angry secret. She died on the *Queen Mary 2*.

The trip had been a gift from Tom's parents for Boop and Pater's fiftieth anniversary. *Don't worry,* Tom's father told him when he broke the news of her death. *All cruise ships are required by law to have morgues on board.* They shipped her body back from Southampton two weeks later. Pater continued the trip as planned, and six months later married Miriam, a widow with whom the couple had dined the night of Boop's death.

My mother wasn't warm, Tom's mother told him at the cemetery. *She didn't express much emotion. Well, I love you.* Then she kissed him on the cheek. *I can't believe my father brought a* redheaded woman *to her funeral.*

"So, how do your parents feel about you being married to, um, someone like Cass?" Jane asked.

He raised an eyebrow at her. Wry was his most appealing look. "They didn't remember her as the housekeeper's daughter, and we didn't feel the need to remind them. We got married at city hall just a few months after I left Realities. The rehab center," he said.

“We had dinner with them once we did it. They liked her a lot. They especially liked that she was, you know, a girl.” Tom cleared his throat and looked down at his hands. When he met Jane’s eyes again, he shrugged and smiled with what seemed like enormous effort.

Jane remembered her glib tone in the pantry, and Tom’s anger. She felt wretched. It was easy to imagine him as a little boy, making some innocuous comment or gesture that raised his mother’s hackles and led to years of observation and correction. *Those are* girls’ *toys! That’s how* girls *wave!* She wanted to find Tom’s mother and slap her.

“Boop and Pater set up a trust for me. The funds would only become available once I got married. To a woman. They were very clear on that. When we got access to the trust, we bought this place. I haven’t seen my parents since then.”

Jane felt sure that Cass had known about the trust. She wanted to ask about it so badly, the desire felt like a stitch in her side. How much money was it? Did they have a prenup? What would happen to Tom if Cass decided to divorce him? Why didn’t guys with family trusts ever offer some of that money to Jane to wipe out her debt?

I’m not a very good person, she thought, not for the first time. And: *Why can’t I be some other way?* She offered to stay up with Tom so he wouldn’t have to stay in the stinking kitchen all alone.

“Thanks,” he said. “That would be nice.”

Jane sat down at the table across from him. It reminded her of when she and Eleanor were just starting to knit themselves together. So she told him about Eleanor, how she would bring something over to Jane's for dinner—a savoy cabbage or a sweet-and-savory grab bag of frozen pierogi, some meat and cheese, some mixed berry, or whatever else was the cheapest at the corner store—and they would cook together and talk so easily, like they were living parallel lives just a few inches apart, with everything that happened to one so immediately comprehensible to the other that it must be okay.

In Jane's memory, they were always sitting at a table together, in one of their apartments. She knew they went places, too, but it was the times when it was just the two of them, inhabiting the reality of their lives but somehow feeling comfortable with it, that stayed with Jane. Eleanor was always doing something with her hands—folding a piece of junk mail into a fortune teller, or plaiting her hair—and Jane found the action comforting, the idea of forward motion while sitting still.

She and Eleanor had the same deep but nebulous ambition—to be free from constant doubt and worry, to feel they had arrived at a place that was a *real place*—with the same bafflement about how to achieve it. They used their want to fuel their love for each other.

Jane had never had a friend with whom she felt on such an equal footing. She wanted good things for Eleanor, which felt akin to wanting good things for herself, because their lives seemed so intertwined. When Eleanor had gotten her first big promotion at work, Jane had gotten into her PhD program. As Jane realized she was out of her depth in grad school, Eleanor's position as associate editor was dampened by the fact that her boss was still making her print out and bind all his emails. Jane's medical debt was a cataclysm, but it was almost the same-sized cataclysm as Eleanor's student debt.

They dwelled together in their fears and their hopes, all of which appeared to them over a shared horizon. It seemed impossible that things would work out for them and unthinkable that they wouldn't, someday.

When Jane was done, Tom asked if she still talked to Eleanor.

"Sometimes," Jane lied.

He looked at her for a long time, his eyes searching. Then he nodded and said, "Good."

He walked over to the stove and wafted some of the steam from the pot toward his face. The horror smell had dissipated, or else Jane had just gotten used to it.

Tom announced that the broth was done and it was time to go to sleep. He replaced the pot's top and hauled it to the fridge.

"Sleep well, Jane," he said, and went up the stairs.

Jane felt a pang of disappointment when he didn't invite her to his room, but she couldn't discern the flavor of her longing.

~

Eating the bone broth the next morning, she was amazed at how good it tasted despite the smell. She was hungry, but not like she had been at first. She added "rapid increase in satiety" to her mental list of the Marketable Pillars of FortPath, along with "omnipresent sexual fog" and "smooth neck." She had only slept for a few hours the night before, but she barely felt tired.

It was the last day of the session, and Jane still wasn't sure if she was staying. She had been afraid last night to ask Tom about her future there for fear of ruining the moment.

After they broke the fast, they gathered outside once more. Cass addressed them from the center of the circle, rotating slowly, holding everyone's eyes for a few seconds.

"Our time together has created such a power inside me. I am deeply invigorated by your life forces. As you return to your lives, hold with you the intentions you set here with me. Hold your intentions in your mind, body, soul, and spirit. Do not deny yourselves the abundance of breath. Cherish hydration."

Did she really just tell us to drink more water and make it sound like some secret of the universe? Jane could already see the *Cherish Hydration* merch: mint-green water bottles with wooden caps, rose-quartz tote bags, possibly yoga-friendly T-shirts if she could find the right font. *Cooking with Water: Recipes to Help You Cherish Hydration and Breathe Abundantly.*

"You are all teeming with possibility. Allow that possibility to flow from you into the world. If you lose your way, remember you are always welcome here. I love you all."

Jane glanced at Tom, who was looking at his feet. She wondered again if he knew where Cass had gone the night before. Cass embraced Josh first. She held him for a long time. When she let go, he was weeping. She moved on to Farren, who wiped her dry cheeks, sniffing theatrically, and then bowed to Cass when her time was over.

She didn't skip Tom, but their physical contact seemed perfunctory, habitual.

Jane was last. *It's just a hug*, she told herself. Cass stepped in front of her. Jane thought of the mirror exercises from high school drama class, when it felt possible that you could just slip out of yourself and maybe into someone else. Like a real-life Instagram.

Cass was better at hugging than Jane was at anything. She moved slowly, like a snake stripped of its symbolic moral freight. It felt like she was transferring some bodily knowledge, straight from her chest. A warmth spread through Jane. She felt safe, swaddled. And she didn't even really like hugs. She wasn't crying, though to cry seemed like a perfectly reasonable response to this feeling, and she felt sorry for judging the people who had.

"I invite you to stay here with us," Cass said in her ear. It was Jane's first whispered job offer. "And bring our message to more people."

She didn't feel happy, exactly, but for the first time in months, she felt still.

chapter 15.

Hammering out the details of the employment agreement proved more difficult than securing the job. Jane didn't know how much money was left of Tom's trust, and there was no good way to find out without seeming mercenary, which of course she was trying hard to be.

Of the three of them, Jane assumed she knew the most about business. At least, she knew that "equity" wasn't what it sounded like, and that things were only worth what you could convince someone to pay for them. She knew to buy low and sell high. She sat down at the picnic table with Tom feeling confident she had the upper hand, insofar as there were hands at all.

"This is just a preliminary conversation, of course," Tom said. "We're going to have to get our lawyer to draw up a contract for you once we figure everything out."

He recognized immediately the source of her nonplussed expression. "I was an i-banker for a second after college," he said. "I wasn't exactly qualified. My father knew someone."

"I actually think that's *the* qualification." Jane had dated two investment bankers. Both were lacrosse-presenting blond men who spoke of their very recent years at Princeton with a level of nostalgia Jane associated with the Greatest Generation, except they were talking about eating clubs rather than storming the beaches at Normandy. They had both been dull at restaurants and careless in bed, but she still had wondered if she could stand to spend her life as one of their rich wives, riding horses and raising cruel sons.

"That was the only job I ever had," he said.

"Well, now you work for Cass, LLC." She made a mental note to research LLCs. Limiting her liability sounded great.

"FortPath," Tom said.

"Oh yeah. We have to talk about the name. It's not a good name. It sounds like a military base."

Tom sighed and looked up at the ceiling. It was stamped tin, blurred from layers and layers of paint. The house was, Jane realized for the first time, beautiful. Looking at it more closely, she finally understood what "good bones" meant. She had always had a hard time seeing potential. It was why she was terrible at thrift store shopping: She needed to see beautiful things presented with fanfare, ideally in a stark white retail space staffed by thin, mean women.

Now that she had committed herself to FortPath, she was pleased to find that she was capable of looking beyond presentation. It made her feel like she had already acquired new depths—spirituality by osmosis.

The house's floors were all hardwood, which her demographic unthinkingly prized, with unusually wide beams, scratched and pocked enough to suggest character rather than neglect. The sink was a schoolhouse trough style Jane recognized from Instagram, and there was a wall of exposed brick behind the six-burner gas stove.

"This house is really nice," Jane said, hoping he got to *so you can afford to pay me handsomely* on his own.

"Cass found it," he said. "She knew a realtor out here. And I sort of fixed it up a little. Well, I ripped up some carpets and I painted it because Cass didn't think the other color flowed well enough."

"Where did you guys live before?"

"New York for a while." Of course Cass had lived in New York for a while. "During Occupy Wall Street."

"Oh wow. I didn't think Cass was, um. Political?"

"She likes energy. There was a lot of energy there."

"Were you camping out?"

"For a little while," Tom said. He looked up at the ceiling again. Jane could tell he didn't want to talk about it, but she pressed on.

"What was it like?"

"It was fine. It was loud. I don't know. It was fine. After the park we stayed there with a friend. Daniel."

Breeziness was his tell. He tried to say *Daniel* like it was just another word. *Bowl. Kelp. Daniel.* He was so determined that it felt like a kindness to let it go, at least right then.

"That's lucky," she said. "Finding an apartment sucks."

"Yeah. Brokers."

"They're the worst," Jane added. She had time.

~

Jane assumed she would go to the lawyer's office with Tom, but when it was time to leave, Cass came downstairs instead.

"Jonathan is a dear friend," she said.

Cass was such a terrible driver that their time in the car felt like an interstitial scene from a hacky sitcom. She changed lanes without so much as a glance at her mirror and braked like she was waking up from a nightmare. *Fear is a powerful illusion fear is a powerful illusion fear is a powerful—* By the time they got to the office, Jane's T-shirt was damp with panic sweat. "Are you getting enough bee pollen?" Cass asked as they walked up to the office, a Victorian house with a small hanging shingle that read JONATHAN M. DAVIES, ESQ., ATTORNEY AT LAW. "I find it helps with body odor."

It seemed possible that Cass had invented negging. At the very least, she had perfected the form.

Jonathan M. Davies was a slight, middle-aged white guy with an elastic face that registered equal parts desire and fear when he looked at Cass, as though she were an expensive and much-longed-for gift that might somehow be a cruel trick.

"Is your family thriving, Jonathan?" Cass asked when they sat down. It didn't feel ominous until Jonathan blanched, and Jane realized they had definitely slept together, or at least done things that wouldn't help his family thrive.

She was impressed by Cass's ability to leverage her sexuality in such a wide variety of situations. She didn't feel sorry for Jonathan. He thought he was entitled to fuck a comically gorgeous woman, and why? Because he had a law degree? Because he still had most of his hair? Jane understood then that they wouldn't be paying for Jonathan's time, and felt proud of Cass.

"Jane is going to be creating with us," Cass said. Jonathan registered Jane's presence for the first time. His smile felt like a bookmark, like if Cass wasn't there he'd let his gaze linger. For the first time, Jane wondered if it was ever exhausting to live in Cass's body.

The idea that inspiring such feelings in others might sometimes be a burden hadn't occurred to her until she felt from Jonathan a mere fraction of the intensity he directed at Cass. Even if it was just a sip, in her case, the way he drank them both in made Jane uneasy. She felt sorry for Cass, until the subject of money came up and she remembered that Cass was also, via Tom, rich. The envy returned.

"We need to discuss her material compensation," Cass continued.

Jane had spent enough time around people who were rich and beautiful to know that not all of them were happy, but she believed with a religious fervor that if *she* were rich and beautiful, *she* would be happy. Jane appreciated the fact that Cass seemed to be making the most of her privilege, even as part of her resented Cass's self-satisfaction.

"Fine, of course. While you're here, though, I'd really like to reopen the conversation about liability insurance. I don't feel comfortable with how unprotected you are at the moment." Jane would bet anything Jonathan had asked Cass to call him Daddy at least once.

"Insurance would demonstrate a lack of trust in both

my own strength and the generosity of the universe," she said.

"Insurance is simply a way of protecting yourself in the event of unforeseen disaster."

"As we've discussed, I choose not to be governed by fear," Cass said. At least it explained her driving.

Jonathan gave Jane a *we're both reasonable people, right?* look that included the slightest wink, and which made her want to act unreasonably. Did he really think that given the choice of allies, she would go with him and not Cass?

"The entire insurance industry is a scam," Jane informed him. "They'll find a way to get out of paying no matter what, so we might as well put our money into something worthwhile. Like ethically sourced macramé."

Cass looked at her with mild surprise.

"I can draw up a standard employment agreement," Jonathan said to Cass. He seemed relieved that his initial assessment of Jane as useless had proven correct. "I always recommend a standard probationary period, for your protection, and—"

"Jane will be our partner."

"Can you give us a moment?" Jonathan said. He was still looking at Cass, but it was clear he was talking to Jane.

"Only if that's what Cass wants," she said. Being on Cass's side of the table was exhilarating. Maybe this was how an athlete felt when her team was unstoppable, or a mean girl in middle school when she and her friends made someone cry. Jane had always seen herself as the beleaguered one, ever virtuous, ever floundering. Sitting with Cass, united against Jonathan in all his overconfident mediocrity, she realized that actual superiority was infinitely preferable to the feeling of superiority casting herself as the underdog conferred.

"Jonathan," Cass said gently. "I feel your fear for me. It feels like love."

"Oh no. I—" Jonathan hoisted himself out of his chair and hovered a few inches above the seat, as if not sitting would give him some plausible deniability if his wife found out.

"But I won't take your fear on. I choose to move through life open-souled. And Jane is our family now."

Only one other person in life had ever claimed Jane as family. Her joy at hearing Cass say this made Jane feel disloyal to her mother. Her immediate euphoria was also clouded by wariness, but she reasoned that Cass wore the label of "wife" as loosely as her caftans, so probably "family" landed just shy of "hairdresser who remembers that you have a vacation coming up" in her taxonomy of relationships.

Jane wondered if Cass would explain everything to her on the way home. Maybe even *everything*, everything. Sitting in Jonathan's office with Cass felt more like a religious experience than any Silence. Cass's powerful benevolence was like a Sunday school story.

"Why did you make me a partner?" Jane asked, once they had gotten back into the car.

"It was what you wanted," Cass said, turning her body fully toward Jane.

"The road, the road!" Jane yelled. Cass turned back and swerved away from the shoulder.

"You try so hard to protect yourself. You don't trust

that the things your heart seeks will come to you. But just now in the office, I felt you step into your power. I believe you have the power to manifest your dreams." She turned away from the road again and studied Jane's face. "But only your most potent dreams," she added.

Cass was the most dangerous kind of person: the kind who believed her own bullshit. They could convince you. Jane had always wanted to belong to something, but now, in Cass's orbit, she wondered if slipping into belief might be this easy.

~

"You don't have *Wi-Fi*?"

Of all the things Jane had learned about FortPath in the past week—sometimes bats came in through a hole in the roof and Tom had to kill them with an atlas before anyone noticed! Cass believed showering with soap robbed her skin of its hydration barrier and only did so when menstruating!—this was the most surprising.

"I have a phone," Tom said. "And there's an internet café in town, for when I need to update the website."

"An *internet café?*" Jane screeched. "Are we studying abroad in 2006?"

Tom rolled his eyes, but agreed to make an appointment with the only local internet provider.

When he arrived the next day, the Wi-Fi technician, Piotr, was entirely immune to Cass's charms. "This house is difficult to find," he said when Cass opened the door. Tom and Jane were in the kitchen making a list of furniture they needed.

Physically, Piotr was nearly Cass's equal. He had shoulder-length blond hair that looked like the magazine clipping Jane's mother used to show her hairdresser to make sure she got the highlights right. His eyes were angled downward, which gave him the effect of being on the verge of a wink, and there were deep brackets around his mouth like he spent most of his time smiling. Smiling and winking.

"We're so glad you found us," Cass said in her full-charm voice. Piotr made a noncommittal sort of grunt. Jane felt a little embarrassed for Cass, and annoyed at Piotr for being so obtuse.

"Where is the phone jack? Out here we need to do DSL. You know what it is? I can explain." Jane and Tom listened as Piotr gave Cass a primer on the rich tapestry of internet connections, from dial-up ("You remember the noise of the connection, like crackling then *zzzapzap!* People always wonder, *It still exists?* Yes. But very slow.") to satellite ("Expensive, because it must come from space."). He was satisfied that DSL was the best option for them. He had installed DSL for many houses like theirs, and everyone was very happy with it ("Even people who have had cable internet tell me, 'Piotr, the speed is the same.' ").

Jane, who had very little interest in the functionality of internet connections in the abstract, was fascinated by Piotr's cheerful indifference to Cass. She almost hated him for it, but she couldn't look away. Sometimes people pretended not to see the very beautiful, but Jane could always spot such active resistance—they laughed too loudly, were too studious in their not-seeing. Piotr wasn't avoiding Cass, he was just treating her like a regular person who needed internet.

“Who was your last service provider?” he asked.

“I’ve never had the internet in my home.” She sounded brusque, and something else. Unnerved? But Piotr was delighted about being the first to usher Cass onto the information superhighway.

“People say, *Oh, life was better before internet,* but it’s because people love to complain. I grew up in Poland, before internet. It was so boring! Now if I’m bored, I find a video, I play a game. People who never have to suffer are the only ones who want to deny themselves this happiness. There’s no reason to be bored. Life is bad enough.”

“I’m never bored,” Cass said. “Tom. Please come help Piotr while I go outside.” Tom dropped his list and hustled into the front hall. Jane trailed curiously behind him.

“Goodbye, Piotr. Thank you for lending your gift to us.”

Jane admired Cass’s grace in defeat, before it occurred to her that Cass might not consider a stranger not explicitly wanting to fuck her a loss.

He shook Tom’s hand and gave Jane a friendly nod.

“Your wife does not like the internet?” Piotr said.

“Not really,” Tom said. “She’s more into trees.”

It took Piotr another forty minutes to finish the install. As he drilled into the baseboards and threaded fat cables, he chattered to Tom and Jane, who learned that he loved Twitter but hated Facebook (“Why do I want my aunties in Kraków to see all of my business?”), could find pirated videos of any professional wrestling match—“including Japanese”—in under five minutes, and considered online dating the greatest invention of the twenty-first century.

Though Jane had been receiving push notifications from her own cadre of dating apps the whole time she'd been at FortPath, Piotr's discussion of something so central to her before-life—and so absent from this one—was an unwelcome intrusion.

Jane had thought about sex constantly since she met Cass—it was a low hum that underscored everything, like the sound of a refrigerator—but she'd barely thought about her single state at all. In the past, Jane had fucked people with whom she didn't want relationships, but the questions of *Could we? Could this?* were always in her mind. Now the idea of sex felt more like how physicists meant *potential* than how leadership books did.

Piotr was still talking. "I meet many, many women. Sorry to offend you," he said to Jane, who was only offended by his assumption of her offense. "Before, I have to go out to a bar, spend time to talk to women and maybe she's not even interested! So I've wasted my time! Now, before I leave my house, I know already."

"What kind of women do you like to date?" Tom asked too loudly, like someone had turned up his volume dial by accident.

"All kinds! That's the best part—like being in a candy store where you can try everything before you buy it." Jane wondered if candy stores had different rules in Poland, or if Piotr had just been stealing candy his whole life. "I can meet a different woman every night if I want. Probably I shouldn't say this to a married man!" He laughed and patted Tom's shoulder conciliatorily.

"My wife is the most beautiful woman in the world."

"Ah!" Piotr blew a kiss toward the router he had just

installed. "Someday maybe I will find a woman I feel this way about, and *then* I will get married." He smiled at Jane, all kindness and no wolf.

Piotr was more at home in his life than anyone Jane had ever met. Maybe that was why he was impervious to Cass's charms—he wanted for nothing. She had nothing to offer him that wasn't a swipe away. Piotr wasn't one of them.

"No, my wife really is the most beautiful woman in the world. A lot of people think so, not just me." Tom was almost yelling now; he steadied himself against the back of one of the plastic faux-Eames chairs. It made a cracking sound like it was about to break, but held steady. Piotr nodded and returned his attention to the modem.

Jane couldn't tell if Tom felt protective over Cass, or protective over his choice of her.

"You have a computer? I am ready to set up your network," Piotr said, with a new formality. "You can choose the name, maximum thirty-two characters."

"I don't know what to call it."

"Can be anything," Piotr said, casually surveying the room, already planning his exit.

"Can you just choose?" Tom asked, a fissure of desperation in his voice. Jane understood. She didn't like doing anything that required her to confidently project herself to the outside world—like wearing a hat. Anyone who saw your network name could assume something about you based on these thirty-two characters.

After Piotr made the necessary arrangements and presented them with a carbon copy of his bill, Tom walked back toward the kitchen without a word to Jane. For a while she tried to think of more things they needed for the house, but got bored before long and went to look for him. He was in the pantry, which she now knew was his Emotion Room.

"Man, how hot was that guy?" she said, trying to keep it light.

They hadn't spoken about his sexuality or his family since the bone broth night, but Jane kept trying to leave him openings in case he wanted to confide in her. She wanted to cement their closeness. She also wanted to know everything about his relationship with Cass.

She loved hearing about the mechanics of relationships, even mundane ones. The deep-worn grooves of snipes and grievances that textured a relationship were endlessly fascinating to her. It was comforting to know that even cruelty could be weathered. The idea of a relationship like Tom and Cass's, one that could survive rehab, familial estrangement, small business ownership, and pretty obvious ongoing infidelity, was thrilling.

"He was handsome," Tom said. "I've never met someone who likes the internet that much."

"He's found his bliss," Jane replied.

Tom smiled in the sad, distracted way he had, like he had terrible news but he had decided to bear it alone for a few more hours.

chapter 16.

They ate vanilla mushroom parfaits with green-tea-marinated zucchini ribbons and pistachio porridge with chia and grapefruit and cashew-zucchini bisque with kelp croutons and kelp rolls filled with bee pollen and kelp broth with mushroom dust and alkalized mushroom water and alkalized turmeric water and alkalized almonds and stone-ground almond butter on zucchini medallions. They spiralized things Jane didn't realize could be spiralized: pumpkin and asparagus and single leaves of lettuce. After only six days, food as Jane had previously understood it felt like a distant memory.

"At the beginning, your body is in discord with hunger. Then your body learns to integrate it. When you integrate the hunger, it means your body knows that the hunger is in service to it," Cass said one night as they ate their zucchini-kelp Napoleons. "I don't hunger, but this is what I've come to understand."

She sometimes sounded like a walking pro-anorexia

forum. The hunger was like a sore tooth Jane had learned to chew around. Sometimes she would feel it like a sharp pain, but mostly it was just there. There were no full-length mirrors in the house, but she could feel her body changing shape.

"Do I look thinner to you?" she asked Tom after dinner. Cass usually floated away after meals. Sometimes she took the car. Sometimes she disappeared into her room or wandered off into the woods. Jane wondered if Cass was visiting different versions of Tom she'd scattered across the tristate area. Jane had only seen her return to the house once. Cass got out of the car holding a stack of magazines. Later, Jane snuck into her room to look for them, desperate to find out which ones they were, but there was no trace of them.

"I have no idea how much anyone weighs," Tom said, and started clearing the table.

"I bet you'd notice if Cass lost weight," she countered, feeling petty in a contagious way.

"Her weight doesn't really fluctuate." He reached under the sink to retrieve the bottle of Dawn he kept secret from Cass. She didn't believe in cleaning products, but Tom had a hard, if hidden, line when it came to dishes.

"You're really good at neutral diffusion, has anyone ever told you that?"

"I'm the child of two WASPs who didn't really like each other," he said. "Neutral diffusion is my most cultivated skill."

"My mom was really into emotional sharing, but it kind of had the opposite effect. I used to scream anytime she said the word *feelings*."

"Ah," said Tom, neutrally.

~

There were pockets of tiny grossness all over the house—a nest of hair on the porch, a ghostly print of a bare foot on the wood floor that kept materializing, even after Jane had mopped. Signs of life where they shouldn't be. Once Jane stayed at a motel where she found a white cotton glove in the shower. It was still the most disgusting image she could conjure, that flat, damp hand draped over the side of the tub.

She explained to Tom that for the clientele they were trying to attract, life could only exist within the immediate aura of an actual living person; nothing sloughed off and left behind.

"We're calling them clientele?" Tom said.

Jane sighed. "I haven't decided yet. I have a list somewhere. But I do know that part of what we're selling is a world without grossness. Not sanitized, obviously. Just someplace where no one is *exactly* human."

Tom looked skeptical. "We're all human, Jane."

They were sitting at the picnic table together making a to-do list for the day. Jane had convinced Cass to give her a three-month "reboot" period before they opened the rebranded FortPath (they hadn't settled on a new name yet). She was terrified of fucking it up, though she wasn't even sure what fucking it up would look like. Her style was usually under-promise and over-deliver, but for once her long-dormant ambition had taken over and now she was on the hook for a Global Wellness Phenomenon.

Success hinged on how moldable Cass was. That Tom and Cass had managed to convince would-be influencers like Farren to come to a dilapidated farmhouse in New

Jersey without even the promise of palo-santo-scented gift bags was a testament to them both, but Jane knew that the discerning clientele she planned to court would require a more polished exterior, starting with Cass herself.

Her brainstorming doc included the aforementioned *gift bags* as well as *reality show appearance* (something Bravo) and *celebrity friend*. The last was the most promising, but Jane struggled to think of a famous woman who would want to invite the physical comparison to Cass. *Celebrity boyfriend* was the obvious solution, but Jane didn't want to bring it up to Tom. At least not yet.

"You don't think we could convince Cass to shower more, do you?"

"More than once I've seen her step in goose poop with bare feet and just wipe it off on the grass so . . . sure, give it a try."

"We need to do something about those geese, too," Jane said.

Tom had started to drop details about life with Cass into their conversations, which made Jane feel like he was actually starting to trust her. Cass never referred to him as her husband, or referenced their marriage in any way. Neither of them ever wore rings.

"Do you have any pictures from your wedding?" she asked.

"I told you, it was just at city hall. Well, I have one." He opened his phone and pulled it up so quickly she felt sure he had bookmarked it.

They were standing on the steps of New York's city hall. Whoever had taken the picture had centered Cass, so Tom was only three-quarters in frame. Tom was holding Cass's hand in both of his. She wore an oversized taupe baby-doll dress with a round neck and a gathered waist. She looked radiant, though not *just-married radiant;* just Cass radiant. Tom, on the other hand, was beaming. He wore a gray suit that fit him surprisingly well, and a slim black tie. He was fully in profile, his face turned toward Cass as she gazed into the middle distance, possibly at whoever was taking the photo.

"You look really happy," Jane said.

"It was a good day." He gently took his phone back and glanced at the picture once more before locking its screen and putting it facedown on the table.

"We definitely need a new table. And new bedrolls. And new soap. And I *know* how Cass feels about soap, but this is non-negotiable." She wanted to ask more about the wedding, but she could tell he'd had enough for the day. She was proud of herself for putting his feelings ahead of her curiosity. It seemed like the kind of thing a friend would do. Jane was almost sure Tom thought of her as his friend, but she still wanted to hear him say it in the same way she used to yearn for men she was dating to define the relationship.

"I'll put it on the list," Tom said.

The list was endless. So far, the only task they had managed to complete was canceling every reservation currently on the books and refunding the deposits, and that was only because Jane was worried about the online blowback if they didn't.

"Can you help me move the table out now?" she said, suddenly desperate to complete something material.

"But then we won't have a table."

"So we'll eat on the floor. I can't concentrate with this

thing in here. It's hideous. And why does it always feel *wet*?"

Tom looked bemused, but he extracted himself from the table. "Okay, how do you want to do this?"

"How did you get it in?"

"Oh, it was in here when we bought the place."

Jane stood at the end of the picnic table and stretched her arms across it. Then she walked to the kitchen door, trying to keep the space between them steady. "I don't think it will fit."

Tom replicated Jane's arm measurement. He looked like a beginner mime performing carrying an ottoman. "So what should we do?"

She thought. "Do you have an ax?"

"Let me check the shed." He jogged outside and returned a few minutes later with a large ax and a small hatchet, both pocked with rust and wrapped in cobwebs so thick they looked like cotton candy.

"Do you have any axing experience?" she asked.

"Only throwing them. Summer camp," he said. "It was better than riflery or sailing."

"In deference to your expertise, you can take the big guy. I think our best bet is to chop it in half lengthwise. Hot-dog-style, if you will."

"I haven't had a hot dog in so long," Tom said.

"We'll get you a pack and stick it in the freezer."

It took longer than she imagined possible because, as it turned out, they were both terrible at chopping, Tom's summer camp experience notwithstanding. The hatchet was far too delicate to be useful for anything except, maybe, sculpting a wooden bust, but Jane swung it dutifully into the meat of the table until her palm, newly free of stitches, burned, and she had to take a break to find one of Tom's ancient gardening gloves.

Tom was making slightly more progress at his end, except he kept getting the blade lodged in the table and having to pause to wrestle it out. After half an hour, he had created a six-inch split in the wood. Jane had created a tiny dent and a small pile of shavings. She offered to take over the real ax.

Tom carved his initials into the table with the hatchet while she worked. After another half hour, she had managed maybe eight inches. At the rate they were going, they would be done in seven hours. It was the most satisfying task Jane could remember. In her previous life, physical activity was divorced from any goal beyond reshaping the body. She didn't even own a real bike—she only cycled to nowhere. The word *productivity* conjured Excel docs and follow-up emails rather than the physical work of changing one thing (table) into another (pieces of table).

Neither Jane nor Tom spoke, or spoke about not speaking. Each one would work with the real ax until they needed a break. Then the silent handoff, and whoever had the hatchet would continue the art project on the other end of the table. Tom carved his initials, Jane made a heart around them. Tom carved a knife stabbing the heart, Jane made droplets of blood oozing into a puddle. Tom carved a concerned-looking face in the puddle, Jane gave it eyebrows and pigtails.

They worked until dusk. Jane had a blister on her palm and shooting pains in her forearms. Her mouth was so dry from the exertion and the silence that she made a clicking sound when she swallowed. They were halfway through the table by the time it got too dark to see.

"Finish tomorrow?" she said. They could have turned on a lamp, but that seemed like cheating, somehow.

Tom nodded. "Kelp macaroni for dinner?"

It sounded delicious.

When Cass came in for dinner, she regarded the table neutrally. She ran her palm over the carvings and over the split in the wood.

"There's violence here," Cass said.

"We couldn't get it out the door," Tom explained. "So we have to chop it in half. We're going to get another table. Jane just thought . . ."

"It wasn't serving us anymore," Jane said, slightly annoyed at Tom for tattling.

"How can we serve the beings around us?" Cass asked. Her voice sounded like a hum.

"It's a picnic table," Jane said.

Cass looked her in the eyes with infinite patience and compassion. "And it fed us every day."

Jane thought about her mother, and Eleanor, and all the unkindnesses, small and enormous, she'd ever done to the people who had fed her, cared for her. She tried to dam the memories by focusing on the absurdity of the word *violence.*

She refused to let Cass make her cry over a moldy table. It was a matter of pride. She returned Cass's gaze as long as she could before she felt the sinus-tingling, then she looked over her shoulder like *Did anyone else hear that?* But it was too late. Cass stepped forward and embraced her as she wept.

This doesn't mean she's right, she told herself, wondering whether it was true.

~

That night, Jane heard Tom and Cass speaking softly through the wall. She had moved her bedroll to the upstairs room next to Cass's. Tom always went to bed after her and woke up before, so she wasn't sure if he and Cass slept together. She wondered if he knew about Jonathan. She wondered if he cared.

She gulped her water so quickly that most of it landed on her chest, and pressed her jar against the wall. She felt a little thrill when it actually worked, and an even greater one when she heard Cass say her name. Hearing what people actually thought of her was both her fondest dream and her most reliable nightmare.

"Is Jane thriving in your presence?"

"I can't tell," Tom said. "Sometimes it seems like she's really *here* but other times . . ."

"She's trapped in the cycle of fear."

"I sort of see her trying to get out sometimes. But then it's like she gives up."

"You understand her."

Tom didn't say anything. Jane didn't breathe. Obviously she was afraid. Fear was a rational response to the world. It was the times she was unafraid that she really ended up looking like an idiot. Like with Byron. She hadn't felt afraid with Byron, but she should have. Cass wasn't afraid because her beauty and secondhand wealth were armor. Jane was larval and unprotected.

It was comforting and somewhat unexpected that Cass spoke identically to and about Jane, but she ached for a new revelation about herself.

"Your spirit is tired," Cass said now. "Are you getting enough turmeric?"

Tom said either "I will" or "I'm willing."

"Are *you* here?"

"I'm here."

"*Are* you here?"

"I'm here."

"Are you *here*?" Again, her voice had a maternal note, though this time it was shaded with concern, not reproach.

"I'm here." Tom didn't sound convincing, even to Jane.

She listened at the wall for a long time, but they were done talking.

chapter 17.

At the end of the month, Jane had to go back to the city to put her things in storage. Her landlord was delighted that she was breaking her lease in the most lucrative New York real estate month. She put off telling Cass she was leaving, half expecting some sort of argument, but Cass just said, "We belong to our belongings," and smiled her serene smile. Jane chose not to remind her about the table.

Tom even offered to drive her, since there was a health food store in East Williamsburg that carried various nutrient-rich dusts Cass preferred. Jane had expected some resistance, somewhere. The ease with which she was slipping out of her old life unnerved her, like touching too-soft skin. It occurred to her that part of the reason to go back was to test the strength of her resolve.

In the car, she was struck again by Tom's excellent driving. Now that she had spent a little more time with him, she had a better appreciation for how unusual his confidence at it was. The two of them may have been the least confident pair ever to monetize spirituality.

Every time she tried a new activity, Jane wondered if it would be her secret talent. She had an idea that everyone had one discrete skill, some more lucrative or obvious than others, and it was just a matter of trying enough things until you found yours. As a kid, her mother had gamely signed her up for a buffet of community center lessons, from jazz dance to woodshop, but Jane never found her One Thing. For a while she thought it was poetic analysis, which wasn't the best, but also wasn't the worst. (Better than being able to make yourself burp on command, slightly worse than being, like Tom, a gifted driver.)

"You're really good at this, you know," she said, gesturing to the wheel.

He flicked his eyes to her and smiled slightly.

"My mother taught me. Driving was her favorite thing. Is, I guess. When we lived in Little Rock, she hated everything about it except the interstates. My father sometimes tried to get her to at least go on scenic drives, but she only ever wanted to cruise 530."

"My mom used to tell me I could be anything I wanted to be, except a rocket scientist or a cabdriver. On our first driving lesson I sideswiped the only car in the parking lot."

"Why not a rocket scientist?" Tom asked.

"I caused the *Challenger* disaster." It was a joke Jane had used before. Tom didn't laugh. "I'm just not very good at math."

"What are you very good at?" Cass's influence on him

came through erratically, as though he were possessed by a very distracted spirit.

"Sarcastic deflection," she said.

~

Few of Jane's friends knew she had left New York—she continued to respond when they texted her, citing work exhaustion if they proposed getting together, which they rarely did. She liked the idea of sneaking away from her life entirely, though it made her sad to think it could be months before anyone noticed. Years, maybe.

At the same time, she liked that FortPath existed outside the sight lines of anyone on whom she had previously relied for affirmation. She was creating something that was completely hers, not performed on social media or dissected in group chats. And when the work was complete, she would have a triumphant reemergence.

Jane had sometimes wondered how long it would take for someone to find her body if she died in her apartment. She and Eleanor used to be each other's designated death checkers. Sometimes if they hadn't spoken in a day or two, Eleanor would text *ded?* And Jane would respond with a skull emoji. While she was still at Relevancy, she'd realized Rand would likely be the one to alert the authorities to her absence. When he got around to it. This was one of the reasons finding a boyfriend had felt so urgent.

But Tom and Cass would know immediately if she died. Cass might also know exactly when she was going to die.

Driving through Brooklyn, Jane was struck by how different everyone on the street was from one another, something she hadn't fully registered when she lived there. It was perplexing how quickly she'd forgotten the diversity of the city; it had only taken a few weeks of being cloistered at FortPath for her to normalize an existence that resembled a mid-1980s J. Crew catalog.

Tom dropped her off in front of her building.

"I'll pick you up here tomorrow at noon," he said.

"Where are you going to stay?" she asked. She had assumed he would sleep at her place. She had imagined them staying up late and talking and maybe sleeping in the same bed in a platonic way, and now she felt silly.

"With an old buddy. From college." Tom said *buddy* like it was a word from a foreign language. *Soupçon. Schadenfreude. Buddy.*

The guy in the car behind them leaned on his horn. "Okay," Jane said, opening the door. "Don't have too much fun."

~

She had paid a reckless amount of money for the storage place to pick up all her things. All she had to do was box them up. It didn't take long; she had never been interested in buying objects of which she was the primary appreciator. When she spent too much on a dress or a coat, it was always in the hope that someone else would compliment her, thus validating the purchase. There was no opportunity for that kind of validation for a vase or a rug, since the men she brought home were rarely inclined to comment on a vase or a rug. The most she could expect from them was a critique of her books.

She looked at every title as she packed them now, trying to imagine the conclusions a stranger would draw about her based on their sum. She had never gotten rid of any of her books from graduate school, so poetry was overrepresented. Now she only ever opened the poetry books when she was trying to find a quote to impress someone. She loved novels most, which was why she never studied them. Academic thought was the most efficient way to ruin anything. She set aside a few titles she thought Tom might like, where average people mean well and then come through okay.

Jane's particleboard dresser had buckled six months in, but she had never replaced it, so she kept all her jeans and T-shirts and underwear folded on a large armchair. *No offense, but that looks like something a serial killer would do,* some guy had told her once, offensively.

Most of her wardrobe was inappropriate for the farm, and though she knew it wasn't fair to curse her past self for failing to anticipate this life turn, she did it anyway. She thought about all the practical garments she had eschewed over the years. Why did she have so many pairs of high heels? Why did she have a leopard-print bodysuit with a boned corset? Why didn't she have one single caftan? She already knew Old PR Jane was useless as a proxy for Cass, but only among the detritus of her former persona did she begin to feel a little sad for the real self she had so disdained.

Jane was prone to fits of reinvention, usually lasting less than a week but sometimes months or more, like PR

Jane and Poetry Jane. PR Jane had been more fun than Poetry Jane, who overused the word *enact* and claimed to prefer films in which nothing happened. Sometimes with enough repetitive motion she could cram something into her permanent personality, like sticking a piece of clay to a ball of different-colored clay and rolling it around in her hands until it was warm and smooth and swirly. Then eventually less swirly, then all the same dull color.

She packed a duffel bag with the most practical of her clothes, including a down jacket and some shapeless sweaters and wool socks. She didn't know what they would do in the winter, but she had already started pricing luxury yurts.

She hesitated over her vast array of skincare products before packing them up for storage, along with her spices. She knew she would need neither red pepper flakes nor snail mucin where she was going, but she still felt a pang for her once-precious serums in their minimalist bottles. Even her beloved dry shampoo was extraneous—her scalp oils were now perfectly balanced from only washing her hair once a week.

When she was finished packing, she undressed and stood in front of her full-length mirror. It used to be a habit of hers, like a weekly inventory, a state of the body. She would pinch the flesh below her belly button and pluck out errant hairs that sprouted from freckles—one day invisible and the next a full inch long—and squeeze the tiny whiteheads at her temples, and consider, not always cruelly, what she saw. The only mirror at FortPath was the one above the bathroom sink. It was the size of a dictionary and was clouded over in inconvenient places, and the bathroom's light was a single bare bulb—she fished a notebook out of her last box of books and wrote down *order new bathroom light*—so she had only the vaguest sense of how much her skin had improved since she'd been gone.

She didn't look like a different person, she just looked like a more skillful rendering of herself. Her lines were more confident, her edges more defined. She once read that Leonardo da Vinci had created a technique that made his subject's skin glow. She felt like she had lived her whole life as a medieval diptych and now she was a sacred baby in a Renaissance painting. She was not only more beautiful, she was also living, glowing proof that she had hitched her wagon to the right Instaguru. Whether it was the turmeric or the zucchini or the light starvation, something was working.

She basked in both her appearance and her acumen for nearly an hour before deciding she should go to the bookstore where Byron worked to try to find the perfect book for her new friend Tom.

Jane's fixation on Byron had dissipated at FortPath, but it rematerialized immediately upon her return. She didn't wish any of her exes well. She didn't wish them ill, either, for the most part; she would just have preferred if everyone she had ever dated liked her the most of anyone they would ever date, up to and including the person they married. The thought crystallized the first time she saw one of her exes' wedding pictures online: *He chose someone else,* she thought, hurt, never mind the fact that they had only gone out off and on for six months, years earlier. Byron's choosing someone else had been more pointed. But now she looked so much glowier.

The glow wasn't only physical, though its physical manifestation was better than Jane could have hoped. It wasn't inner peace, or enlightenment. Jane didn't feel any kinder—she actively hoped Byron would feel bad when he saw her—but she felt closer to completion, like she was finally making some progress on the project of Self.

She dressed in her best approximation of Cass: a plain white tank top and a pair of shapeless flax-colored pants that had never fit her right but now hung from her hips and highlighted the roundness of her ass. It was difficult to tear herself away from her full-length mirror. *If Byron's not working, I'll just get a book for Tom, which is what I wanted to do anyway,* she told herself as she walked to the subway. She smiled to herself, charmed by the outrageousness of her lie.

When she walked into the bookstore, though, he was right there, standing behind the counter reading Goethe in German. *Die Leiden des jungen Werthers.* He lowered the paperback when the door jingled, his face customer-service pleasant. She saw him not recognize her for a moment, then recognize her, then register the difference in her. It was a drama in three acts, or a living gif. She didn't realize how much she would enjoy this.

"Oh, you still work here!" she called out.

"For as long as they'll have me," he said. "Hi, Jane." He sounded wary, which offended her. What did he think she was going to do? For that matter, what *was* she going to do? She had come up with the opening line on the train, but hadn't gotten further than that.

"I'm looking for a book," she said.

"You've come to the right place."

"It's for my dear friend." She had never in her life referred to anyone as her *dear friend.* "He has a weakness for love stories." She was talking like Blanche DuBois for some reason, but at least she knew she looked great. She thought of Cass, for whom coherence was a secondary concern.

"Uh, okay. So, romance? Or something more literary?"

"You're looking well, Byron. You're radiating wellness."

"Oh, thank you. So are too. I mean, you are, too. Also." He was actually looking at her now. Staring. She smiled back at him, hard. How could she describe this feeling in an Instagram caption? *With the Glow comes Ultimate Freedom. Move through the world with the unquestioning confidence of a sentient Sunbeam, casting your Light on others and accepting their quiet gratitude as your due.*

"Jane?" Byron's co-worker Paul had come up from the basement holding a stack of paperbacks, including one Jane recognized as last season's triumphant, groundbreaking tour de force. She wished people would stop writing books, just for a little while.

"Holy shit, you look awesome," Paul said. "Did you get a haircut? When's the last time I saw you?" He once told her that Iza Brecht scared him a little and that he much preferred her as a girlfriend of Byron's. She had always liked him, despite the fact that the egregious asymmetry between his looks and his girlfriend's offended her on behalf of ordinary-looking women. Paul was a medium-attractive guy, thin-ish and on the tall side of average, with nice-enough features and thick-looking brown hair. His most striking feature was a pair of thick tortoiseshell glasses. His girlfriend was a lawyer who paid her way through school by working as a face model.

He put the books down next to Byron and gave her a hug. "Seriously, you look amazing. Not that you didn't always, just . . . you know. Contemporary etiquette! What a minefield, right, guys?" He mimed mopping sweat off his brow in a feint of self-consciousness that Jane might have believed if she hadn't known about the girlfriend.

"You can't offend me that easily," Jane said, though in truth she was just as easily offended as she was flattered. "It's really good to see you, Paul." And it was—Paul's public and enthusiastic response to her was a best-case scenario she hadn't even considered. Paul was staring at her face, possibly trying to figure out if she'd had work done. Byron looked deeply uncomfortable. Jane almost felt bad, but then she remembered how much her mom had liked him when they'd met. *You tricked my mom,* she thought. She picked up a copy of the tour de force.

"Is this any good?" she asked Paul. She liked the feeling of Byron's eyes on her while she shined her glow on his friend.

"It's by that guy who wrote *A Man, A Plan, A Canal, Suicide.* I actually found that one more structurally interesting, but then he said all that antisemitic shit and went to rehab and wrote that memoir about his recovery so everyone kind of forgave him." He spoke enthusiastically about the book for a few more minutes, citing reviews both positive and negative, and an essay in *n+1* about the decline of the third person. Jane remembered how boring she found this sort of monologuing when she and Byron were together.

"I recommend it, with reservations," Paul concluded.

"Great, I'll take it," she said, forgetting that the book was ostensibly a gift for her dear friend Tom.

She stared at Byron as he rang her up. It felt possible she would never need to blink again. Paul stood to her left, thumbing through the book and sighing about how correct his assessment of it was. A blush was blooming on Byron's cheeks. He was an easy blusher, but she still felt victorious. She was certain that she had bested Byron in some ineffable but essential way. More than that, Byron felt irrelevant. She even felt a little sorry for him as he struggled with the register.

If I can figure out how to describe whatever this is in a press release, I'm going to be so fucking rich, she thought.

Absent the consideration of her debt, Jane was slightly more attracted to prestige than wealth—hence the poetry PhD—but standing in a bookstore staffed by two doctors of literature, the financial possibilities of Cass, Inc., came into sharper focus. It was a different kind of prestige, a more fungible kind.

"I don't need a bag," she said to Byron. "Paul, it was *so good* to see you." She gave him a hug. "You, too, Byron." She walked out of the store like it was the end of a montage, took the subway back to her soon-to-be ex-apartment, and ordered pad Thai.

But when the food came, she found the smell too rich after weeks of undressed zucchini. She ate two bites and felt a little sick. She had already packed her garbage can, so she went down to the street to throw it away. Then she stopped in a bodega and bought a pack of cigarettes. She had quit smoking years ago (after the demise of Poetry Jane) but if she couldn't eat takeout, she still felt the urge to give her toxins a symbolic send-off. She smoked three of them out her soon-to-be ex-window, one after another, thickening her sick feeling.

She wondered what Tom was doing. She texted him, *hows it going?* When he didn't respond she followed up: *you said 12 tomorrow right?* And then *ok have a good night!*

She slept badly. She had already packed her sheets and pillows, so she curled up on her bare mattress under a batik blanket she was planning to bring back to FortPath as a possible wall hanging.

A new bar had opened up across the street since she'd been gone, and it seemed to be a popular destination for loud breakups.

Jane pulled up an episode of *Law and Order: SVU* on Netflix and turned the volume up loud, then fell back asleep comforted by the idea that every couple was always having fights that were about everything.

The next morning, she woke up feeling so hung-over she wondered if she had gotten shitfaced in her sleep. She had a viselike headache and her tongue felt too big for her mouth. She got out of bed and shuffled to her fridge, knowing it was empty but hoping somehow she had snuck a jar of Tom's green juice in there without realizing it. She wanted to eat fistfuls of grass and drink an entire creek.

In the fridge was only a box of baking soda, but behind the ice trays in the freezer she found a merciful bag of peas. She ripped it open and filled her mouth with the icy nuggets. She stood there for a minute in her sparse, grubby galley kitchen, mouth full of slowly thawing peas. It was better than the frozen pizza, at least. *The before,* she thought. *All the wellness you seek is a poor imitation of the wellness here. Cass is a glass of perfectly blended juice and you are stuffing your maw with peas. You are a dull-faced girl messing around with highlighter and she is an excess of generous light. You are cut particleboard and she is beveled edges.*

Jane half jogged back to bed, opened her laptop, and started typing. She worked until the movers came. The doc was a frantic stream-of-consciousness thing, but she felt sure that somewhere in there was The Message. She had settled on a name—subject to trademark status: Opeia. It sounded like a pretty whisper or a satisfied exhale.

She couldn't wait to tell Tom about it. *I figured out the name,* she texted him. No response. *Opeia,* she texted. *Like Cassiopeia.*

What was he doing? It was eleven. He was supposed to pick her up in an hour. She put on her flowiest dress (pale pink, drop-waisted, wildly unflattering but possibly in an interesting way) and went around the corner to the natural foods bodega that sold $12 pre-packaged juices that wouldn't taste as good as Tom's but would probably be better than the peas, which she had finished anyway.

When she came out of the store, she noticed Tom's car parked down across the street, with Tom inside it. She was about to go knock on the window when she saw the guy in the passenger seat. He leaned forward and rested his forehead against the glove compartment. Jane walked a few steps past the car so she could see through the windshield. She crouched next to a mailbox, feeling slightly ridiculous but not caring much.

The guy lifted his head and turned to Tom, brushed his hair out of his face so tenderly that Jane instinctually looked away. When she looked back, Tom was touching the guy's shoulder. They looked a little alike. Tom's hair was longer and shaggier, a little lighter. The guy was clean-cut and cute, like a work crush.

Tom threw his head back and laughed. Jane had never seen him laugh so completely. She was jealous of both him and the guy. She often wondered if there would ever come a time in her life when someone else's happiness didn't make her throat ache. Either everyone else was lying when they talked about being *happy for you* or she was even more broken than she assumed.

She didn't even consider Cass until she saw them kiss. It couldn't be a first kiss—their mouths found each other too seamlessly. Did Cass know? The idea that Jane might know something before Cass was alluring, but also a little sad. Even though she knew their marriage allowed for Cass to do whatever with Jonathan, and probably others as well.

She had assumed Cass's extramarital *things* were within the bounds of their relationship rule book both because Tom didn't seem to have any opportunities for his own things, and because he was so clearly the relationship's sub. Now she wondered if she had underestimated both of them. She was jealous of Tom, for the power she didn't realize he had. Being married to Cass and kissing someone else was excessive. It was luxurious.

Tom and the man kissed until Jane's legs started cramping and she remembered her hangover, and her juice. She stood up and leaned against the mailbox, facing away from the car. She drank the whole bottle in three sips and felt a little better. When she turned back toward the car, it was empty, and she had a text from Tom. *i'm outside your door, parked around the corner. u here?*

He must have said goodbye to the guy in the car. With no thought of what she would do if she caught up with Tom's whatever-he-was, Jane jog-walked in the direction of the closest subway. He must have been walking slowly; she passed him before she realized. She stopped, pretended to have something stuck in her sandal. She watched him through her eyelashes. She expected him to be taller. He was slight, shorter than she was.

She followed when he turned in to a coffee shop, unsure what she was doing but unable to stop. "Can I just have a steamed milk with some vanilla syrup?" It was the most pathetic order of all time, and the guy's voice suggested he knew it. She had to admire the confidence—was it confidence?—required to order warm sugar milk in public, to tell a complete stranger *I need care.*

"We don't do flavored syrup," said the angular barista, bored but not unkind. "We have simple syrup."

"That's fine," the guy said. "Thanks." He handed the barista his card, but she waved it away.

Jane wondered if this often happened to the guy, if he activated people's urge to shield him from reality. This was one of Tom's strengths, she realized.

"And for you?" It took Jane a beat to realize that the barista was addressing her.

"Large black coffee." She ordered her usual automatically, though she hadn't had any caffeine in weeks and the pad Thai effect suggested she ought not to start now.

"Three dollars," the barista said.

Everyone in the coffee shop is best friends except me, she thought.

The barista put her and the guy's drinks down on the counter at the same time. When he picked his up, he smiled at her, like maybe friendship wasn't entirely off the table. He paused to check his phone, and smiled a smaller, private smile at something on the screen. Then he walked out the door.

Jane had five texts from Tom.

at your door, where ru?
????
ru ok?
sorry I didn't respond last night, my phone died!
don't be mad

She wanted to feel bad about his spiral, but she had a mean flash of her power, which made her feel terrible again. She didn't want Tom to be sad. She wanted him to be happy with the guy. She wanted him and her to both be equal amounts of happy.

sorry! went to get coffee shh don't tell C. back in a sec

She walked back to her former apartment and found Tom sitting on the stoop reading a Foodtown circular.

"Any good deals in there?"

He looked up. "Two for one on all fungi resins."

She held out her free hand and he took it. She hauled him off the stoop and they went up to her apartment together.

"It's a nice place," Tom said.

"Not really." It was dark and poky and strangely laid out—railroad-style with the bedroom in the middle and the bathroom all the way at the end, off the kitchen. She had been so proud when she'd signed the lease—her first just-hers apartment!—but as soon as she moved in she felt a dull disappointment. For this, she was paying $2,200 a month? She had never had a triumph that hadn't curdled in this way. Yet she wanted the thing even as she expected it to crumble like wet sand when she held it.

FortPath would be different. She would be different. She already was. She had transformed—even Byron could tell. And she had the full force of Cass behind her. And Tom. This would be her final form, she was sure of it.

"I don't know," Tom said. "I think this place is okay. I sort of like the little flowers here." He ran his hand over the wall above where her couch used to be.

"What flowers?" Maybe it was some kind of visualization exercise.

"They're faint but it looks like there was some kind of textured wallpaper or something that someone just painted over. You can still sort of see them."

Jane had lived in the apartment for two years and had never looked closely enough at the wall to register the texture of it as anything more than decades of sloppy paint jobs. As soon as she really looked, though, it was obvious. The wall was speckled with tiny flowers.

"Oh yeah, those," she said. "I forgot about them. They're nice, but they don't make up for the terrible shower." Admitting to Tom that she had failed to notice the one beautiful thing in her apartment was too depressing to contemplate. "I'm ready to go, by the way." She left the keys on the counter and didn't look back.

Jane planned to ask Tom about the guy as soon as they got in the car, but she couldn't even make it around the corner. "I saw you," she said. "With that guy." He stopped walking. He looked so afraid. "I'm not going to tell her. I just want to know who he is."

"It's not like . . . I don't think she would be mad. But I don't want to hurt her." It had never occurred to Jane that Tom had the power to hurt Cass. Or that anyone did.

"Let's go to the car," she said, like she was trying to trick a dog. "And then you can tell me about him."

chapter 18.

The guy's name was Daniel, and he had been Cass's boyfriend first. After Tom and Cass both left Realities, the Yale of rehab, they had come to New York. Cass was interested in the Occupy movement, though not for political reasons. She liked the idea of a thrum of people, a bodily energy disrupting the climate-controlled inhumanity of the Financial District.

All the people made Tom feel claustrophobic and lonely at the same time. At Realities, he and Cass could be alone together. She told him she had thought of him often since he had moved away when they were children. He thought of her constantly, of course, but never expected that she felt the same. She told him she had missed his spirit, which was uncommonly gentle.

The first time he went down on her was in the garbage room off the cafeteria, but they also took walks on the grounds, and had long talks about his sobriety in the studio where she led Mindful Spatialism workshops.

In Zuccotti Park, everyone wanted to talk to her, and she never said no. They slept in a tent Tom had bought from a sporting goods store in Union Square. At all hours of the day, people would scratch at its nylon and Cass would poke her head out the zippered flap and leave with them. Sometimes she didn't come back all night.

Cass was the first one who alerted Tom to his family's wealth. *Your family isn't like my family,* she'd said once, apropos of nothing, when they were children. *Your family is rich.*

In response, Tom had parroted something he'd heard his mother say. *We're comfortable.*

No, Cass said. *You're rich. You're not very comfortable at all.*

Among the Occupy protesters Tom felt both rich and uncomfortable. Tom thought he understood why the protesters were so angry at people like his father, and thought their anger was probably right, but he still hated the noise and the smells and the roughness with which people moved against one another. The only thing he liked about Zuccotti was the People's Library. He was barred from New York's public libraries as a condition of his ongoing probation, and he missed them. The People's Library was the one place where he didn't mind the chaos, contained in precarious stacks and USPS crates.

The weather was getting colder, and one day, Cass announced that she had found a new place for them to stay: with a corporate lawyer named Daniel she had met outside the park. Cass told him Daniel was suffering, and desperately needed her light.

She had told Daniel that Tom was her dear friend, and that he was gay. She said this was a version of the truth, and he didn't question it. It was nice to have someone else define him and still love him. And after all, it had been Cass who had told him he was still mostly attracted to men, after the first time he made her come. He had admitted it was true, but that he loved and wanted her more than anyone else, male or female. She told him she knew that, too.

Tom didn't like pretending to be just Cass's friend, but he trusted her when she said that Daniel's need was greater than his, and anyway he was just happy to get out of that tent. So they moved into Daniel's "luxury FiDi high-rise" (as the framed poster in the lobby called it), Cass in Daniel's room and Tom on a twin-sized air mattress in Daniel's home office.

Once Tom asked Cass if she felt bad about leaving the camp for the 1 percent.

Do you remember the apartment where I lived with my mother?

He did. His mother had sometimes dropped him off there when she needed a last-minute babysitter. It was a one-bedroom, and Cass's mother, Jade, slept on a pull-out couch in the living room. The walls were hung with batik-print fabric and it smelled like the time Tom had set a bowl of his mother's potpourri on fire. Tom had loved it there.

You don't remember it, Cass said, and that was all.

They stayed with Daniel for six weeks. Tom worried he would feel jealous, but Cass treated Daniel pretty much the same as she treated Tom. She still stayed out all night sometimes, in Zuccotti Park and other places where people gathered. Sometimes she went on very long walks, often barefoot.

Tom could tell Daniel loved her, but he also pushed back against her behavior more than Tom would ever dare. *Where have you been? Couldn't you have called? Don't you even understand why I'm upset?*

Cass didn't, or claimed not to. Daniel seemed to think they could have a normal kind of relationship, the kind that involved meal planning and couple friends and accountability. The only thing they seemed to agree on was sex, which, from the next room, sounded like softly crinkling paper and made Tom's scalp tingle.

Daniel didn't pump Tom for information about Cass, but they did start spending more time together while she was out. Daniel worked as a corporate litigator, mostly defending corporations that had poisoned migrant workers. He hated it, and hated himself, but he was hundreds of thousands of dollars in debt from law school and his mother had early-onset Alzheimer's. Only the really evil jobs paid well enough to get him out from under his circumstances.

Tom and Daniel went to the movies together. Cass didn't like movies because she said it made her too sad to sit with so many people in a room together who were choosing to direct their energy toward a screen instead of one another, but Tom and Daniel both loved romantic comedies enough to risk her disapprobation.

Tom realized Daniel was the first person he had ever had a crush on. There had been fleeting attractions through the years, always to boys, usually the ones whose obvious good looks made them unkind. And there was Cass, of course, but *crush* was too ridiculous, too trivial a word to describe how he felt about Cass, had felt about her since childhood. He still loved her. He still wanted her to smile at him and tell him he was okay more than anything in the world. But he had so much fun with Daniel.

Cass doesn't really laugh, does she? Daniel asked him once as they emerged from a fit of laughter about Tom's mispronunciation of every shape of pasta.

She does. She laughs all the time. It was the first time Daniel had approached criticism of her, beyond wondering where she went. Tom was defensive, but exhilarated, too, at the implied comparison between him and Cass. Since childhood, he had taken it for granted that she was Better in every way. It felt good, or at least *interesting,* to contemplate that Daniel might be comparing him with Cass and finding her wanting, even if only in one small way. Later, when he heard them having sex, Tom thought, *But I laugh with him.*

Outwardly, he tried not to engage with Daniel's increasing frustration. *Why doesn't Cass wear shoes? Do you ever feel like sometimes when Cass talks she isn't actually saying anything? Do you think Cass is taking advantage of me?*

Tom felt implicated by the last question, but Daniel never acknowledged that Tom was also a beneficiary of his generosity. He told Tom he loved having him around, that it had been so long since he'd had friends who weren't paid to hang out with him, like the paralegals on his cases at work were.

Cass started spending more nights away. Tom only asked where she had been the first time she came back. She told him that questions were valuable and he should never stop asking questions, but that to expect answers to those questions was to misunderstand the value of questioning.

She told Daniel the same thing when he asked, but instead of nodding apologetically like Tom had, Daniel laughed and told her he was going to try that one next time he had a hearing he wasn't prepared for. Then he asked again, *No, really, where were you?*

She told him she'd needed to feel the pulse of the city through her feet.

Well, just call next time, he said.

After that, Cass told Tom that her relationship with Daniel was toxic. As he knew, she said she was very sensitive to emotional poisons. *Daniel is severely misaligned. I thought I could help him, but I fear he will drain me before I have a chance.*

She said it would be time to leave soon.

Tom didn't think Daniel was misaligned, or toxic, but he trusted Cass. He tried to keep his distance from Daniel, at least when she was around. He would leave the apartment and drift through a nearby Duane Reade smelling shampoos. When she went out, though, he stayed, watching TV on the couch with Daniel after work, cooking boxed mac and cheese.

One night, when Cass had been gone for two full days, Daniel told Tom he was going to end things with her. *She's amazing,* he said carefully. *But we're too different. I understand if that means you have to leave, too, but you don't have to. You can stay if you want.*

Tom leaned across the couch and kissed him. It was the most spontaneous thing he had ever done sober. He did it out of a combination of attraction, gratitude, and the desire to shut Daniel up before he said something terrible about Cass. As soon as their lips touched, he realized the gravity of what he had done. He was too afraid to move, even to pull back, so he just stayed there, very still, until Daniel kissed him back.

Tom had known for almost his whole life that he liked boys, but his liking them had been murky, obscured by a haze of ambivalence toward *liking*. His mother was at her most playful when she asked him which girls in his class were the cutest, and he wanted desperately to join in the fun with her, so he pretended. He never mentioned the boys at all. He met Cass when he was eleven, and liked her more than anyone he had ever known. He didn't even think of her as a girl, really. He didn't think of her as anyone but Cass. Long after his family moved away from Arkansas, even after he had stopped missing her so acutely, she served as proof that he didn't *only* like boys.

Tom and Cass rarely kissed. Mostly he went down on her, which he liked because of how much she liked it, and because of how concentrated the smell of her was down there. It felt like they were sharing a secret.

Even as the kiss with Daniel was happening, Tom felt like he was describing it to some future self. *Like a warm sponge in a bath. Like thick pudding. Like a waterslide.* It was his first real kiss.

Daniel pulled away first. Tom might have kept going forever. They could have died like that, joined at the face. *I really like you, Tom,* he said.

Cass came in then. *The most beautiful souls live in the Bronx,* she said. Tom said he needed to go buy shampoo and excused himself. When he returned an hour later, Daniel was gone.

It's time for us to leave here, Cass said.

Tom hesitated. Had Daniel told her anything about the kiss? Or his offer to let Tom stay?

And I think it's time for us to get married, she added.

You-and-me us? Tom was almost too shocked to realize how happy he was.

Yes. She smiled her best smile, the one that spread gradually across her face like raspberry jam on toast. *It's time.*

What could he say? It was everything he wanted. Daniel was six weeks of ease and laughter and one kiss, but Cass was his whole life. She was woven through everything. It was so much easier to brush Daniel away, like a loose thread. So he said yes.

He texted Daniel that he had to leave with Cass. *She's my family.*

Daniel replied, but Tom couldn't look at it. He deleted the text, and Daniel's number.

They moved into an apartment in Tribeca. Someone else Cass knew somehow lived there when he wasn't in Europe or Hong Kong, buying and selling money. It was furnished like an expensive hotel room, with crisp white sheets and heavy drapes and no sign that a person with specific loves had ever lived there. The apartment's owner had left a note telling Cass to help herself to whatever, signed with a string of X's. Tom wondered what the person wanted or had already gotten from Cass. He wondered whether she could actually want to live somewhere like this, sumptuous and sterile. Cass lit incense from a robin's-egg-blue box. Tom didn't help himself to anything.

They got married at city hall, less than a mile from

Daniel's apartment. The ceremony was over in about five minutes, and afterward Tom didn't feel as altered as he had hoped. Cass encouraged him to tell his parents. They knew only that he had moved to New York with a girlfriend he'd met in rehab.

When he spoke to them, he called her Cassie and said she had been in treatment for an eating disorder (which his mother, Caroline, considered a sign of good discipline, as long as one didn't go overboard). He'd given her a Swiss banker father with a Midtown pied-à-terre, so his parents wouldn't ask questions about where they were staying.

He thought they would be angry about the marriage, but they were only irritated about the wedding. *City hall? She's not using you for a green card, is she?* his mother said. He assured them that he and Cassie were very much in love and that she was a true romantic who couldn't stand to wait any longer. His mother didn't really like that, either, but at least it was more acceptable than Cass being an immigrant. They insisted on coming to the city to take the couple out to dinner.

Tom was afraid they would recognize Cass. She had often hung around their house while her mother was cleaning, and Caroline had nursed a deep dislike for her. She said she found Cass's curiosity disrespectful. *It's very impolite to pry,* she once told Cass, in response to the question *If you could be any kind of flower, what kind would you be?*

It was the first time Tom could remember having been angry at his mother. He loved Cass's questions. The thought that his mother's reprimand might make Cass stop asking them filled him with unfamiliar rage.

Caroline's distaste wasn't unusual—she complained about everyone from their UPS man to Mister Rogers (*I don't think children should be watching a man who speaks to them with such* intimacy *in his voice*)—but she had a good memory for special grudges.

Tom did have some memories of his mother's love. When he was very small, she used to lie next to him in bed describing to him the plots of books he didn't realize were books until years later. When he read *Pride and Prejudice* for the first time, before he was banned from the Brooklyn Public Library forever, Tom realized that Jane Austen's Mr. Darcy was his mother's Mr. Digsby. He was struck by a nostalgia so strong he had to lie down on the floor.

The more time Tom spent with Cass, though, the more his mother seemed to hate her. And hate Tom, too. Even after they moved away from Arkansas, something was different. And though he knew they'd moved back because of his father's job, Tom felt sure that his mother also wanted to be rid of Cass. But she didn't seem to like him any better once Cass was gone.

Tom knew, even at the time, that the truth was she did have reason to feel threatened. He did like Cass more, liked her in an all-encompassing way that left little room for anyone else, even his mother. Caroline had moments of warmth, but Cass enveloped him, made him feel safe and held and beloved. He didn't try to hide his single-minded devotion to her. Now he recognized that it hadn't really been his fault. But also, he thought, maybe it was a little his fault.

Cass told him not to worry about the dinner. His mother had a negative response to Cass's energy, she said, but she was able to cloak her aura. *How did you know she didn't like you?* Tom asked. He had never told her how his mother talked about her.

Your mother wears her wounds like jewels, she said.

Cass wore a wool dress with two seams down the front, and a pair of low heels. Her hair was straighter than usual, and eerily immobile. He had no idea where she had gotten the clothes. He had never seen her in something that hewed to her body. She looked like a different person, one who preferred shorn grass and cut flowers and lacquered surfaces. She looked like someone his mother would admire.

They went to a steak house in Midtown that resembled the inside of a men's-only library, except there were no books, only dark wood and maroon leather and light fixtures made of antlers. All the waiters were very old men who addressed their remarks only to Tom's father.

Cass was perfect, terrifyingly so. Tom had never seen her act any way but entirely herself. Her real voice was a rich alto, but when she spoke to his parents it became lilting and thin. She lied fluidly—she even cited a Swiss boarding school whose name his mother claimed to recognize. Her skill was disconcerting. Tom wondered briefly if she had ever lied to him, but determined that few things she said were concrete enough to be verifiable in either direction.

At dinner, she was only herself when she ordered a mixed green salad and nothing else, but this, too, worked as a character choice.

She told them that since her "little hiccup," which led to her meeting Tom, her parents agreed the best thing for her would be fresh air and rest, which was why she and Tom were planning to buy a house in the country. Tom was so disoriented that he wondered if she had mentioned this plan to him and he'd simply forgotten.

Well, this is all happening quite quickly, Tom's mother said. *But if there isn't anything else you'd like to tell us . . . ?* Tilting her head toward Cass's perfectly flat midsection ever so slightly.

Oh, no! Cass trilled. *I do want children, of course. But not yet.* Tom wondered if this was true, and found that he hoped it was.

Well, that's very sensible of you, Caroline said. *Of course, with Tom's trust, you'll have ample means to start a family. Tom's grandmother set up the parameters of the trust when we went for a visit and he fell in love with her china cabinet. He would sit in front of it for hours and hours, like it was a television. She worried about him. She would have been glad to meet you.*

She reached across the table and patted Cass's hand. *And so are we.*

Tom had told Cass about the china cabinet once when they were children. She let him describe the patterns of different kinds of flowers and the configuration of dishes for so long that he finally interrupted himself, afraid he was boring her.

No, keep going, she'd said. *I want to imagine.* Then she'd gotten him paper and a pencil and asked him to draw it.

Cass was always doing things like that—making him feel okay without making a big deal about the fact that he didn't feel okay in the first place. She was two years younger than he was, but she knew so much more about everything than he did. She seemed to understand that sometimes thinking about things was worse than living them.

Watching his mother touch Cass, Tom felt like crying. The only thing that stopped him was not wanting to remind his mother of the child who had so concerned her. The trouble was that in his memory, his mother had liked hearing him talk about the china cabinet, too. Had she really been appraising him so single-mindedly? Had the playfulness with which she questioned him about girls been entirely calculated? But his mother used to like him—he was almost sure of it. And he used to like her.

One of the things I love most about Tom, Cass said to his mother, in a voice closer to her own. She withdrew her hand and laid it on the back of Tom's neck. *Is how much he appreciates real beauty.*

At the end of dinner, Tom's father promised to talk to the family's lawyer about giving Tom access to the trust. Caroline embraced Cass. She stage-whispered near Cass's ear, "Take good care of my son," and Tom loved her then, for the tacit assumption that he was the precious thing, and the admission that he needed care.

~

Tom didn't allow himself to think about Daniel as they made preparations to leave the city. There was too much to do. Cass was unexpectedly task-oriented. She bought a car, a forest-green 1999 Camry, so they could look at houses. They needed someplace big, she explained, because she wanted to reach as many people as possible. Everyone was lost, she said, and she wanted to lead as many people as she could out of darkness.

What kind of darkness? Tom asked. *Where are you leading them?*

Almost everyone was trapped in a cycle of fear, she explained. Fear is the most powerful toxin in the world, and it exists in everything. Anger is fear. Exhaustion is fear. Illness is fear.

All illness? What about cancer? What about Alzheimer's? he asked, thinking of Daniel's mother.

Some fears are more powerful than others, Cass said. Tom wondered if she'd ever been sick.

Besides fear, other toxins included nightshades, dairy, and wheat—*a bodily catastrophe.* Ridding one's body of toxins was a complex and sometimes painful process. She was called to shepherd as many people as possible through to the other side of fear.

Why was Tom still so afraid, after over a year of being personally shepherded? He couldn't think of an inoffensive way to ask. It wasn't her fault. He was probably a more dire case than most. He was afraid all the time, but his fears felt vaporous, shifting shape as soon as he tried to grasp them. He couldn't get a look at them straight-on, so they were impossible to face.

Cass knew a realtor who showed them houses all over New Jersey, in Tewksbury and Bridgeton and Colts Neck. *Why New Jersey?* Tom asked.

It's a place without fear, she told him. He wondered how much time she'd spent on the East Coast.

Cass knew immediately when a house wasn't right, and often refused to go inside no matter how far they'd driven to get there. The realtor would throw up his hands in mock-despair and smile a little wolfishly, like she was a handful and might have to make it up to him later somehow. Tom hated the realtor so much he tried not to remember his name (Jason Kellerman), but he kept remembering it anyway.

Finally, they found it. *Move-in ready,* Jason Kellerman kept saying. It reminded Tom of a dollhouse his mother had, which he wasn't allowed to play with because it was an antique and not a toy and besides, dollhouses weren't for little boys. Both had wraparound porches with trimmings that looked like lace, and spindly turrets.

By the time they'd moved to Little Rock and Tom had met Cass, he was too old to care about dollhouses, but Cass had a small yellow box of pinky-sized dolls that she let Tom hold whenever he came over. They were worry dolls, she said, from Guatemala. *You tell them your worries and then put them under your pillow at night, and when you wake up, your worries are gone.*

Do they really work? Tom asked.

Cass considered the question for a long time. *Sometimes,* she said. *But not always. You should try them.*

He told her he couldn't accept them, which is what his mother always told him to say, because it was rude to accept things from people in their homes. Later he found them in his coat pocket.

He held them all in his palm and brought them to his mouth and whispered that his mother was always mad at him and he wasn't good at soccer. But even though his worries felt like a huge, dark cloud—a cumulonimbus cloud, like he learned about in science—he couldn't find the words to describe them, even to the dolls.

The next day during gym class, he scored a goal in soccer and Brian Durkee—*Brian Durkee!*—gave him a high five, and he wondered if Cass was a little bit magic.

The next month, his father's job transferred him back to Connecticut and Cass told him to keep the dolls, but they never worked again. One day he came home from school and they were gone.

~

The house was on ten acres of land. Tom had no concept of how much even one acre was, but the word made him think of horses. He wondered if they could get some. He had told his parents that Cassie was a keen equestrian, two words he had never said out loud before.

Cass walked through the house, slow and unspeaking, her arms lifted just a few inches above her sides, which made her look even more like a beautiful ghost than usual. Sometimes she would stop to touch a wall or a doorknob. She rested her forehead against the little circle window in the turret. Finally, she led them outside and said that this was the house.

It has to be this house, she said, which even Tom knew was a bad negotiating tactic. Jason Kellerman looked like he was going to combust with glee.

Well, we like this house, Tom said. *But we have some questions.*

Cass smiled at him indulgently. *What questions do you have?* But of course he didn't have any. He loved the house, too.

Tom wanted to ask for his father's help with the sale, but Cass said that would be like inviting his parents' fear to live in the house with them.

You think my parents are afraid of something? He tried

to keep his voice steady, but he sounded pleading. They hadn't discussed what happened at the dinner. In the intervening weeks, Tom had decided that it hadn't been so terrible. He knew Cass wouldn't agree with him, though, and he dared to hope she had forgotten about the evening the way his mother seemed to have forgotten about Cass.

He and Cass were in the bathroom of the apartment in Tribeca. Cass was in the tub. The only way she could tolerate being in small indoor spaces for extended periods of time was by being submerged in water. She took his hand in hers and held them both underwater.

Tom, she said. She so rarely used his name that it startled him. He looked around, wondering briefly if a different Tom had entered the room.

Your mother and father have never tried to know you. They allowed your grandmother to try to change your essential self with the promise of money. Don't let them do that to you. Take it back, and free yourself from them.

Sometimes, Cass sounded so different from how he'd remembered her for all those years that he wondered if she'd been replaced by a hidden twin. But now she sounded like the old Cass again, kind and certain and entirely aligned with him. Tom was so relieved to have the choice presented to him with such clarity that he almost forgot to be sad.

She had a plan. He had never had a plan in his life. He trusted her. And the house was perfect. The only thing that bothered him was a lingering wonder whether the trust was the reason she had wanted to get married, but he couldn't remember having mentioned the money to her at all before that dinner. It was strange to think about how she would have found that information on her own, but he knew he should be grateful—without her, he never would have gotten the money.

Cass didn't speak to her own mother anymore. When they were kids, Tom loved Jade, who was so different from his parents. She had silver rings climbing the sides of both her ears, like the spiral bindings of Tom's notebooks, and she wore jeans with ripped-out knees. She really listened to Tom when he talked about stupid kid things. She had a glass box of crystals, and she let him hold them one at a time when he came over. Tom sometimes pretended Jade was his real mother.

When they met again at Realities, Cass told him Jade had married a tax lawyer and lived in Newport Beach. She belonged to a tennis club. Cass had a half brother named Bryce she had never met.

She always trusted the wrong intuition, Cass said.

Tom hadn't realized there were right and wrong intuitions.

After they moved into the new house, he didn't stop talking to his parents all at once. But there was so much to do, it was easy not to think about them. There were rooms to be painted and seeds to be planted and wood to be polished. He texted his mother that they were too busy with the house to come home for Thanksgiving, but that they would see her at Christmas. In mid-December, he told her they would be going to Switzerland to see Cassie's family.

He felt an immediate shame at his betrayal, but when he tried to call up a happy Christmas memory with his own family, the best he could come up with was his mother opening a card he'd made her and complimenting his penmanship. *Thomas, are you left-handed?* his father had said when he'd seen Tom working on the card.

Cass made no mention of Christmas, and Tom felt silly bringing it up, silly for caring at all. She spent most of the day outside, like always, underdressed but at least wearing the snow boots he had bought her. Sometimes she took the car, which worried him because she was such a terrible driver, but that day she just disappeared into the trees. She didn't come home in time for dinner and Tom didn't feel like cooking for just himself, so he went to sleep without eating.

He didn't miss his father at all, but he missed the possibility that his mother might someday surprise him.

When he wasn't working on the house, there was writing to do. The manifesto had to be a distillation of *Cass*, presented for the world, but it also had to be coherent enough to convince people to become customers. Cass wasn't illiterate, exactly. She just had a hard time translating her thoughts into written words, and she found the placement of letters on the computer's keyboard inscrutable.

Cass talked to him, uninterrupted, for hours. It reminded him of when they were kids and they used to lie under the trees in his backyard while Jade cleaned, except back then, Tom talked about himself, too.

She had to reach as many people as possible, she said. She didn't like him to write while she was talking, so he tried to remember the things that sounded most important. She spoke in capital letters.

Positive Energy directed outward is the only way to accumulate Spiritual Wealth.

Negative Energy is the Most Lethal Poison.

Our Spirits feel Trapped in Our Physical Forms. We are Responsible for keeping our Organic Vessels beautiful for Them.

Fear is the Darkness that extinguishes Attraction. We must conquer it in order to Claim what is Ours.

Mindfulness of the Spaces We move through, both Physical and Emotional, is the only way to orient Our Spirits forward.

Meditation is a Humbled Silence we offer Our Spirits and the Earth so they may commune apart from Us, and if They Choose, impart to Us the Wisdom They have exchanged.

Phallic vegetables are the most Deeply connected to the Earth.

When they were children, Cass spoke more naturally. She asked questions that had real answers instead of questions about the Nature of Truth. Tom had felt like the exact same person as far back as he could remember. He wondered when this shift in Cass had happened, and whether she'd had to decide on its occurrence. She was still the best listener Tom had ever known—present in a way that erased all worldly context from the scene—but now it was more difficult to access her. The only way in was through the work.

After he had written several manifesto drafts of varying levels of coherence on yellow legal pads, he went to the nearest internet café to see about building a website. At the time, the town was more blighted than quaint. Besides the internet café (Café Logg'on), there was a preschool called Great Tots with sun-faded pictures of unlicensed Sesame Street–ish characters in the windows, a Chinese buffet that was closed Wednesdays and Fridays, and a few houses pressed right against the street with handmade signs advertising some service—palm reading, doll museum, used books.

He hadn't checked his email since they left Daniel's. Almost an entire winter had passed. His inbox was mostly junk—Tatiana was feeling sexuel [sic] and wanted to chat; a store where he had bought pants had some exciting news for him. And then, there was the email from Daniel. It was dated a week earlier. Tom didn't notice how fast his heart was beating until he started to pant, staring at his inbox. There was no subject. The preview line read *I miss you. Where did you go?*

His shirt felt too tight. His scalp felt too tight. He responded to Tatiana—*I think you have the wrong email address*—and went to the pants website. Then he went to a different pants website and bought a pair of overalls, which he thought might be good to wear while he was planting phallic vegetables. Then he googled *How to make a website* and clicked on the first link and entered his credit card information and purchased the domain name he and Cass had finally agreed on—FortPath.com.

He liked it because it sounded safe and strong and like it could be almost anything. Cass liked it because *F* and *P* were harmonious sounds. The website building service kept offering to make the website building easier for him if he paid a little more money, and he kept clicking *Yes,* and it was actually pretty easy. By the time he had entered all the information from his legal pad and uploaded all the pictures he had taken of the house and of Cass (none of himself, of course), he had authorized payment of over $350, which seemed like both a lot and nothing. Money had never seemed real to Tom. He had never been in danger of running out of it in any permanent way. He could always go to the money store.

Cass said she hated money, but Tom knew that she had a kind of money store, too. She had always been willing to barter how special she made people feel. He told himself she never asked for more than she needed. At first, she had wanted to make their weekend retreats donation-based, but Tom convinced her that asking people to pay for food and lodging wasn't motivated by fear. *We have to ensure the health of FortPath as a whole. And a small sacrifice will make people value the experience more. And remember when you paid money for those crystals?* Finally, she had agreed to $250 per person, per session, with a price break for returning students.

The kid sitting behind the counter told Tom that Café Logg'on would be closing in twenty minutes, which meant he had been there for four hours. He breathed like Cass had taught him, from behind his belly button. Then he opened the email.

> I miss you. Where did you go? Are you okay? I'm sorry if I did anything that made you feel weird or compromised your relationship with her. We don't have to be anything other than friends. I just miss talking to you. Please write me back and let me know if you're okay. I'm spending my days defending a chemical company that may or may not have poisoned the children of a small Appalachian mining town.
>
> Love, Daniel

He stared at the email for so long that by the time he clicked *Reply,* the café was closed. The next day, he told

Cass he had to do some more work on the website and went back.

> I miss talking to you, too. I'm still with her. We are in New Jersey, working on a project, a retreat where she can teach people to live fearlessly. I wish you could be here. I am in charge of the food. It's very healthy.
>
> I'm sorry about how I left.
>
> Love,
> Tom

He sounded like a kid writing a reluctant letter home from camp. He wished he could tell Daniel everything—about the marriage, and his parents, and the disconnection he felt from Cass's newly manic sense of purpose, which had intensified since they'd closed on the house—but now that there was a thin line of connection open between them again, Tom desperately wanted to protect it, the only way he knew how: with stilted half-truths.

He closed his eyes and sent the email, then went to the Chinese buffet and paid $6.99 for an all-he-could-eat early-bird special. He gorged himself on gelatinous beef with broccoli and tooth-sucking General Tso's chicken. Cass had been increasingly vigilant about the food they ate. No meat or dairy. No sugar or grains. No legumes or tubers or soy or nightshades. Some fruits were friends and some were foes, but every time Tom tried to predict which was which, he got it wrong.

Before they moved to the house, Cass's eating was mostly a mystery to him. He rarely saw her consume, but he knew she had to be eating *something*. His mother wasn't much of an eater, either, but once when he had a fever he went downstairs in the middle of the night and caught her eating an entire T-bone steak, cold, dipping each piece in horseradish. She was sitting at the kitchen table in the near dark, consuming the entire thing with the same ruthless efficiency with which she parallel-parked.

Cass didn't explicitly forbid Tom from eating the Bad Foods, but when he came back from the Stop & Shop with a frozen DiGiorno pizza she looked at it so sadly that he shoved it to the back of the freezer and promised he would never eat it. *I want your body to be as pure as your soul,* she told him, which he was pretty sure was a compliment.

Now whenever he went grocery shopping, he gorged on samples of sweaty cheese and melba toast. Once he bought a bag of Cheetos and ate it in the parking lot, but when he got home Cass noticed his orange fingers. She told him his aura was manifesting a need for control and prescribed more Humbled Silence. After that, he only ate food that was the color of his skin, like Bugles.

The Chinese food was the most he had eaten in a single sitting since they left Daniel's. Afterward, he felt so sick that he just sat there, staring down at the table, until the owner came over to check on him. He assured her he was fine, paid his check, and walked out the door, only to vomit still-recognizable broccoli all over the sidewalk. Then he went to the cellular store behind the doll museum and bought the newest iPhone model.

He told Cass it was for uploading photos of her to Instagram, which Daniel had loved. *I mostly take pictures of things on the street that look like they have personalities.* Daniel's followers seemed to be eating beautiful breakfasts constantly and doing nothing, but there was one picture of a very beautiful woman in a meadow, extending one hand to the camera, that made Tom think of Cass.

He took pictures of her in the most photogenic places on the property, though the scenery always paled in comparison with her. Everything in frame that wasn't Cass looked faded, like it had been left in the sun too long. Even the sun. He couldn't take a bad picture of her. Once he caught her mid-sneeze and in the photo she looked like she had fallen lightly asleep and was dreaming about something delicious.

Instagram seemed like the correct ratio of Cass's face to his words. He uploaded all the pictures to the @Fort Path Instagram and tried to copy the kind of captions he remembered from Daniel's followers. *Perfect Day—* he wrote under a picture of Cass leaning back on the grass, her head tipped toward the sky. He liked to experiment with punctuation.

He followed every account that had anything to do with meditation or nature or beautiful women who didn't wear much makeup. A few followed him back, but nowhere near the flood he expected Cass to draw. He googled *why does no one follow me Instagram,* and learned about hashtags.

He loved hashtags. He loved that they were a club that anyone could join. You didn't have to prove that you were a #foodie, you only had to adopt the label and you were automatically allowed into the grid. He wrote down hashtags that reminded him of Cass on his yellow legal pad, and started tagging all his posts #mindbodyspirit and #wellness and #well and #meditation and #health and #yoga and #yogagirl and #namaste and #instafit and

#instagood and #instawell and #beauty and #farmlife. And the trickle of followers became a rivulet.

He liked being the mediator between Cass and the world. She often said she wanted to share herself with everyone (something he tried not to think too hard about), but she was still suspicious of the internet. Once, she asked him whether inhaling its waves might be dangerous. He assured her that the internet was perfectly safe—though he wasn't entirely sure if that was true—and necessary for their growth. She accepted this, and Tom learned that she would agree to most things if he cited growth.

It was exciting for him, the flood of interest in Outward-Facing-Cass. He felt like he had found his calling. He had never really thought about what he wanted to be when he grew up, probably because he hadn't realized that "extension of Cass" was a job.

Sometimes the captions he wrote were things he wished Cass would say to him, or things he half remembered her saying when they were children. Under a picture of Cass in a white hemp slip with her arms wrapped around herself and a halo of light encircling her head, he wrote *YOU are on a journey toward the Truth, and only YOU will know when you reach it. Trust YOURSELF to know what your Soul needs every day. If You act fearlessly from your Heart, You won't ever hurt anyone.*

After he wrote a caption, he read it out loud to himself, and imagined she was speaking to him. Sometimes it helped him remember the parts of Cass he really believed in—parts that had nothing to do with hydration and sexual magnetism. The longer he and Cass were married, the more he suspected that her love for him was the exact same as it had been when they were kids. She had always wanted to save him.

Her favorite game back then had been *new mom.* Sometimes an absent Jade was the new mom, and Tom and Cass were both her children, but more often the new mom was Cass herself. Tom usually started by acting out a scene from real life. He would tell her about something he had broken, the top of a porcelain box or one of his father's expensive pens, and she would tell him that it was okay because everything breaks, and suggest having a funeral for it so he could say goodbye. Then the reveals would become imaginary—Tom would tell the new mom he had grown a lizard tail and she would find Jade's sewing scissors and cut a hole in the top of his pants and stroke his lower spine with one finger and tell him she loved his lizard tail. Tom would tell her he had a dream about kissing Brian Durkee and she asked him what it felt like, and did he like it, and could he show her. And then she changed from a mom into something else, and they were kissing, and she said, *I love you,* and he believed it, and not just because believing it was nice.

It was weird, he knew, to think of her as his mom/wife, but sometimes the thought was a comfort. Either one of those titles could be shucked, by negligence or law, but there was strength in the pairing.

Still, he emailed Daniel all the time. They wrote back and forth all day, politely avoiding topics like Cass and kissing and fearlessness. Tom wondered if he could just email with Daniel for the rest of his life, and never tell him about the marriage, and live happily with him as a pen pal, like they were a pair of wartime lovers and the war just went on forever.

Then Cass told him they needed to incorporate bee pollen into their diets before the spring. He would have to drive to the city to buy some, as well as raw kelp and activated cashews and other things the Stop & Shop didn't carry. She couldn't come with him, she said. She was preparing. Lately, he had stopped asking any questions at all.

He didn't tell Daniel he was coming until the morning of the trip, half hoping it would be too late. *I have to come into the city (New York) today for an errand. You probably have to work but if you have time we could grab coffee?*

Daniel replied within minutes. *Broad St. Cosi at 2?*

Tom had spent hours at that Cosi when he and Cass were sleeping in Zuccotti Park. He recognized the woman behind the cash register when he walked in and smiled at her. She smiled back, but blankly, because he was a customer and it was her job. He was early. He ordered two lemonades, because he wanted one and it seemed rude not to get Daniel anything.

Daniel walked through the door exactly at two. When Tom saw him, he felt the way he had read about a girl feeling when she saw her boy. He wasn't sure how boys were supposed to feel. He hadn't read any books about that. With Cass, he felt like he was watching himself from the outside, aware of himself at all times in relation to her. Looking at Daniel, Tom felt more *of* himself than he could remember ever having felt. He felt every fiber of his clothes against his skin.

They only stayed at the Cosi long enough to finish their lemonades, then they went back to Daniel's apartment and lay on his bed together. Tom only briefly wondered what Daniel had done with Cass in that bed.

Daniel admitted he didn't have much experience with men. Tom had never thought of himself as a *man*.

Neither do I, Tom said, so they just kissed until Daniel had to go back to work.

Daniel asked when he would be back, and Tom said *next week* because any longer seemed impossible. He expected to feel guilty, but instead of guilt there was a curious void, as if the events of the day had happened in a timeline parallel to his existence at FortPath. He remembered learning about parallel lines in school. *Even if they extend forever in both directions, they'll never intersect.* At the time he had been afraid of the *forever,* just two lines drifting infinitely in space.

The day Tom went to New York for the first time was also the day the FortPath Instagram hit 7,777 followers. Cass always said seven was the most sacred number, except when she said eleven was the most sacred number. Still, Tom was elated. It might have been the first time he had ever accomplished anything.

Is it time? he asked.

Of course, she said.

Tom bought a bunch of bedrolls from a Romanian website because they were the cheapest he could find, and a clipboard from Staples that made him look official, like a camp director. He planned seven meals he could cook for ten people and made a bathroom sign-up sheet he would later find in the garbage. He contacted a livery cab service that made out-of-town trips, to see if they could shuttle guests to the farm. The woman on the phone sounded annoyed that he was calling about a theoretical job, but told him that *theoretically*, he was within their radius.

Tom had no idea what Cass was planning to do with eight to twelve people for two and a half days, but she seemed unconcerned as ever. Tom announced on Instagram that FortPath was accepting reservations for the inaugural workshop. Transportation from New York City would be provided. Six people signed up. Tom felt like he had built a house from a single tree.

He had to go back to New York again to buy more supplies. This time, he and Daniel got naked together. Tom hadn't been naked with another man since the locker room at his family's country club, where he had dressed and undressed with the speed of an on-duty fireman. Even with Cass he usually kept most of his clothes on. Tom didn't actively hate his body, he just assumed it was embarrassing and went to appropriate lengths to keep it hidden. The idea of someone seeing all of him, and forever knowing what he looked like, felt instinctually catastrophic, like how certain horses know to fear anything that resembles a snake. But Daniel looked at him like he was something rare and precious.

Cass was Tom's world, but Daniel was his secret reward. For what, he didn't know. For not insisting on anything, maybe. For not making a fuss, at least since his enormous fuss at the library, which felt like it had happened to a different person. He didn't think he deserved this reward, but somehow Daniel's presence seemed like proof that he did.

When he had to leave, Daniel didn't ask when he would come back, which made Tom feel both grateful and somehow slighted. If there was no plan, there was no betrayal. Besides, he had work to do.

The guests were much glossier than Tom had anticipated. He expected them to be unkempt, more like the Occupy Wall Street people, unintentional dreadlocks and amorphous cargo pants. The people who arrived at FortPath's inaugural workshop weekend were effortless in a painstaking way. They wore exercise clothes, though Tom was almost certain he hadn't promised any exercise. The women's cheekbones were chrome-shiny. Everyone had very white teeth. They looked appraisingly at the house, which needed fresh paint, and at Tom, but when Cass appeared, they nodded with satisfaction like they had ordered correctly at a fancy restaurant.

Tom's second surprise came during Mindful Spatialism. Mindful Spatialism was an exercise that, as far as Tom knew, was of Cass's own creation. At Realities, patients (who were called "kin") would lie in a dark, quiet room while Cass directed them to envision themselves in different universes; as light, as grains of sand, once as molecules of carbon dioxide being exhaled from the mouths of their grandfathers. There had never been any masturbating, at least that Tom had noticed.

You weren't supposed to open your eyes during Mindful Spatialism, so at first Tom just heard the sounds—the sigh of a drawstring coming uncinched, tentative skin on skin, a startled intake of breath. When he peeked, Cass was embracing one of the girls from behind, holding her hand by the wrist and guiding it into the girl's leggings.

Tom was halfway to the house before he thought about what Cass would think. It looked like he had left out of outrage, but his body felt only fear, like the dream he sometimes had where he realized he was the murderer and he had to get away before anyone saw him. He ran up the stairs to his room and sat under the window, his back pressed against the wall.

When they were kids, Cass told him she had good ideas when she touched herself. *Just below my sacral chakra,* she said, then hiked up her dress to show him.

What kind of ideas? he asked. *Do you just have to touch there once and then you get an idea?*

She didn't touch him, only herself, beneath her underpants. She told him to try, but he was too afraid until later that night, when he was alone in his room. When he did it, he thought of Cass, lying on his lawn. He didn't have any ideas.

That none of the guests lodged the slightest objection to publicly masturbating made Tom feel ashamed of his childhood reticence. He wondered if his whole life would have been different if he had touched himself the first time Cass suggested it. Maybe he would have gotten ideas if she'd been next to him.

The rest of the weekend was, according to the surveys he distributed to everyone, a great success. *Transformative,* they wrote. *Healing. Sensually fulfilling.* Only one mentioned Tom: *The assistant seemed organized.* Some of them wept when they hugged Cass goodbye. They posted obligingly hashtagged Instagrams of themselves posing on the porch.

When the last cluster pulled away, Cass took Tom's hand. *What a beautiful thing we've created,* she said.

chapter 19.

"How long have you been doing this?" Jane asked. They were nearly back at the house. She hadn't meant to sound so accusing, but she realized she had underestimated Tom, which made her feel foolish and unkind. The snipe seeped out of her.

"Which part?"

"With Daniel, I mean." As she asked the question, she realized it must have been more than five years. She couldn't believe Tom had that kind of magnetism. "Is he okay with it? Are *you* okay with it?"

"He's really busy," Tom said.

Jane rolled her eyes. "What about Cass?" she asked. She was surprised to find that she actually cared. She felt protective of Cass in that moment, even beyond her usual knee-jerk identification with the loser in any scenario. Tom flinched, keeping his attention perfectly focused on the road.

"I told you. She's my family."

"So she knows?"

"She doesn't know everything I do, and I don't know everything she does."

"Do you think she would care?" Jane was genuinely curious. The more she learned about Cass, the less she understood. She had the charisma of a cult leader, but not enough of the drive. Maybe more than the flawless skin, this was the secret Jane wanted Cass to reveal to her the most: *How do you just* exist? The fact that Cass would probably welcome the question made Jane even less willing to ask it.

She had assumed Tom was under Cass's thumb, especially after the cunnilingus / bone broth affair, but Tom's story made it clear how dependent FortPath/Opeia's existence was on his kinesis. Maybe Cass didn't have a master plan. Jane wondered if she was the only one of the three of them capable of thinking more than fifteen minutes ahead. The idea that Cass had created an entire ecosystem around her without really trying was even more impressive. Maybe she was the only influencer in the world whose existence *was* as effortless as it seemed. When you could see the seams, at least you could convince yourself that your own lack was impermanent, and improving your station just a matter of a little extra grit. The challenge in selling Cass would be, perhaps, manufacturing some relatable inauthenticity.

"I think she would be unsettled," Tom said carefully. He turned off the two-lane highway at their exit. At the traffic light, he turned to her. He looked afraid, and exhausted. "Please don't say anything to her."

"Of course I won't," she said. "Did you really think I would?"

He raked his hands through his hair, roughly enough to dislodge a few strands. The car's upholstery, a velvety gravitational field, sucked them close. The light turned green.

"No. I'm sorry." But he didn't sound convinced, or relieved, or sorry. They drove the rest of the way in silence.

~

After a few days of companionable labor, Jane assigned Tom the task of sanding and painting the floors, which she had decided should be white. She was busy shopping for furniture online.

"See, this is the exact aesthetic we're going for," she said, showing him the photos of minimal interiors she had bookmarked. "It's easy. And if you don't like it, it's really easy to scrape it off," she lied.

Cass had mentioned something about the toxicity of the paint's smell—for once she might have been using the word correctly—and taken the car.

Throughout her five and a half weeks at FortPath, Jane had assumed she and Tom were both late starters, siblings in inertia waiting for their shoves. Tom's story had made it clear that he had already been shoved. She felt tricked. Not only was he loved—*actually* loved, loved across distance and the bounds of marriage to someone else—he was competent. He was the force behind Cass—the one who had drawn Jane here. Abstractly, Jane would have assumed she would be more upset by the fact of Daniel, but now Tom's acumen felt like the greater offense by far. She thought they were a team, muddling through together, just like she and Eleanor had been. In truth, he'd passed the muddling phase long ago, and Jane had to catch up. No—she had to do better.

She was barely sleeping—there was too much to plan. She was actually *busy.* Before FortPath, everyone around her was "busy." Even if she had said yes to everything, which she never did, she would still have been the least busy person she knew. Being "busy" sounded terrible, but because it was a universal badge of honor, she coveted it.

But now, during the day, with Tom, she completed actual tasks: washing endless windows, patching the bat holes in the roof, ferrying to the dump the inexplicable collection of broken chairs and dented cans and a single Cold War–era globe that had apparently lived in one of the closets since Tom and Cass bought the house.

At night, she worked on the parts of the project for which she wanted sole credit. She created a dummy Instagram (@kelpandhoney) and followed any influencer worth courting or copying. She scoured the websites of upscale spas and sound healing retreats and adult summer camps for tech bros intent on optimizing friendship, and copied down key phrases to use in her own materials—*nurture in nature, release of energetic blockages, detoxifying botanicals.*

When Tom asked if she wanted his help with Instagram and the website, she told him she had it handled.

His wounded look made her feel guilty, which made her want to punish him more.

"You did a *great* job on Phase One of Cass's web presence." She aimed for sweetly patronizing. "Especially for the early days of Instagram. But the platform has changed a *ton*. It would actually take me longer to explain best practices to you. It's easier if I just do it myself."

"But it was working before. People kept coming. And how much could it have changed in a few years?"

"Wait, are you seriously asking how much Instagram could have changed in, like, six years? Okay, that's *adorable*."

She was pleased to see Tom's hangdog expression sharpening to something like annoyance.

"Fine," he said. "Why don't you tell me how it's changed."

His question made her nostalgic for the time, just days before, when their arguments had been spirited and familial. *Pretty sure they added 150 percent more self-loathing,* she would have responded.

Instead, she said, "It's all about Stories now. And nobody likes, like, high-contrast food pictures anymore."

Maybe if he had responded with a joke, Jane would have cracked. She would have shown him the overly intimate pitch emails she was composing to beauty editors and they would have cringed together and he would have pointed out her typos. But Tom left the kitchen without saying anything.

For a moment she was ashamed of how she was treating him, but that was just an echo of her old pity for him. Now she felt like he had tricked her into pitying him. He had a wife and a boyfriend and a trust fund. He didn't deserve any extra gentleness. She opened the old Fort-Path Instagram and deleted every picture that wasn't of Cass, then she deleted Tom's embarrassing captions from the remaining ones, stabbing the backspace on her screen until her finger was sore.

Usually, competition made Jane want to quit rather than risk the ignominy of trying her best and still failing. That wasn't an option now. She had no apartment to go back to, and while she wasn't actually *making* money now, there was the promise of money—the promise of absolution from her debt. And Tom was quietly paying for her COBRA every month. In her desperation, she had bulldozed her way into a far more outwardly desperate situation. That Cass had exerted no pressure on her whatsoever unsettled her more.

She focused on small, achievable projects. For the first time, enormity was within her reach, and she was terrified. Cass was a golden goose, but Jane knew nothing about goose care.

She made a list of everything still wrong with the house, and a list of all her media contacts, including the ones who never responded to her, and of all the wellness words she had ever seen in prestige publications, and of all the adjectives she would use to describe Cass, including the overtly horny ones. She thought about Farren, and the other Scary Women.

The Scary Women wouldn't feel sad about keeping Tom at arm's length. They would argue that *ambition* wasn't a dirty word and that women were socialized to please others and that *Thanks!* was the patriarchy. They would tell Jane she wasn't being mean to Tom, she was just setting healthy boundaries and respecting the limits of her emotional bandwidth.

She couldn't help feeling guilty for dismissing Tom so thoroughly, but the Scary Women weren't afraid to pivot. She had to prioritize her professional goals. And, once she had succeeded, she could always return to Tom. But she wouldn't apologize. Scary Women never did.

chapter 20.

The floors looked like shit. Tom had painted over several dead crickets, whose bodies looked like a tiny reenactment of Pompeii, as well as several coins and a bobby pin. From a distance, they looked fine, and at a previous moment in her life, Jane would have thanked Tom and moved on, because they were floors and who really cared.

"These floors are unacceptable," she told Tom. She resisted the urge to tell him about all the times she had fucked up home-improvement projects, like when she tried to install her own air conditioner and ended up nearly getting kicked out of university housing for demolishing all the sunflowers in the community garden below her. Instead, she told him he would have to scrape off the paint and try again.

Once she had decided to care about the quality of Tom's work, she noticed that every project he completed was similarly slapdash—earnestly attempted but with some equivalent of the painted-on dead crickets. He left streaks on the windows and scrubbed dull patches into the counters with steel wool. He ordered serape blankets that turned out to be hand towels, and when he tried again, he got one that had the stars of the American flag in the corner. Jane usually felt kinship with the incompetent, but she suspected that Tom's fumblings were a symptom of his lifelong wealth, which stripped them of relatability and added to her frustration.

Unbelievable as it was to her, she cared about this. And she was good at it. Her years of life-coveting on Instagram had prepared her to calibrate Cass precisely to the desires of a nebulously dissatisfied Millennial woman with (theoretical) disposable income. It was thrilling to finally discover a talent, even if it was for monetizing her low-grade depression.

She tried to explain herself to Tom while they went over menus together. They still hadn't replaced the picnic table, so they were sitting on the kitchen floor. It was somehow sticky, even though Tom had just cleaned it. "If this thing doesn't feel exclusive and luxurious, we won't be able to build the right kind of momentum."

"What's the right kind of momentum?"

"Well . . . fast. If the right kind of people pay attention, we'll be able to build enough buzz to grow into something really important. Like, a wellness institution. Cass could have her own line of products. *You* could have your own line of products. Tom's Activated Zucchini Snacks. Or something."

"Does she want her own line of products?" It didn't sound like an accusation, but it felt like one.

"She wants to reach the most people possible. Even people who can't come here. So, imagine a woman living in Des Moines." When she worked at Relevancy, Des Moines was always the flyover city where Jane situated her Everywoman. It was northern (which made it easier for clients to imagine the Everywoman wasn't obviously racist), it was relatively urban (so they could think of her life as sort of a low-stakes, practice version of theirs), and it was fun to say.

"She can't come all the way to this place, but she follows Cass on Instagram and all she wants is to find a little piece of Cass's lifestyle where she is. Maybe the Instagram captions have inspired her to take a yoga class, or live more fearlessly. But she wants more. She wants to feel closer to this person whom she has come to see as a role model. If only there was some way to smell how Cass smells, or wear what Cass wears. What if there was a book to tell her how to live more like Cass, in Cass's own words?"

Jane hadn't given this pitch to Cass herself, but only because she knew she didn't need to. Cass got it. Cass intuitively understood about the Des Moines Everywoman, and her desires.

"Cass's own words?"

"Or *my* own words, but *as Cass,* okay? Come on, don't act like you don't know how this works." She picked up the mostly empty yellow legal pad in front of her and flipped through it page by page to avoid having to look at him. "Or are you just mad that the role of Cass will be played by someone else?"

She was furious at the implication that she was ruining something instead of creating it, and ashamed that he might be right. Her only recourse was to make him feel as bad as she did. If only she felt bad, it demonstrated weakness. If they both did, she was a Scary Woman with a soul.

"You don't even believe in her," he said.

"Oh, we're back to this again? Okay, Tom, you're right. I wasn't a *true believer* like you. I admit it. But *I'm* the one who's trying to take Cass to the next level, and *you're* trying to keep her small."

"She was never small." There was no triumph in his voice, no *aha!* That was how she knew she'd lost the conversation.

"You need to clean this floor again," she said. "It's disgusting."

~

Usually after she behaved badly, the shame kicked in instantaneously. She braced for it, but felt only more righteous anger. Why was Tom trying to sabotage her? He was already enmeshed with Cass, plus he was rich. Jane was the one with something to prove. And a -$97,000 net worth. Despite the sympathy she felt for him after hearing about his repressed childhood and shitty parents, his trauma was abstract where hers was urgent. She told herself it was petty, really, his insistence on taking her vision from her.

She had to consolidate her relationship with Cass. Jane found her lying on the lawn, exhaling loud, rhythmic huffs. "It's important for us to be on the same page going forward," she told Cass, without announcing herself or waiting for an acknowledgment. "In order to reach more people, we have to align our messages. We should meet every other day so I can fill you in on what I've been doing." She loomed there, purposely casting a shadow over Cass, until at last she finished her huffing and sat up.

"All right," she said. And that was all. Jane walked back to the house, trailing clouds of glory.

She told herself the check-ins weren't solely to wrest intimacy from Tom. She wrote down every agenda item she could think of:

- negative brand implications of group masturbation
- key moments for founder's narrative
- rebranding options
- Cass last name??

Just before the hour of their first check-in, it began to hail, so Cass invited Jane to sit beside the tub while she soaked. Though Jane worried it would set the wrong tone for her anti-masturbation agenda, she was too interested in what Cass looked like naked to refuse.

The nudity turned out to be a letdown; her stubbly mons pubis, the outlines of her ribs, her slightly skewed nipples, were all too ordinary, too much like Jane's own. She focused on Cass's still-immortal face and the sound of the pinging hail as she gave her pitch.

"Release is essential to my work," Cass said, cupping water in her hands and spilling it over her breasts. The left one was bigger. "People have no understanding of the power of valves. That might be the greatest gift I offer them."

"What about screaming? Or like . . . saying mean things about their parents?"

"Is there something you'd like to tell me about your parents?"

"What? No. I mean, my dad's an asshole but that's not . . . It was just an example. Of another kind of valve," Jane said.

"My father took me from my mother when I was a child. The last time I saw him was at the airport when he brought me back. I think he jumped bail."

Hearing Cass say *jumped bail*—and for that matter, *I think*—was jarring. It felt like an unwelcome intrusion in the narrative Jane had spent weeks trying to articulate in her promotional materials. She knew the appropriate reaction would be sympathy for Cass, maybe even gratitude for this newfound vulnerability, but instead she was vaguely repulsed, again, by Cass's humanity. This wasn't the Cass she'd been sold.

"Why did he bring you back?" Jane said. She told herself she wanted to connect with this new Cass, but she realized she actually wanted to get out of the room as quickly as possible. The air was too close. Even the thought of accidentally brushing arms with Cass made her itchy.

"He had enough of me," she said simply. She leaned one elbow on the side of the tub and looked past Jane. "He did take me. But I chose to go with him. It was after Tom left. I was nine years old and I felt like my atmosphere had changed, but no one else's had. Everyone else could still breathe normally, even my mother. But the air around me was toxic. Every breath was a struggle. I thought maybe if I went with him, it would fix things."

Jane wondered if there was a single right thing to say. Cass's childhood sadness made her own seem puny and dull. The fact that Cass had overcome that sadness so spectacularly stung in a puny and dull way, too.

"Was the atmosphere better in Aruba?" Jane asked after leaving the silence too long. It was the only thing she could think to ask. A second after she spoke, she remembered that it was Tom who had told her that part of the story, not Cass.

"How did you know about Aruba?"

"Didn't you just say Aruba?" Despite her past dependence on lies, Jane was a terrible liar.

Cass put her mouth to the water between her legs and took a loud, slurping sip. Then she leaned back and slid under the surface, eyes open.

"Tom told me," Jane said when Cass reemerged. "It was a long time ago."

"Curiosity is a gift." Her voice had returned to its unreachable register. Jane didn't realize how tense her shoulders had been until they relaxed. An hour earlier, she was trying to find a point of connection with Cass. She didn't know what had changed.

"Back to the masturbation question, then." She could only forge ahead, a Scary Woman with an inviolable agenda. "In the future, we could consider a vertical with a focus on the power of sexuality, but the pilot program needs to be unimpeachable."

"Who is trying to impeach us?"

"No one," Jane said. "Everyone." She was a little surprised Cass knew the word.

"Are you releasing regularly?" Cass sat up very straight and stretched her arms over her head.

Jane thought of the box of elaborate vibrators from her former client C-Sweet languishing in her storage locker. The only time in recent memory she'd tried to get off without electricity was during Mindful Spatialism. "I'm fine," she said. "I'm very released."

She relaxed her shoulders, which were inching up toward her ears.

"If you build a brand on group masturbation, you're asking for a takedown in *The New Yorker.* Well, *The New Yorker* if you're lucky. It could be much worse." She realized she had a tendency to throw in references she didn't expect Cass to get. "Before I came here, someone told me it was a cult. That's what I'm trying to avoid. We can be *cult-y,* but you can't ask anyone to call you Mother and you can't have concubines, and you can't lead with a circle jerk. You said you wanted *everyone* to come here. This is how you reach them."

Cass twisted her wet hair into a knot at the nape of her neck and stood up, putting Jane eye-level with her dripping crotch. "Fine," she said. She stepped out of the tub and left the bathroom, leaving a trail of water behind her.

Jane dragged her fingers back and forth through the bath that Cass hadn't bothered to drain and considered her victory. She was never sure if Cass's capitulations were an indication of her true belief in the things she said, or the opposite. Did she have so much confidence in her overall philosophy that she was willing to compromise on the details, or was everything she espoused open to negotiation?

Jane saw a lone pubic hair stuck to the side of the tub and added *research bikini wax trends* to her mental to-do list. Despite their conversation, she was almost certain someone would see Cass naked, and she wanted to be ready.

chapter 21.

Tom didn't seek her out anymore. He wasn't pouting, but there was a new quiescence to him, like an animal playing dead. She listened at the wall at night to see if he was going to break his stillness with Cass, or tell her about Jane's outburst, but he never did either.

She sent him to the city to pick up the new table from a man in Bushwick who made live-edged tables out of lightning-scarred trees and refused to sell them to anyone he didn't meet in person.

"You want me to go alone?"

"I have too much work to do here. Is that a problem?"

His wariness suggested that he thought it was a test, but she meant the implicit offer of time with Daniel as a kind of peace offering. Besides, they really needed the table.

He was gone for five days.

It was much simpler to keep his absence from Cass.

Jane said he was in town running errands, then taking the car into the shop. Cass rarely ate beyond a handful of activated cashews or a bowl of undressed microgreens, so the lack of a cook went unnoticed. Jane consumed an entire bottle of honey one afternoon, out of sheer boredom. It gave her a terrible headache, but it seemed to cure her lingering grass pollen allergy.

She envied Tom for having somewhere interesting to go, and for being able to keep it a secret. She was pretty sure her envy for everyone would go away when her vision had been realized. Sometimes she was furious at Tom, though she knew that fury wasn't really hers to claim. She was the least of what he had abandoned. Other times she just missed him. She knew he was okay—he responded to her text messages (*i am ok,* again and again). She knew what he was doing. She had sent him to do it. She hadn't expected him to be gone for so long, but she was pretty sure he would come back eventually. After all, his wife was here, and all his shirts.

Finally, Cass said she needed the car as soon as Tom returned. Jane said Tom had an appointment with Jonathan, the lawyer, and offered to call Cass a car. "He might be a while."

"Tom doesn't see Jonathan," Cass said.

Jane was sprawled on the sheepskin rug, pretending to work on the impossible press release. "I must have misunderstood," she said, in a terrible approximation of casual. "He might have said a different name. And thing."

"Where is he?"

"I sent him to pick up the new kitchen table. It's taking a little longer than anticipated."

"Is that your true truth?" Cass's denial of the existence of lies made for some interesting linguistic maneuvering at times like this.

Jane clicked on CASSISMS.doc, which she always had open, and made a quick note. Then she closed her laptop and stood up, so she and Cass were nearly eye-level. It didn't actually make her feel more powerful, but Cass was such a graceful sitter that it was better to begin on high ground, where at least Jane didn't have to look at her own legs.

"I think . . . this has more to do with your journey with Tom than my journey with either of you. He'll be back soon. You can talk to him about it then."

Sometimes, neutrality was the worst kind of betrayal. She knew as soon as she finished speaking that she had broken something small but possibly essential, somewhere deep in the machinery of the house. She didn't yet know what would come of it, but she felt it, like biting down too hard, bone on bone.

Cass smiled her shaken Etch A Sketch smile, the ghost of an expression, which Jane usually found more gratifying than her full dazzler. It suggested an invitation to a private pleasure. This time, it unnerved her. She wanted Tom to come back. She needed to ask him about the taxonomy of Cass's smiles and so many other things: the equally intriguing taxonomy of Cass's smells and how she was pretty sure Cass only ever went to the bathroom outside and if so, did he know if that included poop? And did he think they could convince her to at least dig a hole so if any guests were wandering around the woods they wouldn't step in a pile of Cass's feces?

And she wanted to ask him about his five days with Daniel. As far as she knew, she was the only person in his life who knew about Daniel. Though she envied their connection, it was better to be a confidante than an outsider.

Cass stood watching her, still as a heron. She didn't move even when they heard tires on gravel. It took Tom decades to come inside. Jane saw him out of the corner of her eye, but Cass didn't break eye contact, so Jane couldn't, either. She hoped Tom would say something to break the spell, but he just stood there.

Jane broke first, because she hated standing. She lifted her arms over her head and sighed loudly and, she hoped, yogically. "Did you get the table?" she asked, twisting toward Tom.

"It's in the car. It took a little longer than I expected. Because it wasn't ready. The guy had to finish it. Sorry about that."

"Can't rush an artisan, I guess," Jane said. "I'll help you bring it in." She took a few steps toward Tom, but he didn't make any sign of movement. She caught him gently by the wrist and gave him a little tug through the door.

"I didn't think she would notice I was gone," he said once they were in the drive.

"She didn't, until today. Like, just now."

"Oh," he said, as if he was disappointed to have his grasp of his own significance validated. Which Jane understood.

"You know you were gone for five days, though."

"I know. I'm sorry."

The apology only annoyed her more. "Why did you even come back? I mean, Jesus, I'm working really hard here," she said.

"I know. I'm sorry."

"What are you sorry for?" Cass had come onto the porch. "An apology without specificity is constructed from fear."

"I'm sorry I was gone for longer than Jane expected."

Cass walked down into the drive and stood in front of Tom, very close. Jane's high school drama teacher had once said two characters onstage should only be facing each other in full profile if they were about to kiss, or fight. Tom and Cass looked like they might do either, or both.

"Why were you gone for longer than Jane expected?"

"The table took longer than I expected." Tom stared unblinking into Cass's eyes.

"Why did the table take longer than you expected?" Cass sounded curious, but not probing, like she was listening to an acquaintance tell an interesting story that had nothing to do with her.

"The table maker ran out of screws," he said, his voice so steady that Jane almost missed the absurdity of the claim.

"Why didn't the table maker anticipate how many screws he would need?"

"The table needed more screws than usual."

"Why did the table need more screws than usual?" Despite the persistence of Cass's questions, there was no tension in their exchange.

"It's a big table."

"Why didn't the table maker account for its size when he was gathering his supplies?"

"The hardware store didn't have enough of the kind he needed."

"Why didn't he try a different hardware store?"

"I was with Daniel."

Jane was surprised he'd said it, mostly because she'd forgotten that Daniel was the problem to begin with. She'd forgotten about everything besides the white noise of the scene.

"Who is Daniel?" Cass said, like they were having a normal conversation again.

Tom glanced over at Jane, as if to make sure she was still there. He shifted his weight back and hooked his thumbs into his belt loops. "We lived with him in New York. You guys were—I mean, you and he were dating, I guess." Now that they were speaking normally, he seemed nervous.

"I don't think this person impacted my energies in any meaningful way. I don't remember him." She crossed her arms over her chest, something Jane had never seen her do before. If not for that, Jane would almost have believed she had no memory of a person whose apartment and bed she'd shared for weeks.

"That's not true," Tom said. His voice was steady but a little impatient, like he was speaking to a misbehaving child.

"This person was a disruption. Your absence disrupted not only your work, but *our* work. Do you think that's acceptable?" The words should have sounded like a reprimand, but Cass's voice was gentle. Jane wondered for a moment if she had underestimated Cass's connection to Tom. Then she remembered Cass telling Tom *I love you, and everyone*. Tom, she reminded herself, could be anyone. Including Jane.

Tom looked at his shoes and rubbed the back of his neck. Then he tilted his head up to the sky, Job-like. Jane couldn't tell if he was contrite or righteously angry. He didn't say anything. She looked at Cass, who was looking at Tom, who was looking at a cloud.

Cass turned her head slightly to meet Jane's eye. "Do you think Tom's behavior is acceptable?"

Scary Women had the courage of their convictions. Jane wondered if this was something she could learn, or if she could find her courage in someone else's.

"No, it's not acceptable," she said. "It's not acceptable, Tom. We're trying to create a new paradigm, and we need absolute commitment."

She wouldn't have been sure, even moments earlier, if she could do it. So far her Scary Woman aspirations had been mostly abstract, but now here she was, unapologetically setting aside her relationships for the sake of her career, leaning in so far she was basically kissing the ground. She felt a little pride, followed immediately by guilt.

This wasn't the worst kind of betrayal. Which still made it a betrayal. She had forsaken Tom, and she had used the word *paradigm* to do it.

"You've done a violence," Cass said. She had closed her eyes, and Jane wasn't sure who she was addressing until she opened them and crossed behind Tom. She embraced him like a full-body restraint, pressing her cheek between his shoulder blades. "You've done a violence to us."

"I don't think you know what you're doing." He was almost whispering. "She wants to make you a *product*. She doesn't understand what you do here at all."

Oh, Jane thought. *Me*. She hurt more than she had any right to. Brand-building wasn't an endeavor that allowed for much righteous indignation. But then, neither did most jobs. Not even poetry—people only pretended it did. Anyway, PR was a kind of poetry. Capitalist poetry.

Tom hadn't said anything so wrong, though she disagreed with the part about her not understanding Cass's mission. Cass's mission was to live the exact life she wanted to live.

"I can't control what the world receives of me," Cass said into Tom's back, her voice like a hum. "Only what I offer to the world. We are all gifts. We can only present ourselves with perfect generosity. Jane's work will help me give of myself more generously."

"What she wants to do is the opposite of generosity. I should have told you before. I just . . . I liked her, I guess."

Jane knew that this was not the moment for pride, but she felt a little pride anyway. Tom had always thought she was a shitty person, but he was drawn to her despite her rotten core. Was this charisma?

"He and Daniel have been sleeping together for years." The words had barely formed in her mind when she spoke them. The note of triumph lingered in her mouth, like something spoiled. Tom didn't look at her. She realized he would certainly have told Cass even if she hadn't.

"Jane," Cass said, unwrapping her arms from Tom. She walked to Jane and took both her hands. Tom looked away. "Tom and I need to connect apart from you. Please leave us."

"Where should I go? And for how long?"

"Go into the trees. It's very peaceful there. You can return when it's dark." She led Jane onto the grass in the direction of the tree line. "Goodbye."

When they were together, Byron had undertaken a project to read the Bible cover-to-cover. Sometimes he would read her passages, which she loved. It made their relationship feel ancient and sacred. Mostly the words didn't move her, but there was one verse from Leviticus that she found devastating: *And Aaron shall lay both his hands on the head of the live goat, and confess over it all the iniquities of the people of Israel, and all their transgressions, all their sins. And he shall put them on the head of the goat and send it away into the wilderness . . .*

Byron was academically excited to explain to her the origin of *scapegoat*. Jane couldn't stop imagining a little potbellied goat sent into the wilderness alone, bearing the weight of sins it couldn't possibly understand, bleating piteously. She thought it was the most devastating thing she had ever heard.

She thought of the little goat now as she trotted off into the woods. She knew she wasn't an innocent, but the knowledge did nothing to stanch her self-pity. Sometimes Scary Women lost friends because the friends couldn't handle their ambition. She'd read a profile of the woman who founded an empire of women-only salad restaurants, She Leaves, in which the founder described falling out with her best friend over unfulfilled maid of honor duties. Of course, the profile had come early enough in the founder's ascent that she didn't have a PR rep savvy enough to shut down the anecdote.

Jane had never been a bridesmaid, though she and Eleanor had sometimes sent each other pictures of horrible dresses with the promise *ur bridesmaid dress.* Tom and Cass's not-fight made her think of her own non-falling-out with Eleanor. As she followed the footpath through the trees, she missed Eleanor so sharply that it felt like a cramp.

Eleanor's sister Phoebe had died unexpectedly, of a brain aneurysm, and Jane hadn't *been there for her.* She hated the cliché for both its vagueness and its precision. But she wasn't there. She flew in for the funeral, of course, in the immaculate Chicago suburb where Eleanor grew up.

Afterward, she texted *How are you??* every week or so, always with the double question mark to show that she really cared, and let herself off the hook when Eleanor responded *ok,* or didn't respond at all. She invited Eleanor out, but always to some kind of party, anything with a din and a buffer of people. Eleanor usually declined, and sometimes suggested a walk or dinner with just the two of them, but the timing never quite worked out.

Jane kept thinking she would get back in touch when time had diluted Eleanor's grief, made it less defining. The two of them had always been on the same level, but Phoebe's death had elevated Eleanor to a different plane. She seemed more serious, more important—being with her made Jane feel small. Trivial. All the bad things she had ever experienced had become cosmetic in comparison with Eleanor's bone-deep devastation.

After a few months, Jane told herself that she'd done everything she could. Taking a break from Eleanor's grief was a form of self-care, actually. And besides, Eleanor barely seemed to notice. At some point Jane set a daily *Call Eleanor* reminder on her phone. After the sixth snooze she changed it to a weekly *Text Eleanor* alert. It took her five months of inaction to delete it completely, at which point she was so used to ignoring it that she felt barely any guilt at all.

She'd met Byron months after she and Eleanor stopped speaking, and in the throes of the new obsession she almost forgot she was missing something. She was more successful in not thinking about Eleanor, and she was grateful to her subconscious for doing her that favor. Now, she knew, she would have to avoid thoughts of Tom, too. She wondered if everyone's pasts were such minefields of regret that only the most boring memories—solo lunch at an airport Chili's Too, a rushed networking coffee that never yielded a job—were safe from guilt.

Jane had seen Cass disappear into the woods dozens of times. It always seemed distinctly like her territory, and Jane had been too afraid to explore it without Cass's invitation. Jane's feelings toward nature were benevolently neutral, and the woods were pretty enough, in a generic East Coast nature-y way. She remembered Cass's story about the trees—*We are not your great friends.* Jane had tried to work versions of the story into the origin narrative she was crafting, but it was too bizarre.

She walked for a while, trying to appreciate the trees that all looked the same to her, until she came to a green shed made of corrugated sheet metal set a few yards off the path. There was a small white flower face painted on its door in lieu of a knob, which looked sort of sweet, but also like a clue on *Law and Order.*

There were two small windows on the side of the shed, just above her head. She could just barely reach them when she stood on her tiptoes, but it was too dark to make anything out inside. When she pushed the front door tentatively, it gave like a screen. She felt her pulse quicken, though she wasn't sure if it was from fear or excitement, or both. Once her eyes adjusted, she saw a camp lantern on a wooden crate. She tapped it on and found herself in the clubhouse she'd dreamed of as a lonely kid. It smelled like moss and pennies and, faintly, like a Bath & Body Works.

On the floor was a nest of blankets and bedrolls she recognized from the house, and clusters of fat, colorful candles. The walls were almost entirely covered with batik sheets, save for one square layered with magazine clippings. Jane had the *Law and Order* feeling again as she approached it. The clippings were mostly photos of people Jane recognized—reality stars and A-list actors—as well as jewelry, other evidence of abundance. There were a few words, too—all positive. RADIANT. FIT FOR A QUEEN. GLOW.

Still, it took her a moment to recognize the sum total as a collage, of the sort she might have made in middle school. She looked more closely, to see if there was some hidden artistry she was missing. Maybe it was a commentary on middle school collage? She ran her hands over its surface and had the sense memory of smelling a purple glue stick, pretending to get high.

There was a second crate in the corner, this one crammed full of magazines: *Us Weekly. W.* Even *Vogue,* in whose pages Jane had promised to place Cass. Jane picked up the June 2011 issue of *Cosmo* (Cameron Diaz was on the cover; Cass had excised her grin) and flopped down on the blanket nest. She felt like she'd finally been invited to the popular girls' seventh grade slumber party, fifteen years too late.

Though Jane hadn't grown up with siblings, her desire to talk to Tom about this place felt sororal. *Mom's being weird.* She wondered if he knew about the shed. The realization that she would probably never know was more painful than she expected, like a doubling of only-childhood.

She realized, too, that it was possible Tom had no idea about the shed's existence. He seemed to have no snooping impulse, and she couldn't imagine Cass advertising her devotion to mass-market femininity. Jane was surprised, but mostly she was in awe of Cass's ability to hide her shameful parts so completely. This was much more impressive than being idiopathically unembarrassing. That Cass's effortlessness required the effort of decorating and maintaining a separate structure made Jane feel closer to Cass, almost protective of her. *Cass—she's just like us!* This, in turn, made her sorrier for her betrayal of Tom.

The shed had trapped the heat of the day. She rolled onto her belly and flipped through the magazine, pausing on "78 Ways to Turn Him On." It was only seven years old, but now the list would be called "78 Ways to Feel Your Sexiest," with all the same advice. When she was a teenager, Jane read in *Cosmo* that a good way to subtly signal interest to a man was to trace the edge of her ear, slowly, with her fingertip. It had never even remotely worked, but she still did it sometimes, like an unthinking sexual genuflect.

Reading descriptions of physical contact made Jane realize how long it had been since she had been touched in an unambiguously sexual way. Her date with Adrian had been more than two months ago now. She had rerouted all her romantic desperation into her pursuit of Cass Industries, and now an old *Cosmo* was turning her on.

Last time she had been in Cass's bed she had only lain there. This time, she reached up her T-shirt dress, imagining her fingers belonged to the square-jawed ginger on page 54, or the androgynous South Asian guy opposite him. And Cass was there, too, but somehow the man was still touching her. Maybe Cass told him to? She flipped to the next page with her free hand.

> When you're getting hot and heavy, look him in the eye and tell him to be gentle. Pretending to sound a little scared will only make it sexier!

"Be gentle," Jane whispered.

> Touch him behind the knees—helloooo secret erogenous zone!

"Please be gentle." She brushed the backs of her knees with her fingertips.

> Take off your panties and use them to tie back your ponytail!

She pulled down her underwear and threw them across the room, then tossed the magazine in the same direction. She closed her eyes, and this time she saw Cass standing over her, smiling down approvingly. *Release. Release.* She tried to release herself from herself, her incessant, terrible thoughts, the thousands of small badnesses that made her up. She imagined her hands as Cass's hands, guiding her to release, turning her to light.

chapter 22.

When she woke up, it was dark. She felt sticky, like she had been lightly glazed in honey while she slept. The lantern had burned out, so she groped on the floor for her underwear. She did her best to arrange the blankets as she remembered them before leaving the shed. The moon was bright enough that she found the path easily. When she reached the house, the windows were dark, and the car was gone.

The next morning, she found Cass in the kitchen, sitting at the lightning table, her hands curled around a cup of steaming water.

"As you know, I don't advise drinking water warmer than body temperature," she said without looking up when Jane entered the room. "This is a rare indulgence."

It occurred to Jane to be horrified that she had contrived a profession that required her to live alone (were they alone?) in a house with a woman who referred to hot water as an indulgence. Then she got distracted by the skin on Cass's forehead. It was duller than Jane had ever seen it, and grayer, like a piece of paper that had been vigorously erased.

She glanced out the window and saw that the car was back.

"Were you out all night?" she asked. It was part curiosity, part an assertion that unlike Tom, sometimes Jane would ask questions.

"Yes. I took Tom to the city. He'll be staying there. His journey has led him elsewhere, and I wish him peace." Her voice cracked just slightly on *peace*.

Jane hadn't really expected Cass to give her a straight answer, let alone one freighted with real emotion.

"Do you, um . . ." She cleared her already-clear throat. "Want to talk about it?"

Cass looked at her for the first time. "Do *you* want to talk about it?" she said.

Later, she would wonder what would have happened if she'd said yes—if Cass would have laid bare her relationship to Tom and her grief over his leaving, her secret insecurities. Maybe she would have taken Jane to the shed, and they would have collaged together and talked about the people who had left them and the people they'd left. She would wonder if Cass had been offering her, in that moment, the rarest offering she had—reciprocal emotion—and if Jane, in saying *Not really,* had not only closed the door, but disappeared it.

Even in the wake of the shed revelation, Jane didn't quite know how much of Cass's *whole deal* Cass herself believed, and she was afraid of being tricked into revealing more of herself to someone who revealed nothing in return.

In that moment, when Jane said, *Not really,* Cass nodded, her shoulders lowering half an inch as if she'd been bracing for something and the danger had retreated. She stretched her arms across the table like spilling water, then got up and left the room.

Jane waited a few beats before going upstairs. Cass's door was closed, but Tom's was open. He had taken everything from his room except the sheets, but he'd stripped the bed. Jane gathered up the bundle of (distinctly un-Opeia) green flannel and took it to the outside garbage can, which she planned to hide in a woven teak storage bin she'd once seen in the SkyMall catalog. She scrunched the sheets up and stuffed them to the bottom of the can, replacing the rubber lid with a satisfying *slap.*

When she got back upstairs, she realized that there were no extra sheets in the house, so she ordered herself an expensive linen set in Pantone 13-1106 TCX (Sand Dollar) and added a matching one for Cass to unify the aesthetic. Then she moved all her stuff into Tom's room and sat on the stripped bed scrolling through Instagram until all the slim white shoulders and delicate collarbones and bold eyebrows and sun-blond hair blended together into one übergirl, drinking a matcha latte in every sun-drenched subway tile-backsplashed lemon-hoarding open-plan kitchen in the world.

But not Cass. Cass was different. Though Jane was molding Cass into a timely archetype, the woman herself was beyond type. This might be, Jane realized, the closest she could get to being a true believer.

~

A week before the soft launch, Cass asked Jane to meditate with her for the first time since Tom left ten weeks earlier.

Jane had been running on adrenaline and clarified mushroom tea. She hired a handyman she found on the hardware store bulletin board to paint and install gable vents in the attic because the exterminator she hired to deal with the crickets told her the house was too damp, which was why the crickets "had the run of the place."

She hired a web/textile designer named Armo Raspberry to update the Opeia site, but fired her after the second time Armo Raspberry blamed coding errors on the moon's position, then broke down in tears over the phone and begged Jane to reconsider because she was in the middle of an expensive health issue. After that, she hired a web-designer-full-stop named J Koe whose work was impeccable and about whose personal life Jane learned nothing.

She wrote a style guide for herself so she wouldn't forget which beliefs she had attributed to Cass, and wrote all the press material and website copy and captions and then took corresponding-enough photos of Cass and banked weeks of Instagram content, which she would only occasionally tweak due to sensitivity issues around world events. Opeia wouldn't engage with world events in any meaningful capacity, though of course its official position was that love, life, and nature were good, and hate, destruction, and cynicism were bad.

She formed a tepid alliance with Jonathan based on risk aversion and mid-level pragmatism, and, most important, got liability insurance behind Cass's back. When he patted her elbow and told her she was better for Cass than "that husband of hers," she allowed her pride to eclipse her guilt.

She bought a book about the Ayurvedic kitchen and another one about macrobiotic cooking and made a list of all the things raw zucchini could become (mostly ever-thinner ribbons of raw zucchini). She wasn't a very skilled cook, but the cooking Tom had done seemed to be more about preparation and arrangement of expensive ingredients, like being an interior decorator of food. Still, she researched chefs she might hire if they made enough money to bring on more full-time staff.

She had her eye on a rangy vegan with seventy thousand followers (@theuncruelkitchen). He would look perfect next to Cass in photographs, and his numbers suggested both striving and desperation. Besides, he had an Indigenous Canadian mother and a Japanese father, and Jane was growing a little concerned about the overwhelming whiteness of their project. *Diversity* was a core value that Opeia supported, of course, but beyond searching for (not white) hot people on Instagram, Jane had no idea how to put it into practice. She wondered if she should add something to the bio, like *Beauty knows no color.* Or *Hate has no home here.* That way, they had some plausible deniability if their commitment to inclusion was ever called into question. (People still wanted exclusivity, of course, but they wanted it to be the quiet part.) Jane assumed Cass was putting some kind of diversity vibes into the ether, anyway. She appreciated the existence of vibes as a catchall for the issues she didn't feel like addressing head-on.

She hired a photographer to take professional candids of Cass at work—Cass sitting cross-legged on the lawn,

Cass leaning over a bowl of kelp porridge at the live-edged kitchen table, Cass tenderly jerking off a zucchini in the garden—and enticing shots of the property with which to illustrate her press invitations.

Jane was furiously scrubbing the lightning table—which, like its predecessor the picnic table, somehow had a perpetually sticky residue—when Cass came in and proposed a session of mindful reflection. Jane made a mental note to bring up Cass's irritating habit of giving standard meditation different names every time she spoke about it. It was no way to build a brand.

They sat under the big tree (Jane still thought of it as the cunnilingus tree) facing each other. Cass gazed deeply into her eyes for a long time, which Jane was by now long past being either unnerved or turned on by. Maybe now that her fascination with Cass had been dulled by corporate intimacy, Cass was presenting herself to Jane. Maybe at the moment of orgasm—Cass's, of course—Jane would feel powerful, like she had the privilege of generosity. Maybe that was why Tom did it for all those years.

Just as she was getting turned on again, Cass spoke.

"I've been waiting for you to become conscious, but there's still something blocking you."

The words stung more than Jane wanted them to. She assumed that the spiritual realm had always been hers to reject; it had never occurred to her that spirituality could reject her. It was like when someone she didn't like that much broke up with her. She had the same frantic feeling, the desire to buy herself more time to win something she had been in the process of casting aside.

"There's been a lot of work to do to get things ready. I'm not sleeping much." Jane wanted to force Cass to speak directly, and the best way to do that was to feign obtuseness.

"Your spirit's eyes are closed even when your body is awake."

Since Tom left, Jane's desire to maximize the profitability of Cass had overshadowed her desire to be spiritually fulfilled. She wasn't always sorry he was gone, but when she missed him, she wondered why Cass couldn't have made him stay. She worried Cass was weaker than she seemed. But somehow, the more unsure she felt about Cass the Person's power over her, the more convinced she became that Cass the Corporate Entity would be a financial success.

If Cass had real spiritual power, she wouldn't be palatable to everyone. Religions that required too much of their adherents would remain niche. Adrian had warned her that Cass was a cult leader, but now Jane saw that she was much more Prosperity Gospel than Heaven's Gate.

She still wondered if Cass knew more about her than she knew about herself, though. She still held out hope for insight.

"How can I open my spirit's eyes?" she asked. *How can I be the person you want?*

"I don't know," Cass said.

Jane gave a shiver, despite the day's close heat—*Someone walking over your grave,* she'd heard once. Now she pictured Cass, gliding through a graveyard in washed silk.

Jane couldn't remember ever having heard Cass say *I don't know* before. She'd have thought it would humanize Cass, but it was the opposite. She was so out of practice at not knowing—not just saying the words, but inhabiting the state of unknowing—that she sounded alien.

"Well, what do you propose we do about that?" Jane felt dread, but the Scary Woman would pivot to project management mode. "Because our press preview is in a week and I don't really have time to do anything but, you know, work."

She had managed to keep her voice steady while speaking, but now she held her breath. She was afraid of Cass's prognosis for her spirit's eyes, the existence of which she had never considered. She tried to summon the confidence of unbelief. Or belief.

What she really wanted to ask was whether she could have more time. How did everyone else just know? Was there an unspoken belief deadline? Why was Jane the only one still flailing in ambivalence? She wanted to ask Cass for more time, but she couldn't form the request.

"I'm tired," Cass said—another thing Jane had never heard from her. She stood up and walked toward the woods.

"Enjoy your collaging!" Jane yelled with an irresistible impulse of unkindness, sounding just like the girls who had tormented her in her own collaging days.

Cass stopped, but she didn't turn back. Her shoulders remained perfectly relaxed. "Thank you," she said. "I always do."

~

They spoke only when absolutely necessary for the next week, and neither of them mentioned the spirits' eyes, or collages. Jane kept her headphones in all the time, something she had previously avoided doing, she realized, so Cass would be impressed by her ability to sit in the silence of herself. Now she could at least admit to herself that work was much easier with a soundtrack of strangers recapping reality shows she hadn't watched.

The press preview that weekend was the high point of Jane's professional life. Maybe her unprofessional life, too. She'd sent an initial invitation to a dozen editors and influencers, with a dozen more on the back burner just in case. When every one of her first-round picks accepted, Jane had felt a pang for her younger self—it turned out, popularity was exactly as fulfilling as she had always imagined.

The force of Cass's charisma reached terrifying heights that weekend. Jane even saw an editor swoon—a slight but perceptible buckle, like a skyscraper in a high wind—after Cass grasped her hands and told her that her etheric body had a powerful eroticism.

After the guests published their ecstatic praise, the deluge of reservations was so powerful that they repeatedly crashed the website. (J Koe apologized repeatedly for the lack of foresight, but Jane was too excited to bother unleashing Scary Woman on them.) The price for a weekend workshop was now $1,200, which none of the reviews cited as a drawback. Jane wondered how much more she could have gotten away with charging for the promise of radiant wellness.

chapter 23.

"You have the Welcome Smudging tonight, and tomorrow the Heart Center Keynote at eleven-thirty and the VIP Connect and Commune from twelve-thirty to three-thirty. Then you're back up here to meet with the *W* writer from four to six, and the Women's Nourish Mealshare at six-thirty."

It had been almost a year since Opeia's press preview, and Jane was ready for the next phase. The Well Zenith was the largest semiannual wellness summit on the East Coast, and Cass's billing was unthinkably high for a newcomer.

Cass didn't appear to be listening to her, but it didn't really matter. The Zenith was providing two handlers who would make sure she didn't wander off into Central Park while Jane was meeting with potential investors. It was better to stay behind the scenes at these things, to maintain the illusion that Cass was a self-contained universe.

Cass had accompanied Jane to the first few meetings, but her physical presence was a distraction. Inevitably, the investors directed all their questions to her, and were alarmed by her answers, most of which emphasized the importance of community and connection. Once, in response to a question about scalability, Cass told the room that though she had never been pregnant with a fetus, her body had always teemed with the possibility of life.

Though Jane's pitch clearly laid out their finances and plans for expansion, the investors were left with a sense that Cass was the wrong kind of disruptor. They usually still tried to fuck her, of course, and some succeeded. But it was much better to let her gaze out over the proceedings from the PowerPoint screen.

Cass was standing at the window of her eleventh-floor hotel room, looking out over the treetops of the park. The place was generically luxurious in a way that suggested a complete absence of ill health, but no kind of wellness. Jane loved that the sheets smelled like nothing, even when she buried her nose amid the seven pillows. The Opeia house was always heavy with the smell of "Cass's signature scent," an essential oil blend of lavender, eucalyptus, and cedar that Jane had concocted online. Their guests loved it.

"I'm sharing an evening meal with Tom and his lover, Daniel, tomorrow," Cass said now.

Jane thought of Tom constantly, obsessively. He was the last person she met before she shucked her previous self and became this more powerful Jane, and she was partly glad for any thinning of the ties to her former life. It was only the fact that she had won that prevented her from contacting him. The worst part was that missing him didn't even distract her from the other people she missed—Eleanor, her mother; they had all collapsed into one large lack.

"Of course, Tom's spirit and mine are eternally connected. Tom says his spirit is connected to Daniel's. It's time for me to meet Daniel."

"You dated Daniel. That's how he and Tom met."

Cass tilted her head window-ward for a moment, then turned back to Jane. "I honor Tom's truth," she said.

Jane sighed loudly. Since Cass had told her she didn't know how to open Jane's inner eyes, she availed herself freely of spiritual insubordination. Cass had never returned to the question of her consciousness. Jane wanted badly to ask but refused to do so, which felt close enough to spiritual progress.

Besides, Jane had never looked better. She now swaddled herself in muted natural fibers that both draped and clung, and looked like they might be suitable for either yoga or pottery or attending a celebrity home birth but were, in fact, suitable for almost nothing besides projecting an aura of self-satisfaction. Jane scoured the internet night after night for these clothes, and paid for them amounts of money she would never admit to anyone. Not even to the online therapist she started texting when her mother told Jane she was marrying Dave, and Jane told her mother she couldn't come to the wedding because she was too busy, and her mother told her that she seemed like a different person lately and she had liked the person Jane was before. But now, when she walked into meetings, men drank her in so brazenly that she felt almost uneasy.

Her skin seemed to fit her better, too, like she'd taken it to a highly skilled tailor, and her face had become a slightly different, more pleasing shape. She was higher gloss, higher thread count. Before, she had been a diffusion line, a castoff of her own true image, created in haste. Now she was the real thing. If she still missed Tom and Byron and Eleanor, if her old fears of her body expensively failing and never being anyone's favorite and accidentally telling the entire truth about herself out loud lurked in the shadows, if she still couldn't bear to sit with herself during Humbled Silence, well. That was fine.

She knew that Opeia Jane was as much a performance as Poetry Jane and PR Jane had been. But despite her professional commitment to authenticity, Jane didn't understand why she wasn't supposed to commit to a self that was objectively more successful than her *authentic* one. Was the kind of spiritual change she and Cass promised any better than Method-acting a version of yourself that the whole world preferred? She saw the contradictions everywhere in her work. As Opeia Jane, they didn't bother her at all.

"I need you at the Women's Nourish Mealshare until eight-thirty," she told Cass. "You can meet them after that."

"I'm going to go gaze at the water," Cass said.

"Do you need me to tell Tom you're pushing your meeting?" Calling it a meeting felt good. Jane had meetings without Cass all the time.

"I'll speak to Tom."

"Fine. Go to the reservoir in the park. The water's nice there. Very gazeable."

Cass gave a gracious half smile and walked out the door, leaving Jane alone.

Over the last year, Jane had assumed some sort of closeness would form between her and Cass, if only through relentless proximity, but they remained firmly co-workers. Cass and Tom's relationship—marriage—wasn't *close* in a way that made any sense to Jane, so she told herself that maybe the distance was fine, cool and mysterious even. She didn't actually want to be closer to Cass, but she was disturbed by Cass's total dismissal of her soul's potential. She always excused herself from Leaving Day at Opeia, when Cass embraced each guest and told them, individually, how proud she was of their progress.

So Cass and Tom were still in touch. Jane assumed Jonathan was handling their legal disentangling, but she had never asked. She imagined registered legal correspondence referring to The Parties, or terse emails on the Client's behalf. She wondered what they had said to each other before Tom left. She wondered so often, it might have been the central question of her unfinished dissertation.

Jane had no plans for the night, which suddenly seemed like a problem. She still had some friends in the city, people who would occasionally text her congratulations about a glowing piece of press, usually followed by an ostensibly sly request for comps, which she always accommodated. Everyone who came loved Opeia, even her most analytical, everything-is-both-a-construct-and-a-poem grad school friends, which made Jane think less of them.

After going over Cass's schedule for a fourth time and texting her very explicit directions to the Welcome Smudging (it was in a ballroom on the mezzanine, but Cass took an inability to find something as the universe inviting her to explore), Jane went back to her room for a nap. When she woke, it was dark. She weighed the optics of going to the hotel bar to have a drink. She hewed closely to the Opeia diet except when she wanted to refute someone's conception of the Opeia diet as overly rigorous and possibly anti-feminist, and above all *no fun*. Cass had agreed to do the same, at least with journalists, so they didn't end up with a vaguely mocking profile in which she referred to raw cacao nibs as "an indulgence" and became the internet's collective eye-roll for the day.

If Jane went to the bar, there was a chance she would meet someone. Probably the sex would be bad, which wouldn't matter if he was attractive enough. She hadn't seen any attractive men at registration, though, and the Zenith had booked 75 percent of the hotel. If she didn't meet anyone, she would have to stay at the bar for at least the length of one drink so it didn't look to anyone like she had gone there specifically to pick up a man, and failed. She would also have to have a drink, which would make her feel like shit in the morning. If she ordered only a club soda and did meet a man, she would lose her most reliable opener in situations like this, which was to lightly disparage the wellness industry as she took a sip of her dirty martini (which she hated), and tried to cock one eyebrow.

Maybe she could text someone already in her phone. In the months she had been coming back to the city with

Cass, she often met people. Once she even saw Adrian at a restaurant with a couple who might have been his parents, but he didn't recognize her. He looked older than she remembered, in an undistinguished way, like a former child star.

The men in her phone were less appealing than the possibility of a new man, in part because she already knew exactly how uninteresting she found them all. They were dull in everything but their skin. Because she met them at Zeniths and Happenings and Gatherings for wellness, they were sinewy and hydrated and glowing. They also knew who Jane was, and admired her. Sometimes they wanted to work with her. Sometimes they wanted to ask her questions about their own burgeoning brands.

Sometimes, though—often, even—they seemed to want *her*, and their wanting stood in for what she once thought of as connection. The connection was how she felt when a man reached for her with certainty. He didn't have to say anything at all. It was better if he didn't.

She didn't think of it as a sacrifice, putting aside the possibility of a relationship for the relative certainty of Cass and Opeia, because she knew that the work she was doing would make her a more desirable partner in the end. She didn't fault these future men for theoretically preferring the New Jane to all the old ones. She was ready to be the impressive one.

She would go to the bar, she decided.

She dressed in the Zenith equivalent of going-out clothes: a butter-yellow jumpsuit with a deep V-neck and a low crotch and patch pockets at her thighs. It made her look like a kindergarten teacher in a romantic comedy that imagined kindergarten teachers could afford $500 jumpsuits. She considered a wide-brimmed hat, but decided she didn't have the energy for a hat guy just then.

The bar smelled like mop water and Diptyque, which was somehow greater than the sum of its parts. She didn't see anyone else from the Zenith there, just a couple on what looked like an early date and a cluster of men in suits. She ordered a glass of white wine and sat at the bar. She concentrated on her posture and the taste of the wine. She inhaled deeply, exhaled pure self-possession. She was not here out of desperation. She didn't even have to pay for her drink, as long as she charged it to her comped room, though she probably wouldn't. There was a slim chance Cass would see, and Jane didn't want to have to wonder which, if any, of her sermonettes over the next few days were about Jane's two to three glasses of wine.

These days, for the first time in her life, she felt powerful. Not the *Stand in Your Power* powerful the Zenith was peddling, but actually powerful: the power of being the person in the room other people were glancing away from their conversations to look at. She wished she could talk to someone about it. She wanted to ask if she was doing it right, if it was supposed to feel different from this, better. She didn't expect she would still feel quite so much like herself.

She finished her glass of wine and scanned the room again. The couple had gone, and the cluster of suits had thinned to just three, one of whom was in the process of leaving. Of the two remaining men, one looked like the neighbor on the sitcom about the thoughtless schlub married to a hot shrew. He was short and white and had features that looked unfinished, like someone had quickly sketched him, intending to finish later.

The other man was good-looking in a way that suggested polo shirts and family badminton tournaments, and he held Jane's eye when he caught her looking at him. He raised his eyebrows, which she took to mean that she should wait for him, so she ordered another glass of wine and ran her finger around the top of her glass until she decided it might be crossing the fine line from sensual to gross. Finally, he came and sat down next to her. Up close, he was both handsomer and blander.

"Hi there," he said.

"Oh. Hi," she said, like she was a little disappointed but willing to overlook it. Which she was. One of the things she loved about her newfound sexual power was that she no longer had to feign enthusiasm.

"I'm Preston."

"Jane."

"You here with the conference?"

"The Zenith. Yes. Are you?" Jane assumed men in suits were involved at some stage of the proceedings, but they usually had the grace to stay hidden.

"Oh, sure. It's a major space. Huge growth potential. We're taking some meetings, exploring our options. But we don't have to talk about work." Preston smiled below the cheekbones and Jane weighed whether physical validation from someone like him was even worth the effort.

"What should we talk about?" Jane asked, her voice flatter than she intended. It was a genuine question, though. She couldn't remember what people talked about when they weren't talking about work. She had really never had hobbies beyond Instagram scrolling and light skin picking, and while she kept an eye on current events to make sure Cass didn't say anything topically insensitive in interviews, her world had shrunk to the exact dimensions of Opeia.

Preston seemed as stymied by the question as she was. "What are you drinking?" he said.

"Wine. White wine." She was disinclined to give him any help. Probably they should just fuck and get it over with. "Do you want to come upstairs?" She regretted the offer almost as soon as she made it.

"Uh, wow. Yeah." He drank the remaining half of his beer in two gulps and signaled to the bartender for the check. Now that he had displayed a reasonable level of enthusiasm for seeing her naked, she didn't feel the need to actually have sex with him, but there was no graceful way to extricate herself at this point.

This is my choice. I chose this. I am choosing this.

In the elevator, he kept smirking. When they got to her room, she unzipped her jumpsuit and stepped out of it as soon as the door clicked closed, even before she took her flat woven mules off.

"Shit," he said, admiring her from his perch at the end of the bed. "You've got an incredible body." And then she was able to like him, at least enough for the next hour.

He kept asking *Is this what you like? Is this what you like?* in a way that sounded like a statement of faith and brooked no disagreement. He stopped touching her and just looked, and shook his head like he couldn't believe his luck, and after a while she wanted to tell him to cut it out. She looked better than she had before, *good* even, but she wasn't exceptional. She wondered what he would do if he ever saw Cass naked. Probably die.

She extracted herself from under him and straddled his thighs, pushing him back onto the bed. She was exhausted all of a sudden. She wanted him to leave.

"Is this what *you* like?" she said, gripping his dick a little too hard and guiding it into her mouth.

She still loved the charge of knowing someone wanted to fuck her on sight, but the actual fucking was such a hassle now that she didn't need it anymore. Her power no longer required genital contact to activate it. At the moment of Preston's climax, Jane found herself wondering whether she'd ever actually liked sex.

"How long are you here?" he asked afterward, trailing his fingers over her shoulder a little too tenderly.

"Thursday morning."

"Got any plans for tomorrow night?"

"I'm in meetings all day tomorrow," she said, reaching for her phone on the nightstand so he would stop touching her.

"So am I," he said. "But not at night."

"I might have a drinks thing. It's still TBD. I'll let you know." He gave her his number and she put it in her phone.

She knew there was no connection with Preston. His obvious interest forced her to admit to herself her hope that there was. Even the word *connection* was embarrassing. It was so obvious. She was lonely, of course, but no lonelier than she'd ever been. And loneliness was the human condition.

"My physical vessel is absolutely aching for rest," she said. Sometimes she liked to affect a bit of Cass to unsettle people.

"So should I . . . ?"

"Thank you for sharing yourself with me, Preston. Have a peaceful night."

When he was gone, she looked at the blond wood digital clock and saw that it had only been forty-five minutes.

chapter 24.

Jane woke up the next morning at five, as she almost always did now. She used to have bitter reverence toward morning people, but now that she was one, she took no pride in it. She felt only irritation at her efficient body for robbing her of a few extra hours of unconsciousness.

There was Sunrise Yoga in Conference Room C, which sounded terrible but which was at least *something*. She checked the TV guide channel just in case there was a rom-com coming up on TBS, but seeing only *The 700 Club,* she dressed in her status yoga gear and slouched down to the lobby.

Though she had, at various points, been employed as a yoga teacher, Cass knew virtually nothing about yoga beyond the names of a few poses. That, combined with her aura of White Woman Yoga and her essential Cassness, had been enough to land her teaching jobs through the years. When Jane was setting the final itinerary for the press weekend and asked Cass if they could include a yoga session, there was a tiny fault in her voice when she agreed that led Jane to ask her for a demo. After ten minutes of moving bafflingly from Balasana to Dandasana to Sukhasana to downward-facing dog and back again, Jane told Cass that maybe they could back-burner yoga because yoga was a little played out anyway, and Cass had the good grace to look relieved.

Conference Room C was nearly full. As was almost always the case at these wellness summits and health conventions and spiritual aesthetics symposia, the crowd was overwhelmingly white. She wondered, as she often did, whether the issue was more the conferences' lack of interest in diversity, or not-white people's lack of interest in paying through the nose for something so absurd. Or both.

Jane unrolled one of the provided yoga mats near the back and struggled through forty-five minutes of sun salutations and flow led by a woman who introduced herself as Tà. At the beginning of class, Tà suggested they each set an intention.

"Whether that intention is gratitude, or strength, or successful networking," she said, her voice betraying zero irony. The room stirred with possibility.

I intend to crush it in these meetings, Jane thought. Then: *Am I a person who says* crush it *now?*

At the end of class, she thanked Tà, and asked if she would ever be open to collaborating with Opeia.

"Oh my God, I hope this isn't weird but I am, like, *obsessed* with Opeia. I just read Cass's interview on *Shwell* and I was just like . . . she's the real deal."

The *Shwell* interview had been conducted over email,

which meant that all the words had been Jane's. She didn't mind—the key to letting go of the anxiety of attribution was writing only things you found ridiculous.

She took Tà's contact information and went back to her room to prepare for the day's meetings. She could only remember scheduling three of the four, but her pitch would be the same no matter what. For now, they were fine without outside investment, but Jane wanted to hire more help—a consultant for her long-planned line of physical Opeia products, for one—and get a pied-à-terre in New York. She also had to figure out insurance for when her COBRA ran out, and insurance for Cass. And she still had $85,000 of debt left, but her progress was much steadier now that her life felt within her control. She didn't need to buy things to make her feel powerful. She just was powerful. Besides, beyond the debt, her only expense was wardrobe.

Her most common stress dreams now were Cass dying, or falling seriously ill, or getting adult cystic acne. She worried about shrewd potential investors pointing out that their entire business model was inextricably linked to a mortal, but maybe once they encountered Cass it seemed impossible to them that she would ever die. Jane hadn't considered the fiduciary downsides of mortality until a few months after she'd yoked her entire life to Cass's, but now she thought about it all the time.

What would happen to the seconds-in-command of the girlboss empires if the girlbosses themselves were somehow wiped out en masse, by a targeted comet or a tainted batch of adaptogens? Would the Janes of the world rise up in their stead, the mammals after the dinosaurs, or were they more like tapeworms, destined to perish without their hosts? Jane preferred to keep her knowledge of the system's fragility at a healthy distance.

Sometimes she could imagine Cass aging into a Lauren Hutton–ish version of her present self, unmarred by chemicals and radiant as ever, but it seemed equally likely that one day she would just dissolve into a vapor. Jane had watched the fashion influencers she followed in her twenties pivot seamlessly to motherhood, but it wasn't clear what a woman could become after that.

Her first meeting was with a female venture capitalist who had invested heavily in Innr, a company that made feminist douches that turned out to cause pubic baldness. Innr had embraced the side effect and pivoted away from feminism. They recently launched a line of nipple tinting creams called Nipstik.

The venture capitalist was a genuine Scary Woman. Her face was so sharp it looked like it would shatter if she lay down too hard, but her no-makeup makeup was impeccable. Jane wondered if she had a full-time glam squad on staff, as invisible as their work. The woman was dressed "casually," in perfectly tailored wide-legged jeans, a black T-shirt, and what looked like Birkenstocks, but the outfit's breeziness was clearly a trap designed to lull fools into a false sense of camaraderie. Jane knew better; the Birkenstocks were a designer collaboration, and the T-shirt probably cost a grand.

The woman's face remained neutral as Jane gave her pitch, detailing Opeia's stunning rate of growth in the past ten months, the fawning press they had received, their demographic breakdown and plans for expansion, and plenty of interstitial photos of Cass in various poses and outfits.

She had cobbled together her understanding of a pitch from the internet, *Shark Tank,* and a podcast hosted by a billionaire venture capitalist and a soothing-voiced former public radio anchor. But pitching to women was harder than pitching to men. It was easier to confidently tell men that you knew exactly what women wanted. They seemed to find it plausible that she had unlocked the secret to the acquisition of the white female customer aged twenty-four to forty-five with an annual income of over $100,000, who spent at least $200 a month on skincare. It was more difficult to tell a woman who fit that demographic that she was just part of a monolith.

At the end of the pitch, the woman nodded twice and folded her hands on the table in front of her. "Correct me if I'm wrong," she said. "But there's nothing proprietary here."

"The Opeia program is entirely Cass's creation," Jane said. "She's the product."

"Hm," the woman said, thrusting Jane right back into Rand Hagen's office. "Well, she's very pretty, I'll give you that."

Jane had never heard anyone call Cass "pretty." The dismissal was terrifying. She wanted to leave this meeting immediately. She wanted to find Cass and stare at her for a few hours to reassure herself that this woman's assessment wasn't true. That she was just jealous. That Jane hadn't banked her future on "pretty."

"Well, I won't take any more of your time," Jane said, smiling fiercely. "*So* nice to meet you. Enjoy the rest of the conference. I recommend the Sunrise Yoga with Tà." She gathered her laptop and her minimalist, fair-trade leather bag, shook hands with the gratifyingly nonplussed investor, and left the conference room, banging her elbow against the door on her way out. She hoped if word got around, her minor tantrum would make her seem man-difficult rather than woman-difficult.

Before this, she hadn't worried too much about the fact that none of her pitch meetings had yielded actual money. The podcast told her it would take time, and besides, no one had actually said *no;* they'd said *Let's circle back in Q3* and *Keep us in the loop* and *Talk to my assistant about avails for a visit.* Now she wondered if this Scary Woman was a portent of future rejections.

The next two meetings went fine. They were both with only men, one of whom wore fashionable overalls and spent a quarter of an hour talking about his commitment to breathwork. They asked questions she could answer easily and nodded a lot and made smiling eye contact with one another and told her they would absolutely be in touch. But still she left certain she would never hear from any of them again.

She hadn't experienced this type of disappointment in nearly a year, but there was something cellular about it—her body recognized it. Maybe if you spent long enough as a loser, you would always be a palimpsest of loserdom, and any disappointment would call forth the desperation just under the surface.

In the lobby, she watched a cluster of young women

taking turns being photographed by the Zenith sign, each one holding her hand to the side of her head, elbow pointed upward, a pose whose ubiquity had replaced the hand-on-hip of Jane's youth. She envied their apparent unselfconsciousness for five seconds, until she remembered that they all wanted to be Cass. And that they would probably settle for being Jane.

She caught sight of herself in a mirrored wall. Her new physical self was not an illusion. She had created her own destiny. She knew she sounded like an embroidered throw pillow and she didn't care. She told herself she wasn't a loser. She was wearing a sold-out-everywhere Panama hat that *New York* magazine had dubbed The Hat.

Jane considered using the time before the last meeting to research the people she was meeting with, but it hardly seemed worth it if they were only going to dangle their capital in front of her then jerk it out of reach. Instead, she paced the lobby, trying to remember how to forget herself. She saw a calligraphed sign for the VIP Connect and Commune and decided to reassure herself of Cass's extraordinariness instead.

A VIP ticket cost an extra $300 on top of the Zenith's already exorbitant fees, and entitled the holder to a different-colored badge, two extra juice tickets, and ten minutes of one-on-one time with one of the featured presenters. Cass's time slots had filled up faster than any of the others, including a woman who had starred on a beloved teen drama in the early 2000s and now ran the most successful crystal start-up in the country.

The room was divided in two with a modular partition. The VIPs waited their turn in the holding area, some clutching notebooks so they could jot down the wisdom for which they'd paid handsomely, others checking their faces in their front-facing cameras to make sure their photos would be fit for posting.

Jane flashed her own badge at the crowd wrangler and slipped behind the partition to find Cass. Each presenter was seated at a bistro table laid with a bud vase, a carafe of water, and two small cups. Did that mean every VIP had to use the same one? This sort of tiny logistical fuckup was common at the conferences Jane and Cass attended, and she collected them like sea glass.

Cass was seated across from a very pale girl with a peacock-blue scarf wrapped around her head and sparse eyebrows. She was bad-thin, like someone had forgotten to put anything between bone and skin. She looked like a collapsing tent.

"I've been reading your blog," the girl was saying, her voice very quiet. "And it's helped me so much. My insurance wouldn't pay for another round of chemo but I've been doing the mushroom teatox."

Jane had a vague memory of cobbling together *teatox* benefits from wellness blog SEO terms—*Immune Boosting, Resentment Clearing, Spine Aligning*—but she was almost sure she hadn't said anything about cancer.

"I feel so much better now," said the girl. Her breath was shallow. Jane looked around to make sure no one at Zenith was recording this.

"You've let go of your fear," Cass said. She stroked one of the girl's pipe cleaner arms. She wove her fingers together with the girl's.

"Yes."

"You have the clearest aura I've ever seen."

Tears rolled down the girl's face and neck. People around them must have been talking, but the only sound Jane heard was the splat of tear on tabletop. They kept looking at each other, hands entwined like lovers. They breathed together, their bistro table expanding and collapsing with them. After what felt like eons, the crowd wrangler tiptoed over and told Cass in an agonized whisper that she had another VIP waiting. Cass and the girl stood up and embraced. Cass rubbed her back and whispered something in her ear.

Jane backed out of the room, tripping over a power strip and a wrangler. She didn't want to take her eyes off Cass. She went up to her room and turned the hotel's TV channel on loud. She searched *Opeia + Cancer* and *Opeia + Chemo* and *Opeia + Doctor* and made sure she hadn't said anything legally actionable. All her claims were too vague to hold up in court, more poem than promise.

It was nice, really, that Cass had given the girl such comfort. And hydration was good for you. That was a scientific fact. And mushrooms were full of antioxidants, which were definitely important, and maybe even cancer-fighting. Maybe the girl would get better and they could get her to do #spon posts. Then Jane remembered her painful arms and reined herself in.

She told herself that the encounter left her unnerved only because it was unnerving to be close to death. That she and the girl were both victims of the same cruel system, and that Cass offered comfort and empowerment to the uncomforted and disempowered. Jane had found power in Cass, too, though not comfort. Now that she spent her days packaging spiritual fulfillment, she could never consume it. Jane envied the girl, who had experienced a genuine closeness to Cass. She had sought comfort and found it. Cass had welcomed her without suspicion.

Most of the time now, Jane took it for granted that Cass knew, at least a little bit, that it was a combination of beauty and charisma that allowed her to play at being a spiritual leader. That the things she said, even when they were true, would have no effect if pronounced by an average-looking woman. Sometimes, though, when she saw the way Cass was with other people, it all seemed unbearably real. Jane didn't want to sell Cass to hopeless cancer patients—she wanted to sell her to dull-skinned thirty-somethings with too much disposable income. People who deserved to be relieved of their excess money.

She glanced at her phone and realized she was almost late for her next meeting. Before the success of Opeia, jobs had only ever been a distraction for Jane. They prevented her from the urgent task of contemplating what her life should look like. She had never trusted people who claimed to throw themselves into work, but now she was one of them.

She understood what people wanted from Cass. The glow was no small part of it, but more than that, it was the certainty. Jane's job was to create an environment in which Cass could be infallible. This was what Tom hadn't understood—every little nest of hair and skewed macramé wall hanging chipped away at Cass's certainty. She wasn't supposed to be attainable—attainability was for Mormon lifestyle influencers and Hallmark Channel stars.

Jane wasn't sure anymore if she'd ever had the capacity to believe in Cass fully. Now that her financial circumstances were more similar to Farren's, and so many of the others who fully gave themselves to Cass, Jane was too close. She knew that beauty and charisma and the light delirium brought on by forty-eight hours of hunger wasn't a spiritual revelation. She had hoped, briefly, that proximity might reveal something she didn't know, but it had only revealed that those who gave themselves most fully to Cass were those who already believed their lives were 99 percent correct—a belief affirmed by the steady growth of their wealth and by the algorithm and by *The New York Times* Style Section. Cass didn't offer a gut renovation—she was more like the new cabinet hardware that tied an already lovely room together.

So often Jane wanted the world to prove her wrong about the things that seemed obvious to her, but it rarely did. And if she'd ever stood opposite a window of belief, she'd traded it for this: creating belief for others. It sounded almost noble, at least more noble than the other part of the truth, which was that she'd traded it for the certainty of a comfortable life. But none of this changed the fact that Jane was her best self when she was selling Cass.

~

When she saw Preston, she thought she must be in the wrong room. She wondered if he was there because she hadn't answered a text he'd sent earlier (*any word on*

2nite?), and felt briefly afraid. Then she recognized the other men as the ones from the bar last night, and realized that they were her meeting.

Preston wasn't the one in charge, which was a relief but also made her a little sad for him. The short, sketch-faced man from the bar introduced himself as Jeff Portis, head of wellness initiatives at the Vitalia Healthcare Group, part of the RainbowCare family, the same family to whom Jane still owed $85,000.

"We've always prided ourselves on providing our members with the highest-quality medical care available," Jeff began when Jane had taken her seat. "In today's market, that doesn't stop at doctor's appointments and prescription drug coverage. We're hearing more and more that our members are interested in a more holistic approach to health."

Jane wondered if "holistic" now encompassed out-of-state surgery. She nodded thoughtfully.

"We're developing a new membership tier—a white-glove, person-first tier—which will include access to a variety of partner wellness facilities, from acupuncture practices to, well . . . to places like Opeia. We think you have real potential to thrive within the RainbowCare family."

"Wow. Okay. So . . . you guys want to pay for all your members to come to Opeia?"

All the men chuckled. "Obviously, not *all* our members. This benefit will be available exclusively to our Diamond Plus members."

One of the other men cleared his throat and gave a little shake of his head.

"Ah, excuse me. The tier name is still pending legal clearance," Jeff said.

"So we would be, like, a licensed healthcare provider?" Jane asked, imagining the volume of paperwork the proposition would require.

"Ah, well. What we're envisioning is more of an . . ."

"You'd join RainbowCare as a full member," Preston cut in. "Opeia by Vitalia Healthcare Group."

"It's much more streamlined that way," Jeff said. "Like a family."

Jane nodded, like this was a reasonable way to describe a family.

"We're in the early stages of the initiative, but we've been very impressed by your operation. We sent a scout to one of your weekend workshops—sorry about that!" Jeff raised his hands in mock surrender and grinned. "She said it was just terrific."

"What did she like about it?" Jane asked, more perplexed than curious.

"We have a copy of her report you can read. Anyway, we all remember how fantastic she looked when she got back." The other men around the table nodded emphatically. She was glad to see that Preston, at least, looked a little sheepish.

"The point is," Jeff continued. "We think you all could be a great fit for our members."

The same man who'd objected to the reckless use of Diamond Plus rapped the table twice with his knuckles and scowled.

"Right, of course we're still in preliminary fact-finding mode here, so we're talking purely hypothetical, best-case-scenario here," Jeff said.

"So . . . you would buy us," Jane said. "And then what?"

Jane tried to sound impassive when she asked the question. An acquisition would mean an end to her debt. She had been working toward this moment for months, but its arrival still left her breathless. Her reality had shifted. She wondered if she could get away with leading the group in a sun salutation, so she could have somewhere to put her jubilation.

"If you joined the RainbowCare family, we would take over all the financial aspects of the business—all the boring stuff. You and your partner would be free to continue the tremendous work you've been doing out there, and let us worry about the big picture. Of course, you'd both draw competitive salaries, with top-notch benefits."

"Diamond Plus?" Jane asked. She looked at a spot at the center of Jeff's forehead so she wouldn't have to meet his eyes.

It seemed like a question a Scary Woman would ask, because she knew her worth and she would always walk away from the wrong deal. This was something Jane admired about them, even as she'd come to realize that she would never be one of them. She was too easily wounded. Too aware of her own softness. But every day she was getting a little better at faking it, and maybe one day the idea of armor would become real. Like the Velveteen Girlboss.

Jeff laughed at her question, a little too loudly, and after a beat, the rest of the men followed.

"Jane, you're just great," Jeff said. "I knew we were going to get along."

Jane smiled and nodded as she stood up from her

chair, trying to tame her euphoria into something more appropriate for a hotel conference room. She kept saying the word *acquired* in her head. To be acquired suggested permanence and an end to accountability. Being acquired was the ultimate example of things falling into place—building something and then washing your hands of it in exchange for money. True belief, on the other hand, was a custom luxury item—costly, but with almost no resale value. The benefit of being the belief architect instead of the believer was that you could always walk away.

chapter 25.

Jeff gave her a thick, glossy dossier titled *RainbowCare: A Family of Health.* "Talk to your partner," he said. "My assistant will be in touch about a follow-up touch-base."

Before Jane had even gotten back to her room, his assistant had already sent an email to set up a meeting with Jane and Cass, and requesting the Opeia pitch deck as well as whatever NDA they would need to sign. *Shit. Was everyone supposed to be signing NDAs?*

She knew they would come through with an offer. The acquisition made much more sense than her attempts to convince people of a scalable, infinite Cass. There was no program, nothing of Cass herself she could impart to others. She tried to imagine Cass teaching a roomful of Casses-in-training how to inflect their voices just so when they told a dying girl she had a clear aura.

But thinking about the girl made Jane remember how she said that her insurance denied her coverage for chemo. Hopefully it wasn't Vitalia insurance. Maybe she could ask what their policy about denying coverage for chemo was. Maybe she could even get Vitalia to cover the girl, too, as part of the deal. It seemed like the kind of spontaneously generous thing Cass would do, and it would make for a great Instagram post.

As soon as she started to think of the acquisition as an inevitability, she felt much better. It wasn't, after all, as if she'd *invented* health insurance, and she couldn't take any kind of stand against it simply by refusing money. If anything, once she had money, she could finally upgrade her sporadic donations to Planned Parenthood and the ACLU to recurring monthly gifts. Maybe she could secretly pay off strangers' medical debt. Maybe Cass would run for office and Jane could make sure her policies were Good.

The thing that concerned her most was how quickly she'd decided. She knew if she asked Cass, Cass would say something maddeningly inconclusive about sitting with an energy or breathing into the discomfort. The decision was hers alone.

Was it even a moral dilemma if you said yes to the immoral part immediately? Because it was immoral—she was certain of that much. On the other hand, doctors participated in the health insurance system, too, and they couldn't all be ethically compromised. Or maybe they were, but everyone had decided that was fine, and anyone who didn't think so was a sucker. By signing on with Vitalia, Jane would just be making, had already made, a choice to participate. But she was opting in to survive. It wasn't even called selling out anymore. It was called *hustle*.

If she didn't feel good about doing it, exactly, she felt a strange sort of pride at becoming a person who could do it anyway.

That was funny, she texted Preston, and added a wink emoji because it seemed like he would be into that.

whoa I swear I had no idea.

I hope it wasn't too weird.

no it was cool

She weighed her phone on her palm. She was hungry; all she'd had to eat all day was the Zenith's signature turmeric elixir. She didn't want to go to dinner with him, but it seemed like the most efficient option. Inviting him up for sex would be faster, but then she'd have to get dinner later. Or worse, he might suggest ordering room service and she wasn't sure she'd be able to resist.

Her phone pinged again. *Want to grab dinner?*

He suggested a vegan restaurant a short walk from the hotel. His deference to her imagined dietary restrictions irritated her, as did the fact that he couldn't meet until eight-thirty. She ate a bag of Peanut M&M's and a stunted tube of plain Pringles from the mini bar while she flipped through the dossier, which contained no actual information, only testimonials from partners about how smoothly their operations ran as Vitalia members.

RainbowCare has taken billing off my plate so I can focus on what's really important: the patients. The text overlaid a photo of a woman in a white coat beaming as she held a stethoscope up to the bare chest of a small boy, also beaming. It made Jane think of the popular riddle from when she was a child: *A boy and his father are in a car accident and are both taken to a hospital. When the boy goes in for surgery, the surgeon exclaims,* I can't operate on this boy! He's my son! *How can this be?*

Her mother had been so disappointed when Jane couldn't figure it out.

~

Preston suggested they meet at the restaurant, since he was coming from another meeting. Jane imagined the same group of men delivering the same presentation with the same level of corporate enthusiasm to a more poised and qualified version of herself and was afraid. *This is how you lose the upper hand.* As if she didn't already know.

The place's interior looked just like Opeia, from the painted wood floors to the hanging air plants in individual burlap pockets, to the communal tables, whose bench seating ensured that even getting up to pee would require negotiation with strangers. Jane wished they had gone to one of the seventeen steak houses in the neighborhood instead.

Preston was already seated at the center table. He examined a turmeric shaker and turned it upside down, accidentally dumping out a little golden pile in front of him. He used the blade of one hand to carefully sweep it all into the other. When he had made several passes over the table and seemed satisfied with his efforts, he tilted his head back and swallowed the turmeric from his hand. He was still coughing when the host led Jane over.

"Allergies," he rasped when he had recovered. "Hey."

"Hi," she said, smiling a tiny doll smile. "How was your meeting?"

"Great," he said. "I drank about a gallon of cucumber water."

"Not better than *our* meeting, though, right?" She put on a pout.

"You kidding? No way."

She decided to leave it there until they ordered appetizers, at least. She learned that Preston owned a home in Cleveland ("The nice part," he said, without elaborating), enjoyed both golf and live music, and was considering switching from an iPhone to an Android.

"So, this *acquisition* thing," Jane said after their orders were in and she had a cardamom-barley-mezcal cocktail to sip flirtatiously. "Can you tell me anything else about it? I've never been, like, *acquired* before. Would you pay a lot of money for us?" She rested her chin on her fist and batted her eyes to show him she was no threat.

"Oh, *so* much money." He grinned.

"Ohmygod, like *how* much money?"

Then Jane heard a familiar voice behind her. "You know, Cass met my parents at the restaurant right next door to this one."

She whipped her head to her right and saw them: Cass, Tom, and Daniel. Her heart thudded in her temples. Preston looked concerned; she tried to smile at him but only her mouth would cooperate. Her eyes darted toward the door.

"Low millions, probably," Preston said. It took her a

second to recall the context. By the time she did, the host had already led Cass, Tom, and Daniel to the communal table.

Tom saw her first. "Oh," he said, hovering over the bench. He sounded like he'd just been flattened by a wave of exhaustion. Jane's face burned. *Oh.*

"Jane," Cass said. "You're nourishing your body."

For Preston's benefit, Jane forced a smile. "Of course," she said. "Cass, this is Preston. We had a meeting earlier today about funding for Opeia. And we slept together last night." Preston's mouth trout-gaped, but Jane knew if she didn't say it now it would only come out later, in a much weirder way.

Daniel whispered something in Tom's ear, and Tom laughed like a grouchy kid who's been tickled. Watching them made Jane lonely. She felt sad for herself. More distantly, she felt glad for Tom.

"Uh, great to meet you, Cass. I've heard a lot about you, of course," Preston said. He turned to Tom and Daniel. "Are you guys part of the incredible Opeia operation, too?"

"I'm a lawyer," Daniel said.

"Hey, Jane, I thought we were just talking here. No need to get lawyers involved!" Apparently, Preston's default discomfort mode was sitcom misogynist.

"Ha-ha," Daniel said, with the weariness of someone who's heard too many lawyer jokes.

"Hi, I'm Jane," Jane said. She wondered what he had heard about her.

Cass sat down next to Preston. "Tom, Daniel. What a beautiful opportunity this is." Tom and Daniel conferred with their eyes. Daniel sat next to Cass, and Tom came around the table and took the seat across from Daniel, leaving a person-sized space between him and Jane.

"So, how do you all know one another?" Preston asked.

Cass clasped her hands in front of her chest and smiled. "Tom is my former legal husband and spiritual partner, and Daniel is his lover," she said. "Daniel is also my former lover, though the memories of that time didn't meaningfully imprint on my life's map."

"And Jane, how did you and Cass get hooked up?" he asked, with impressive impassivity.

"Oh, you know. Instagram," Jane said, as she did whenever anyone questioned her role in the Opeia origin story. She thought she saw Daniel raise his eyebrows slightly. "And I'm *so glad* I did. My life's map was leading me to Cass all along."

She looked at Preston with as much warmth as she could muster. Under the table, he pressed the side of his foot to the side of hers. He was sweet. She felt nothing for him. It was necessary to keep him on her side, though, not only for the sake of the acquisition, but also because in Tom's presence, her guilt over how things had ended between them threatened to overwhelm her. She needed someone here who liked her. Even if what he liked was only a carefully selected, not entirely truthful segment of her.

"Can I get some drinks started for you folks?"

Daniel ordered a glass of biodynamic orange wine, Cass asked for body-temperature water (the waiter nodded knowingly), and Tom requested unsweetened natural ginger ale. Jane remembered his time in rehab, and realized she had no idea if he was sober. There was so much she didn't know about him, and would never know. He was probably great at a party where you didn't know anyone. He would hang out with you by the food and laugh at everyone with you and not make you feel bad about being incapable of mingling. She wished they could be friends again. She shook her head once, like maybe it would dislodge the memory of how she'd treated him. Tom looked at her as though he knew exactly what the tic meant.

She ordered another cocktail, though she was already feeling the effects of the first.

"So, Tom," Preston said. "You used to work at Opeia?"

"I did, back when it was FortPath. A lot has changed since then." He didn't sound bitter at all, just factual, which was almost worse.

"It wasn't *that* different," Jane said. Her scalp felt very hot. She picked up her water glass and held it to the side of her head, attempting casual. "I mean, it was the same basic idea when you guys started it. Wellness. Fearless. Mindful. Cass. Et cetera."

"It's always been important to me to reach as many people as possible," Cass told Preston, lightly touching his shoulder.

Their waiter returned. Jane hadn't decided what to order, but everything sounded terrible and close reading was getting harder by the sip, so she asked for the first thing her eyes landed on: fermented kale salad with tofu skin croutons and sweet potato pockets. The word *pocket,* at least, was appealing.

Cass and Preston were talking quietly. She held one of his hands in both of hers. Jane felt a distant twinge of annoyance, as if on someone else's behalf. Tom and Daniel were both on their phones, possibly texting each other. The old destructive urge came upon her. She wanted to grab the phones and smash them, and grind the broken glass under the heels of her $400 babouche slippers (created by an artisan named Joshua Harrison whose website claimed he had a lifelong love of Moroccan culture and had completed a weeklong *stage* with a legendary cobbler in Marrakech).

"So, Daniel," she said. "You and Cass used to date, but she doesn't remember? Is that weird?"

"It's not the weirdest thing that's ever happened to me," he said lightly.

"Daniel gives off a very gentle vibration," Cass said. "Like a gnat on the surface of a pond."

"I think Daniel's vibration is pretty strong," Tom said. Jane saw his arm flex and knew that he'd squeezed Daniel's knee under the table.

"Actually, Pond Gnat was my nickname in high school." Daniel and Tom shared a private smile.

"My nickname in high school was The Boca," Preston offered. Even Cass ignored him.

"Okay, but come on, isn't that sort of wild? To fuck someone repeatedly and have them just not remember?" *Why am I doing this?* she wondered to herself, though she already knew the answer. She wanted Tom to scream at her, to tell her exactly how shitty she was being, and had been. And then she wanted to apologize, so they could be friends again.

"Well, I have to admit I wasn't bringing my A-game," Daniel said, infinitely calm. "Sorry, Cass."

"Presence in the moment is all we owe our sexual

companions," Cass replied. She was still holding Preston's hand.

"How did you and Jane meet, Preston?" said Tom, playing the gracious host.

"Preston works for a company that wants to acquire Opeia."

"Wow, what?" Tom turned to Jane for the first time. "What company?"

"Ah, hey, Jane? This is all pretty preliminary, so if we could cool it with the disclosures to anyone on the outside, that would be . . . awesome." Preston sounded annoyed, which caused Jane's attraction for him to flare for the first time all night.

"I actually still own a third of Fort— . . . of Opeia," Tom said. "So I'm not on the outside."

The mezcal had given the evening a faraway feeling, like it was all bundled up in fiberglass insulation and there were no real consequences for anything she did. Still, she had a moment of clarity: It was important not to let Preston know how shocked she was by this disclosure.

She was angry at Cass, but she was furious at Tom. He'd taken something that was rightfully hers and was keeping it, unused, in his sneaky little pocket. What was he planning to do with it? That she knew it was actually she who had taken something from him only compounded her anger. In addition to true love and generational wealth, Tom had a third of the business she had built up from practically nothing. Of course he didn't want to be her friend again—he already had everything.

"Oh, right on. Silent partner," Preston said. "Well, I guess . . . I can just bring you up to speed?" Jane felt his beseeching eyes on her, but she wouldn't turn away from

Tom. "So, I work for RainbowCare, one of the major health insurance providers in the country. And we're looking to expand into the boutique wellness field for some of our new prestige offerings. We're talking to a lot of different providers, but my team leader is really impressed by your operation. So that's . . . where we are."

"Health insurance provider? Jane, come on." She hated Tom's *let's be reasonable* tone, but at least he was finally admitting to having known her. Then she realized that as a part-owner of the business, Tom caring was much more dangerous to her than him not caring.

"Sorry, didn't you once tell me your *boyfriend's* law firm defended, like, fruit companies that poisoned migrant workers? Did I make that up?" Jane said, hoping to appeal to Cass's occasional social conscience and discredit Tom.

"You told her that?" Daniel said quietly.

"Hey, we're the good guys," Preston said. "We *help* people who have been poisoned."

"Yeah, but only if the antidote is *in-network,*" Jane spat, forgetting which side she was on. "Ha-ha! Little health insurance joke."

For a moment she imagined a world in which she and Tom and Cass were still working together—a shambolic threesome that baffled outsiders but still managed to function. Jane and Tom would scrap over Core Values, but in a fun, sitcommy way, where the barbs never pierced the skin. They would turn a small but respectable profit, enough for Jane to pay off her debt and save for retirement and buy expensive hats sometimes. They wouldn't say they were like a family, but it would still be true.

Cass put her arm around Preston and whispered something in his ear. Whether or not it was intentional damage control, Jane was grateful.

Their food arrived, and they all focused intently on the dams of wet vegetables in front of them. Even Cass, nibbling a sheet of nori, appeared cowed by the chaos. The restaurant's soundtrack of rain-forest white noise under Spanish guitar seemed to be getting louder. Jane's kale tasted like lake fish, somehow. She ate it all. She was quite drunk, but in a way where she knew she would remember everything in the morning.

The restaurant staff cleared their plates in silence. Before their waiter could ask about the check, Preston extracted himself from the table and announced that he had an early start and had to get going. He threw down an inexplicable hundred-dollar bill, gave Jane a rough kiss on the cheek and Cass a slightly gentler one, and jogged out the door.

"You're really trying to sell Cass to an insurance company?" Tom said when he was gone. "Even after how badly you got screwed over by yours?"

"I'm not *selling Cass* to anyone. I'm trying to clear the obstacles from her *work*. Anyway, you fucked it up. Preston's probably gonna tell his boss we're a liability after this. I guess you didn't need a few million dollars, but my parents didn't buy me a house."

"But you'll be solving your problem by putting even more money in the pockets of a company that *created that problem.*" He sounded incredulous, like this was the first he was hearing of capitalism.

Here was the fight she thought she wanted, but now she was too exhausted to put up any resistance. She just felt ashamed.

She told herself she didn't care about Tom's disapproval. She hadn't created the problem. She hadn't led a particularly generous life before, but she had been meek and passive and unthreatening, which people sometimes mistook for kindness. Generosity, she thought, was best suited to the very poor or the very rich. Once she had more money, she would focus on becoming the kind of person Tom initially mistook her for. Until then, she had to focus on herself.

And she was so much happier now. She regularly ignored emails. Strangers looked at her like they wondered where her money came from. She slept with men and then lost interest in them. Sometimes, as with Preston, she lost interest even before the sex. She was the object of so many meeting requests. She had pulled herself up by Cass's bootstraps, out of the mire of PR middle management and into a position of actual worth. She had enough power that, by middle age, she could afford to be generous.

The crying came on with almost no warning.

She hung her head so her tears dripped down onto the table, like the dying girl's had. "I just wanted to help." She had wanted many things; "to help" was somewhere in the mix.

"I know," Tom said, because what else could he say? "And I don't actually care if you sell FortPath. As long as Cass is fine with it, I'll sign whatever I need to sign, okay?"

"I'm sorry I made you leave," she said. "I'm sorry I tried to take it away from you."

Tom ran his hand over a lightning scar on the tabletop. The table was identical to the one he had brought back from New York right before he left. Maybe the artisan had started outsourcing them.

For the first time, Jane wondered what happened to Tom the week he was gone. Had he slotted Daniel right into Cass's spot? Had Daniel begged him to stay? Done something to convince Tom to walk away from the last decade of his already untethered existence? Didn't it feel like an awful lot of pressure to Daniel, to become Tom's new everything? Or maybe Tom wasn't looking for a new everything. Maybe he had outgrown the idea of an everything.

Tom was quiet for so long that Jane wondered if he would simply leave the restaurant without responding to her, leaving her in this torturous liminal space forever. Finally, he said, "It wasn't mine, anyway."

It wasn't mine. As if that had ever mattered to anyone. As if desire could be reasoned with, and hunger a matter of whose name was written on a lunch bag. Tom found something he wanted more, that was all. His need had found a reciprocal object in Daniel, while Jane's was in pursuit of something that, she sometimes feared, would only create more need.

Tom and Daniel looked at each other across the table with such unbearable tenderness that Jane had to look away. She buried her face in her hands. But the tightness in her chest was already easing. She and Tom were the same. They had each taken what they wanted. That was all.

She didn't know if he had actually found fulfillment with Daniel, or if he sometimes felt a gasping loneliness in the morning. She wasn't sure which one would make her feel better.

She didn't want to stop crying immediately, but she felt her eyes drying. Even split three ways, a few million dollars was enough to change her life. In a good way this time. And how much money would RainbowCare give her to continue working at Opeia? No matter how much they offered, she would ask for more, of course. And she would insist on the Diamond Plus insurance.

She wiped her face with the napkin in her lap and took a few shuddery breaths.

"You released," Cass said finally.

Jane nodded. Something had released. When she lifted her head, Cass was gazing at Tom.

"Cass, how do you feel about selling?" Jane knew she probably shouldn't press her luck, but it felt crucial to calibrate her hope. "Because I think RainbowCare could help you reach a lot more people." The words felt familiar. "They would literally send people to us. People who really need your help."

"Preston's energy was muddled, but healing. Very green."

"Right, I noticed that, too," Jane said. "I mean, I think he really cares about helping people, you know, get well. I think this would be a good thing for you. I really do."

Tom was dragging a dipper through the ceramic pot that had accompanied his vegan cheese plate. He lifted the dipper and watched the agave syrup slowly drizzle back down before finally looking up at Jane. Just as she was wondering whether he, too, was thinking about the afternoon in the pantry, he smiled, his own version of Cass's ghost smile.

"I don't subscribe to the false binary of *goodness* and

badness," Cass said. "All things are both, and neither. And I never worry for myself. I am protected." It was, on the surface, a ridiculous claim, but it might also have been the most self-awareness Cass had ever demonstrated. "And you have a great capacity to protect yourself."

Jane didn't know whether it was an incisive compliment or a brutal insult. Cass *was* protected, but Jane had to do it herself? Jane was small and ungenerous where Cass was love and light? Like many things Cass said, Jane knew she would be turning it over in her head for longer than she'd like.

"Jane, I think Tom, Daniel, and I will leave now," Cass said. "The universe clearly intended us all to meet, but now it's necessary for us to part."

Daniel was the first out the door, then Cass. Tom was the only one who looked back.

As soon as they were gone, the staff descended upon the table, the force field of polite inattention collapsing. Jane put the meal on her Opeia credit card, planning to pocket Preston's hundred, but she couldn't find it anywhere.

As she walked back toward the hotel, she texted some of the men in her phone, the ones she barely knew, and who only knew her as Opeia Jane—Dan Wine Bar, Blake Tinder, Clinton Cargo Shorts. When she got back to her room, she lay down on top of the covers and set the phone beside her head. Just as she had started to drift off, she heard the chime of a response. She kept her eyes closed for a few minutes, wondering who it might be.

chapter 26.

For the fifth time that morning, Jane brushed her hair, then bent forward and scrunched it in her fists to make it look artfully tousled. The guests would arrive any minute, on the luxury mini bus that had long since replaced the livery cab. Jane always welcomed the bus herself, but she had two assistants—both named Kayla—who took care of the mise-en-scène. They were so confident and efficient that they made Jane a little uneasy. They spoke adoringly to Cass and professionally to Jane but the other day she'd overheard them discussing her *toxic positivity* after she told them not to complain about their benefits package in front of the guests.

The only time she got nervous about Arrival anymore was when she saw a familiar name in the Guest Dossier that Kayla B. prepared for her. They'd had a few mid-tier influencers, a supporting actress from the show about a magicians' agency, and the ex-wife of a disgraced congressman. But the guest whose arrival Jane was anticipating that morning was only famous to her: Caroline Bradstreet.

Jane had been almost certain the woman was Tom's mother, but she googled her just in case. There were a few images of her standing beside a nondescript, vaguely Tom-looking man at galas, from a magazine called *Shoreline*. She had the beginnings of the death-mask face common to all rich white women of a certain age, but she had her son's posture. Jane opened the hidden folder on her phone where she kept the only picture of Tom she had, one she'd taken the day they demolished the table. He was standing in front of the kitchen door, holding the tiny hatchet and grinning. Though Caroline's prop was a glass of white wine and her expression more of an impatient grimace, the planes of their faces were identical.

Jane was anticipating her arrival with a mixture of dread and excitement. She wasn't sure if Caroline had booked the trip in the hope of seeing her son, or if her appearance had anything to do with Tom at all. Money made the world smaller, she now knew.

Given how many man-hours had gone into denying her claims for $111,000, Jane was amazed how quickly the higher-ups at RainbowCare approved the acquisition. Preston's estimate had been conservative—all of a sudden, she had money. When she was writing the check that would clear her remaining balance—resolving her years-long burden with a few strokes of a pen—Jane felt giddy with power. It felt like a magic trick. *Poof! No more debt! No more financial shame! No more anguished phone calls with insurance agents!*

She spent that weekend in the city because she craved human proximity. In search of a spiritual backdrop to her euphoria, she took the train to the Cloisters. After nearly an hour of willing herself to be moved by medieval art, she wandered out to a bench overlooking the Hudson River and the New Jersey Palisades. It was there, in view of her new home state, that she sank fully into her victorious relief. She stayed until the sun set, then went back to her hotel and slept for eleven hours.

Not only was Jane debt-free; now she was *comfortable.* But after the initial high of her new solvency wore off, she mostly returned to her baseline level of dissatisfaction, though the looming dread she felt had turned inchoate.

True to his word, Tom signed everything that needed signing within hours of receipt, with no comment. Jane hoped there would be some legal requirement for the three of them to come together in a mahogany-paneled boardroom, but she didn't see him after the night at the restaurant.

After Opeia joined the Vitalia Healthcare Group, their demographic shifted subtly. There were more older wives of investment bankers, fewer digital nomads. The Cartier Love bracelets shared wrist space with Cartier Tank watches instead of with rubber bands and friendship bracelets. (Though Jane asked everyone to remove their watches and place them in top-of-the-line safes at Welcome, in deference to Being Present.)

In her moments of guilt about her role as Frictionless Wellness Provider to the Very Rich and White, Jane told herself that perhaps the high premiums these women paid to Vitalia somehow offset the costs for people in the lower insurance tiers. That maybe she was, in some small way, helping make the system more equitable for everyone. Just because trickle-down economics was a lie didn't mean trickle-down health had to be.

The new people were less ashamed of their boredom, less committed to performing ceaseless wonder. They treated Jane as staff, not a Scary Woman. She found it comforting, though she hated them. They loved Cass, of course; she moved easily through class membranes. Their customer care liaison at Vitalia reported that they had the highest member satisfaction scores of any of the white-glove wellness care centers. More than one guest called the sleeping arrangements "charmingly Spartan."

Jane had very little contact with anyone from Vitalia; she understood that their approach was hands-off unless there were complaints, so she worked hard to ensure there were none. She didn't like to be reminded of the benefactors of her new circumstances, or the perpetrators of her old ones. She tried not to wonder too much about the decisions she would have made absent the debt.

She bought a one-bedroom apartment in the West Village, where she'd dreamed of living for years. The day she closed, she took a walk around the neighborhood and when she passed Magnolia Bakery, she remembered that the genesis of the dream was watching *Sex and the City* in high school. The people in her co-op were mostly women, over seventy, and single due to their spouses' deaths, either untimely or timely. She didn't spend much time there, but it was a nice place to mention.

Sometimes she drove to the city just to take a very long shower. On a whim, she paid someone to hang toile wallpaper in the bathroom, because when she was a kid she thought toile was the height of sophistication, and because it didn't remind her of Opeia at all.

~

Jane walked downstairs as the bus pulled up. She had the urge to run, but she never deviated from her routine once the guests arrived. Opeia Jane was her best self yet. It still took some effort to maintain, but she felt much better since she stopped attempting humor. Jane recognized that out of the context of herself, she probably wouldn't have liked Opeia Jane, who instructed people to be tender with themselves, and described breath as healing. Other people seemed to like her, though. She didn't command as much reverence as Cass, but she basked in the spillover. And eventually, she was sure, that would be enough.

As the women disembarked, Jane greeted each one by name, and Kayla N. offered them a cucumber-green algae tonic. Caroline Bradstreet was the last one off the bus. She looked appraisingly at the property and gave a tiny nod, more probationary than approving.

"Caroline," Jane said when she stepped down. "We honor your presence here, and your commitment to yourself."

Caroline's skeptical look reminded Jane of how Tom had looked at her the last time she saw him, though Caroline's was likely because Jane had addressed her with such familiarity. The look was so powerful that Jane had the urge to correct herself, though she had a policy against using formal titles. She gave Caroline a beat in case she wanted to discreetly ask about Tom, but Caroline accepted her tonic without comment and followed the others into the house.

When Cass arrived for Welcome Invocation, Jane watched Caroline's face closely, but there was no flicker of recognition, and Cass treated her with the same generic intimacy she did everyone.

Jane had imagined Caroline might have a revelation about Tom, a breakthrough that would lead, perhaps, to a heartfelt apology and a slow mending of the relationship and, eventually, over-earnest Mother's Day Instagram tributes. If Tom could ever figure out how to use Instagram properly.

Instead, Caroline was unfailingly polite and composed. She was a courteous participant in every activity, like an adult at a child's birthday party. She made small talk with the other guests at meals and sent her compliments to the chef. She participated in Humbled Silence and Mindful Spatialism, but she didn't weep or shake or falter.

On the last day, Jane approached Caroline at her sleeping area while Caroline was packing her things. She had been practicing what she would say in her head all morning.

"Caroline. How was your stay with us?" she asked, clenching her jaw into a smile.

"Everything has been lovely." Caroline paused her folding and looked up at Jane with restrained impatience. Jane marveled at her posture, perfect even while crouched on her organic cotton shikibuton.

"Good. Excellent. I wanted to ask you . . . Cass mentioned that you two might have met before."

"No, not that I can recall," Caroline said. She didn't sound like she was lying. She also didn't sound like she was trying to recall anything.

"She said it was maybe a few years ago." Jane had told herself it would be unprofessional to mention Tom, but Caroline's smooth stone façade was a provocation. "She said she was a friend of your son's."

Caroline stood up slowly and stood facing Jane. "No," she said. Her voice betrayed nothing, but she leaned in just a little too close. "I suppose she didn't make a strong impression on me."

Caroline smoothed her already-smooth hair with her palm and took a step back. "Your girls will get my things, yes?" she said on her way out the door.

A few weeks later, Jane found her review on their website:

> To Whom It May Concern:
>
> While the level of professionalism left much to be desired (physical contact bordered on legally actionable), the facilities were clean, if slightly reminiscent of a prison farm. I do not feel I benefited tremendously from sitting quietly for several hours while a stranger told me my body was made of light. Perhaps my appreciation of metaphor was not sufficient for the exercise.
>
> Nevertheless, I would recommend this experience based on the marked improvement in my skin's texture and appearance. In that sense, the chief aesthetician was more than satisfactory. Though the group activities were unorth-

odox, bordering on ridiculous, I admit that I felt a certain peace after my time at the Opeia Center, and both my dermatologist and facialist noted my "healthful glow." I have attached "before" and "after" photographs to this review for your reference.

Regards,
Caroline Bradstreet

Jane read the review a few times, looking for some coded reference to Tom, but after a while she accepted that Caroline was just another one of the many wealthy women to whom she and Cass had given the gift of increased beauty privilege, if only for a few weeks. Maybe some of them would use their powers for good. If Cass felt any particular way about her demotion from healer to aesthetician, she didn't confide in Jane, and Jane didn't ask. Cass had cared for Tom, in her way, and now she had cared for his mother, too, in a way that was both more fungible and less valuable to Caroline. Caroline could understand the kind of care Cass performed now, so it was no longer a threat.

But maybe it was all the same, anyway. Maybe this was what spiritual enlightenment felt like—a momentary quieting of the desire to be someone else, because you've altered the indifferent face a stranger gives you on first glance to an expression of warmth, or interest, or welcome. And that must mean you're a different person, after all.

In both of the photos Caroline had included, she was looking straight into the camera, standing in front of the same floral wallpaper, possibly in a house where Tom had once lived. The glow was familiar enough to Jane that she rarely noticed it now, but the second photo of Tom's mother was so luminous that it took her a long time to close the window. Before she did, she saved it in her hidden photos folder, for later.

acknowledgments

Anyone who gave me an encouraging word (or glance) in the past five years deserves thanks for this book. In the interest of brevity, I'll stick to those who touched its pages directly. (Still, for those many, many kindnesses: Thank you.)

Marya Spence and Clio Seraphim are the agent and editor of my absolute wildest hopes. Thank you for seeing what this book could be, and for your unerring guidance in steering it there. My gratitude is beyond the limits of language (despite how much work you've both put into refining my language). In addition, thank you to everyone at Janklow & Nesbit and Random House for their vital work throughout the publishing process.

To the three people who read this book, in part and in whole, more times than was even remotely reasonable of me to ask—Mary Childs, who bestowed on me the full force of her earnest belief; Thomas Gebremedhin, who heard the very earliest idea for this book, dismissed me from our walk immediately to go home and write it, and sent me typically pitch-perfect notes on its opening scene that very night; Sara Martin, who treated the book like a Book when it was barely an anecdote and who made me want to write more pages just to send—your generosity, wit, and wisdom sustained me and nudged me forward even when I was at my most petulant.

Other essential readers included Rebecca Bengal, Jonathan Gharraie, Anna Godbersen, Anne Heltzel, Thessaly La Force, Caroline Gaynor, Lizzie May, James Molloy, Alexis Pancrazi, Nadja Spiegelman, Tony Tulathimutte, and the members of the inaugural CRIT workshop. Thank you for both the buoying praise and the kindly stated, almost always correct criticism.

Michael Cunningham's infinite knowledge about the wild world of publishing (and just about everything else) was invaluable, and a great comfort when I needed it most.

My mother, my very first reader, never stopped cheering my writing, from dreadful poetry to slightly-less-dreadful poetry to maybe-okay-ish poetry (and even some fiction). For her, I wish I had finished this book slightly earlier, but I suspect she'd tell me to forget about that.

Finally, thank you to Robbie and Frances: one makes everything easier, the other makes everything harder. Both make everything better, always.

about the author

Jessie Gaynor's work has appeared in McSweeney's Internet Tendency, *The New Yorker, WSJ Magazine,* and elsewhere. A senior editor at *Literary Hub,* she has an MFA in poetry from the Iowa Writers' Workshop, where she was a Rona Jaffe Foundation fellow. She lives in Richmond, Virginia, with her family.

jessiegaynor.com